Praise for *The Funny Moon*

"A long-term relationship gone stale, a summer of searching, celebrity cameos, and a comic sensibility…The pace is consistent and the tone light…A brisk, humorous story of a middle-aged couple in an unmoored marriage, stumbling toward safe harbor."

—*Kirkus Reviews*

"Set in a small New England college town, where tongues do wag, *The Funny Moon* is a whimsical, romantic—and touching—romp about finding your true north."

—Meg Lukens Noonan, author of *The Coat Route*

"Janet Evanovich meets Wallace Stegner—a very funny, very well crafted novel."

—C. B. Clemency

"Highly entertaining…funny, insightful and true."

—Lorenzo di Bonaventura, producer of the *Transformers* film series

"*The Funny Moon* is a rare mix of humor, pathos, and surprise, which will draw you in, sweep you along, and keep you laughing."

—Christopher Merrill, author of *Self-Portrait with Dogwood*

"A delightful comic (and cosmic) romp with vibrant characters, poignant midlife awakenings, and magical surprises."

—Sera Beak, author of *The Red Book*

"A wildly entertaining journey through a maze of mid-life and marital madness, with a couple of quirky seekers, and the most hilarious sex scene ever."

—Marisa Smith, playwright

"Natural and unforced, multilayered and perfectly keyed…with characters rendered in vivid, quirky 3-D and scenes so well played, they unfold the way you don't expect. The writing is strong and assured, with the feeling of a handmade wooden boat, simple and beautiful, nothing to add and nothing to take away."

—Dave Greeley

The Funny Moon

To Marion,

Nothing brings her down
Never seen a frown

Just a smile
All the while
All about the town?

XO Chris

The Funny Moon

A Novel

Chris Lincoln

Rootstock Publishing

Montpelier, VT

For Cecy

May ~ The Flower Moon

"Flowers are the earth's way of laughing."

—Ralph Waldo Emerson

1

Claire loved Wally, but lately she didn't like him very much. Sometimes, when she thought of him, she shuddered, as if sucking on a sourball. Other times, when she looked at him, she felt as if she were having an allergic reaction.

Her friend, Roz, said, "You've been married for twenty-five years. It happens."

"It will be twenty-six in October," said Claire. "And how would you know? You've never been married."

"I've seen what marriage can do to people." Roz fluffed her hair. "Plenty of married men have hit on me."

A thought flashed through Claire's mind, and before she could rein it in, she blurted, "Are you saying Wally hit on you?"

"God, no!" Roz said, and laughed. "The only thing he wants to hit is a golf ball. Or haven't you noticed?"

Claire smiled weakly at her friend and looked out the large picture window of the café where they sat sipping their weekly coffee. The café was the lone alternative to the Starbucks just down Main Street and favored by all the independent thinkers, anti-corporate liberals, and tree-hugging hippies who lived in and around the small New Hampshire college town of Hancock, on the Vermont border. Roz wasn't a full-fledged liberal like Claire, having made her fortune in commercial real estate in Boston before retiring early and moving back to her hometown a few years ago. Claire had met Roz soon after her return, through the dog rescue shelter where they both volunteered, and their political differences were quickly overcome by their mutual love of dogs of all shapes and sizes. It was Claire who insisted they patronize the café on behalf of social justice, and Roz didn't argue. A poster in the window announced that unlike the corporate behemoth down the street, the café was locally owned and operated, paid a livable wage and didn't report to its shareholders—just to its customers. All of which resonated like a warm hug with Claire.

"See that man over there?" said Roz, lifting her chin toward a rumpled figure in wireless glasses seated in an alcove. "He's been eyeing me like a cinnamon cruller."

Claire looked over. The man, seated in front of a laptop, appeared to be in his midforties, attractive, with a gray-flecked beard, curly brown hair and handsome face. He wore a faded plaid shirt, blue jeans and a well-worn corduroy sport coat. "Probably a professor," said Claire.

"A professor with *tenure*," said Roz, holding her spoon and licking the length of it. "Total financial security."

"Control yourself, Roz."

"I'm not thinking about me. I'm thinking about *you*."

"I'm married."

Roz turned her gaze to Claire. "You didn't say *happily*." She lifted her chin toward another table. "How about a younger guy?"

"Enough," said Claire.

Roz raised an eyebrow. "The way Wally behaves, he counts as a twenty-something. Maybe even a teenager. You're enabling him, you know."

Claire looked down at her coffee, took a deep breath and sighed. She couldn't argue with that. She paid as many of the bills as she could, while Wally's once thriving creative services ad business slowly tanked. Her own business as a certified massage therapist and energy healer was thriving, but her work couldn't cover everything.

"Wally hasn't been the same since his father died," said Claire.

"When was that, three years ago?"

"More like two."

"Before you know it," said Roz, "ten years will pass. You'll be sixty and still married to an overgrown boy."

"He took such great care of his father. Especially at the end."

"I'll give him credit for that," said Roz.

Claire sipped her coffee. "He can't stop wondering what it's all about."

"Like he's the only one?" Roz leaned over the table toward Claire. "He needs a wake-up call!" She squeezed Claire's hand. "It's not the end of the world. Lots of husbands turn into adolescents."

"It's not funny, Roz."

"Scratch the surface of any man and you'll find a boy."

"He has a good heart."

"Maybe . . . but he still needs a good swift kick in the ass."

"What am I supposed to do?"

"Kick him out."

"*What?*"

"It's for his own good—*and* yours. He'll either wake up or he won't. Either way, you'll be better off."

"I can't kick him out. I still love him."

"Yeah, but do you *like* him?"

Claire turned to face the sunlight streaming in through the café window. *Did she really want to answer that question?* She leaned into the sun. After the long winter, she relished the warmth of May, when the weather finally felt more like Atlanta, where she had grown up loving the spring with its blooming azaleas and dogwoods, colorful blossoms and bright sun. Northern New England had no spring. Just a long cold winter, followed by mud season, and then, almost overnight, an explosion of green as summer seemed to arrive instantly.

Kick Wally out? Then what? Claire sighed and ran her fingers through her hair. When she first met Wally, her hair had been long and silky, a light brown streaked blonde by the sun. That was twenty-nine years ago in Greece. Now her hair was short and streaked with gray. Raising two boys would do that to you. Roz told her she should dye her hair, that every woman over forty-five should dye their hair, but Claire refused, partly because Wally said she was a natural beauty who didn't need any phony hair coloring. Roz said Wally just wanted to get into her pants. Roz said lots of things. Sometimes Claire didn't want to hear them. But this time she wondered if Roz had a point. Had she been too patient and kind? Too forgiving and supportive? Wally seemed worse than ever, living in his dream world. Would he really shape up if he were shipped out? *Could she actually do that?*

"I've seen other wives do it," said Roz. "It's always for the best. Things move forward, one way or the other."

"I'm not kicking him out," Claire said.

"You are such a martyr. Such a Catholic schoolgirl—always bending over backwards."

Outside the window, Hancock's Main Street was coming to life at ten in the morning. Cars streamed past, some drivers slowing to look for parking places, others impatient to get through town on their way to the medical center, the food co-op, a business meeting or a trip on the interstate. The sidewalks were filled with college students headed to and from class and other pedestrians on errands or social visits, all of them looking relaxed and happy, enjoying the May sunshine as much as Claire.

"It's just so extreme," she said, turning to Roz. "Kicking him out."

"Extreme situations require extreme action."

Claire sipped her coffee and looked back out the window. A tall, lean figure on a motor scooter was preparing to turn down Main Street, the rider's lanky frame completely out of scale with the machine beneath it, his knees flared out to the side like wings. He wore a black ice hockey helmet and a high school letterman's jacket—maroon with white leather sleeves—both of which looked vaguely familiar to Claire. She couldn't tell at first, but it appeared the rider was carrying something on his back. A bag filled with golf clubs! *Oh, for cryin' out loud.*

"Is that guy crazy?" Roz said, spotting the same rider.

"Maybe," said Claire softly.

The scooter turned the corner onto Main Street, but the rider's head did not turn with it. Instead, it stayed focused on the shapely figure of a lovely coed standing at the crosswalk.

"Oh shit!" Roz cried.

The scooter hit a car pulling out of a parking space, catapulting the rider off his seat. He flew through the air, golf bag on his back, and soared over the car's trunk before disappearing from sight.

"Oh my god!" Roz said. "Did you see that?"

Claire wished she hadn't. She leapt to her feet to make sure the rider was okay.

"What an idiot!" said Roz.

You don't have to tell me, thought Claire.

Roz raced out of the café. Claire thought about joining her, but she was tired of cleaning up messes like this. It was exhausting. She watched the commotion outside, where a pedestrian began directing traffic and two college students scurried over to collect the golf clubs littered across the pavement. The car's driver, an elderly woman with silver hair, had gotten out to see what hit her. She stood by her open door, looking down, a shocked expression on her ruddy face. A middle-aged couple rushed past her to attend to the rider. Doctors, perhaps. The town was full of them, thanks to the Hancock Medical Center.

Roz bustled back into the café.

"It's Wally!" she cried.

"I know," said Claire.

"He's bleeding. On his cheek. But he's talking and moving just fine."

Claire looked out the window, torn between relief and rage. The couple had helped Wally to his feet, each holding an arm, propping him up. He lifted a hand and adjusted his hockey helmet, smiling and nodding at his two attendants. Blood trickled down the side of his face. The woman dabbed the blood with a handkerchief and handed it to Wally, who pressed the cloth against his cheek, stemming the tide. He stepped forward to speak with the little old lady whose car he'd hit.

"Maybe you're right," Claire said with a sigh.

"Of course I'm right," said Roz, patting her hand. "If he wakes up, you can take him back."

"And if he doesn't?"

"There are lots of fish in the sea, sweetheart."

"I'm not interested in other fish."

"Not a big, handsome tuna? With a treasure chest full of money?"

Claire shook her head.

"Look at him," said Roz, looking back out the window. "Is he the luckiest fool ever? He could have been killed."

Claire watched Wally bend down and embrace the little old lady, who smiled at him and patted his shoulder before getting back into her car and driving away. The two college students handed him his golf bag with his clubs, and he shook their hands with a big grin. Then he shook hands with the couple that had helped him and pulled the handkerchief away from his face to show the woman how the blood had stopped. He pressed his hands together in a gesture of thanks and bowed his head. The man who had been directing traffic rolled Wally's scooter over to the sidewalk and put the kickstand down. Wally thanked him, too, while the crowd of people who had witnessed the accident slowly dispersed. Among the last to depart was the gorgeous coed who had triggered the whole incident. Wally smiled at her, too, and Claire was surprised when the girl smiled back. She gave Wally a wave and a coy look, and then she strutted off, swinging her hips like a salsa dancer.

"I guess if you can stop traffic, it goes to your head," said Claire.

Roz snorted. "In twenty years, she'll be married to some jerk who's cheating on her."

"That's a happy thought," said Claire, and then she had a thought of her own: *In twenty years, I'll be seventy-one. Where did all the time go? What am I waiting for?*

"Another coffee?" asked Roz.

"Well, I'm not going out there."

"I'll get you a refill and a chocolate mousse cupcake. They cure everything."

Roz patted her hand and rose from the table. Claire gave her a weak smile and turned back to the window—just in time to see Wally climb on his scooter and ride off, golf clubs on his back, hockey helmet on his head. The bike looked far too small for his tall, angular body. Look at his knees sticking out to the side! It was as if he had taken a child's toy and decided to go on a joyride. And really, wasn't that the whole problem?

2

Claire didn't see Wally again until later that evening, following her massage and energy work with Betsy McArthur. Betsy was eighty-six and resilient as a birch. She might bend, but she never broke. Claire admired her spirit as she battled the aches, pains and other challenges of old age. The appointment ran late, as usual, because Claire always took extra time to fill people in on everything that had occurred during the session.

"Your chakras were all wide open when we finished," she told Betsy.

"Well, that's no surprise. You *are* the best, my dear!"

"I have nothing to do with it," said Claire. "I'm just a facilitator for the energy of the universe."

Betsy always loved to hear if any entities showed up during a session. Deceased relatives, angels, spirit guides. She welcomed them all. "Did we have any visitors today?" she asked.

"Yes," said Claire, "a man showed up. A bit portly, with brown hair and black glasses."

"Did he have a big nose? And small ears with hair spilling out?"

Claire laughed. "Yes, he did seem to have some hair sprouting from his ears. And his nose was quite prominent."

"That sounds like my Andrew. A younger version, of course—when his hair was brown, instead of gray."

"He said he's always with you. Always watching out for you."

"Well, when he was alive, he could be a real nuisance that way. Always sticking his nose into my business. Quite controlling, my Andrew. A good husband, mind you, and a very good provider. But really, quite bossy."

"He thinks you need a dog walker for Casey."

"Oh?"

"And I spoke to Casey about it."

"You did?"

"Yes. He appeared as well."

"Isn't that remarkable? Honestly, I had no idea you could converse with a dog."

"Actually, I've been doing animal communication for a while now, and it's going quite well."

"What did Casey say?"

"He agreed with your husband. A walker would be a good idea."

"I see."

Claire sensed Betsy's apprehension. "It could be good for both of you," she said. "Casey can be pretty hyper from what I gather."

"Well, he *is* an Irish setter. Full of life."

Casey had radiated nervous energy during Claire's chat with him. As Betsy lay peacefully on the table having her chakras dowsed, Casey jumped around in the back of her car, parked down in Claire's driveway, letting out an occasional bark. His unruly behavior led Claire to speak to him very directly. "Cut out the barking," she told him. "And at home, stop racing around knocking priceless heirlooms to the floor. You need to show you're happy in more constructive ways, Casey. And no matter what, do NOT jump on Betsy and knock her over. She is your meal ticket and she loves you dearly."

"You'll always be Casey's first love," Claire assured Betsy. "And his love will just grow stronger if you let him blow off steam on a walk every afternoon."

Betsy looked uncertain.

"You don't want him running around and knocking things over, do you?"

"No," said Betsy. "Last week, he barreled into the kitchen and almost knocked *me* over."

"Then you really should get him a walker. He needs the exercise and will be much better behaved." Claire wrote down a number for Betsy to call—a dog walking service, run by an entrepreneurial Hancock College student who had helped another one of her clients.

"Do NOT wag your tail when the walker arrives," Claire had ordered Casey during their talk. "No licking, no happy noises, no outward expression of affection whatsoever in front of Betsy—do you understand?"

"Yes," responded the Irish setter, with a hyperactive twitch of his head. "I get it."

"Once you're out that door and walking around the pond, wag to your heart's content. Rub up against your walker's leg. Smile. Flirt. But don't make Betsy jealous or you'll be done walking before you can say, 'Where's my leash?'"

"You humans. You make everything so complicated."

Now Betsy looked at Claire with her lively blue eyes and said, "You can tell Casey *and* Andrew that I'll take it under consideration—hiring a walker. But the final decision is mine. Andrew is quite dead, after all, and I am in charge now. And you might remind Casey that he is the dog and I am the master!"

Claire smiled. "I'll pass that along to both of them."

"Don't misunderstand," said Betsy. "I appreciate that Andrew is still watching out for me. But sometimes you have to let go and just move on."

"Yes," said Claire, and thought of Wally. *Could she just let go and move on?*

"Well," said Betsy, patting her knees, standing up. "I'm off to the Hancock Inn for a drink with Luther Carroll. A girl has to stay in circulation, you know. Can't hide your light under a bushel! I'll see you in two weeks, my dear. Don't do anything I wouldn't do."

Claire led Betsy down the sloping path to the lawn, holding her gently by the elbow. Along the way, they passed the labyrinth Claire had built underneath the maple tree just below the studio. Betsy stopped and cast an admiring look at the neat spiral of stones that finished at the base of the tree. Claire had created the labyrinth so her clients could walk through it on their way to and from their sessions. But it was the rare person who took the time to walk through the stone-lined pathway to the center, where they could sit on a bench built around the trunk of the maple tree and contemplate their life. People were on such a tight schedule, coming and going, they lacked the time to walk the circular pathway, quiet themselves and unwind before entering her studio. And then, following a session, they felt so relaxed from their massage and energy work that they felt no need to walk the circle for additional peace and comfort. They were already embracing nirvana.

"What a lovely piece of sculpture," Betsy said, squeezing Claire's hand. "Just remarkable."

"Thank you," said Claire.

"I'd love to walk it with you sometime. When I don't have a date!"

Claire escorted Betsy across the lawn toward her car, Betsy bent over slightly, watching her step. Claire looked up and saw Wally sitting on the deck of the house, a beer in one hand, Casey's collar in the other. He must have just pulled in on his scooter because he still wore his letterman's jacket and his hockey helmet. She could see the scrape on his cheek from his crash that morning.

"I thought your dog might like a little fresh air," he called to Betsy. "He was pacing like a tiger in the back seat."

"Oh!" said Betsy. "Isn't that nice of you." She patted Claire's hand and leaned in. "Isn't he a sweetheart," she cooed.

He can be, thought Claire. *But right now, he's behaving like a knucklehead.* Look at the bands of tape on his fingers—blisters from working on his golf game instead of his business. Lost in a dream world.

Wally stood and tossed a tennis ball for Casey, who tore off after it across the lawn. The setter retrieved the ball and trotted back toward Wally, his eyes shining.

Betsy smiled at Claire and said, "I've kept you at work too late. *You* should be playing with your husband, not my Casey."

"It's fine," said Claire. "It's always good to be with you, Betsy." Claire often wondered what eighty-six would be like for her. Unlike Betsy, she would not have a late husband's money to keep her comfortable. She couldn't massage people forever. Her body was already starting to feel the strain. Fortunately, doing energy work and animal communication was not as physically taxing and still provided welcome benefits for her clients. Claire felt fortunate to have her unusual gifts. She was like her grandmother, Mama Betty, who had the ability to communicate with spirits. But unlike Mama Betty—who said of her talent in her rich Southern accent, "Honey chile, who wants to talk to dead people all the time?"—Claire let this ability flow through her when she did her energy work because the messages were often reassuring for her clients. And her goal was always to help, just as she hoped talking to Casey would help Betsy. Part of her wondered if these abilities would ever abandon her, but another, deeper part of her knew just the opposite was true—they would only grow stronger as she continued to work with them. She might very well be earning a living at ninety, channeling messages for people and their pets, a crazy old lady who could communicate through the ether by approaching the next dimension with an open heart and a healing intention.

Wally led Casey over to the car and tossed the tennis ball into the back seat. The setter dashed in after it, smashing against the far door, and when he reappeared, he stuck his head out the window, triumphantly clutching

The Funny Moon   13

the yellow tennis ball between his teeth. Slobber swung from his gums and he smiled madly at Wally.

Two loonies made for each other, thought Claire.

"Good boy!" Wally said, patting his head.

"I think he likes you," said Betsy.

"Well, I like him," said Wally.

Betsy turned to Claire. "You are the most *adorable* couple. I wish Andrew Jr. and his ex-wife got along so well." She climbed in behind the wheel and looked up at Claire. "But that woman was a scorpion, and he's better off without her." Betsy started her car. "See you in a few weeks!" She waved out the window as she pulled onto the dirt road and accelerated, a column of dust rising in her wake.

"What a character," said Wally, smiling at Claire.

Claire said nothing. She just turned to walk back across the lawn toward the studio.

"Where are you going?" Wally said.

"To clean up."

"I'll cook dinner."

"I may be a while."

"Okay. We'll eat when you come in."

Claire felt her stomach tighten. "I'm not really hungry."

"Then you can have a glass of wine and celebrate with me. I broke 80 today!"

Claire wheeled around and glared at him, her hands on her hips. "I am *not* celebrating your golf game. Joe Morris called earlier. Did you know our insurance is about to be canceled?"

"I talked to Joe this afternoon. It's all taken care of."

"And the bank called, too, *Wallace*. Just before Betsy came. Evidently, you have an overdue payment on a business line of credit? Since when did you have a business line of credit?"

"Since twenty years ago."

"For twenty-five thousand dollars?"

"I had a lot of good years—as you may remember. They never adjusted the limit. And I've never used it—until recently."

"Well, it's overdue." Claire crossed her arms beneath her ample bosom. "I know Cathy Freeman at the bank. It was embarrassing."

Wally shuffled his feet. "I didn't think you needed to know. It's my business account."

"She's calling *our* house!"

Claire heard Roz's voice ringing in her ears. *Kick him out! He'll either wake up or he won't.* Her throat tightened. "When are you going to wake up, Wally?"

"Wake up and smell the coffee?" he said with a smile, trying to coax a laugh. "You know I'm a green tea guy."

"Then wake up and smell the *goddamn* green tea!"

"Yelling will only close your chakras."

"I'm *serious!*"

Wally stopped smiling.

"You ride around on that *stupid* scooter, ogling college girls and crashing into old ladies' cars."

Wally blanched. "Who told you that?"

"I *saw* it. With Roz. We were having coffee in the Dirt Cowboy."

"Oh," said Wally, and hung his head.

"Ever since your father died, you're like a big lost boy."

"I'm not lost."

"Oh no?"

Wally adjusted his hockey helmet and looked up at her. "I'm going to write my novel."

His novel? How many novels had he written? Three? Four? None of them had been published, despite some close calls. "Haven't we already been through this?" she said.

"It's going to be good, Claire," he said. "I've learned what I need to do."

She bit her tongue so hard she nearly tasted blood. After all her support and understanding in the wake of his father's death, after twenty-five years of marriage, after raising the boys together and being patient while he practically stopped working, now he was going to fix everything by writing another novel? When was enough enough? Why was he so removed from reality? He had always been eccentric, and she had always loved him for it. Loved his creativity and his cleverness, his unconventional way of seeing things. Even his looks were unusual. He was handsome, but not in a classic way. His nose was too big, his forehead too high, his ears different sizes, making him look cockeyed once you noticed. But his cheekbones were sharp, his mouth a pleasing shape, and his jawline remained firm and strong at fifty-five. His blue eyes could shine like beacons, filled with intensity, or flicker softly like candles, melting her. Real weapons, Wally's eyes. She didn't dare to look into them now. She needed to stand her ground.

"You know," she said, looking up into the fading evening light, "you're not the only one wondering what's left in life."

Wally tugged on his helmet strap.

"And you're not the only one who's lost someone they love," she added.

"Claire—"

"I'm spending the night in the studio," she said, cutting him off. "I need some space."

"Claire, come on."

Walk away, she told herself, *stick to your guns.* She turned for the studio.

"I'll make you a margarita."

She kept walking.

"We can have a drink and wrestle."

"Wallace!" She turned and glared at him. "I'm *serious!*"

He held up his hands in surrender, and she started walking again. She didn't hear another peep from him until she reached the end of the lawn and turned up the slope to the studio. That's when he called, "I love you!"

She waved a hand behind her, shooing him away, blinking back tears. Marching up the slope, she was determined not to let him see her cry. Once she entered the studio and closed the door behind her, she gave in. Tears poured down her cheeks as she collapsed onto the daybed. *Oh Wallace! You big, stupid, confounding fool! Don't make me do this!*

3

After a long, restless night, Claire woke exhausted, dreading what came next. In her darkest hours, she had decided Roz was right—she needed to kick Wally out. Otherwise, what would change? She would only continue to feel frustrated and, ultimately, be pulled down with him. She rose from the daybed, having slept in her clothes, haggard and anxious. *You can do this.* Stepping over to a window, she straightened her hair in the reflection and was jarred by what she saw—streaks of gray, bags under her eyes, a slight bulge under her chin. She tapped the beginnings of the double chin with her fingers, eager to make it vanish. She was growing older. Was she growing any wiser?

Through the windowpane, she saw Wally emerge from the house with a large duffle bag slung over his shoulder and carrying a big cardboard box in his hands. She watched him put the box and the bag into the bed of his pickup truck and step into the garage to find a long plank. He lowered the tailgate and made a ramp with the board, and then he wheeled his scooter into the bed of the truck and secured it. He added his golf bag to the cargo and returned to the house.

Was he doing what it looked like?

She hurried out of the studio, down the slope and across the lawn, her mind racing and heart pounding. *He couldn't be.* He came back out, carrying his laptop and a power cord, his golf shoes and a toilet kit.

"What are you doing?" she said.

"I'm leaving. I'm going to Bear's."

"You can't leave! Not before I kick you out!"

He climbed into his truck and closed the door. "Watch me."

"I've been so patient with you, Wally!"

"No, Claire—you've been so disappointed," he said with a wounded look. "And yet, despite your imperfections, I still love you."

He put the truck in gear and pulled away.

"Wallace! You are *not* leaving!" she cried as he headed down the driveway. "I am kicking you *out!*"

He stuck his head out the window. "Beat you to the punch!" He honked twice and drove out of sight.

She swung her foot, kicking a vicious spray of gravel in his direction. *Go to Bear's! What do I care!*

Half an hour later, Claire found herself standing at the entrance of the labyrinth, a half-eaten chocolate bar in one hand, a cup of peppermint tea in the other. Filling the kettle, her hand had trembled so terribly that water splashed everywhere and she dropped the kettle into the sink, metal clanging on metal, making a racket—just like the noise in her head and the commotion in her heart. *Beat you to the punch!* How like Wally to seize the upper hand just when she finally had the courage to throw him out. He pulled the rug out right from under her! How many times had he undercut her over the years? With small things and seismic shifts? Like wanting to leave the ad agency in Boston right when she was in line for a promotion at the Museum of Science. Yes, she was also pregnant with Josh, which complicated matters further. But still. It was all about Wally and his desire to write novels instead of ads, and the irony was, after moving back to his hometown, he still wrote ads because he still had to make a living. But he also got up early and wrote his novels, and one was good enough to secure an agent and another was optioned for film. But no film was ever made and no books were ever published. They were responsible for raising two boys, so Wally built up his business and Claire went to massage school. Like everyone else, they compromised. The dreams of their twenties shifted into the goals of their thirties, which slid into the realities of their forties, and now, in their fifties, with the boys grown and gone, with Wally's father dead, somehow all hell had broken loose. Whatever happened to the man she married? The Wally full of hope and promise? The funny, charming guy who was able to read her mind, sense her feelings and make her laugh? His touch could still send an electric shock through her— which was why he suggested wrestling yesterday, as she marched angrily to the office. He knew how often this magical connection had saved him in the past. It was a form of chemical warfare, the way they blended in bed. *How aggravating!* Looking back at the forks in the road, she wondered how their lives might be different now. She hadn't wanted to throw him out. She just wanted her old Wally back.

She stood at the entrance of the labyrinth and set her intention: 'Bring me clarity and give me peace.' But as she walked the spiral path, instead of growing calmer, her mind began to race. Tension crept into her neck and shoulders. And clarity and peace felt as far away as China.

'Let go and let god,' she began to repeat like a mantra. 'Let go and let god.' She kept walking and soon heard herself thinking, *Let go and let Wallace get his act together. Let go and let me win the lottery. Let go and let the garage burn down so we can file an insurance claim and replace that decrepit piece of crap!*

She stopped walking altogether. She took a deep breath, followed by a sip of tea, and gazed up at the maple branches overhead. 'Calm down,' she told herself. 'Take a deep breath. *Relax.*'

She started walking again, and when she reached the center of the labyrinth, she sat on the bench at the base of the tree. Inhaling deeply, she concentrated on circulating her energy in the microcosmic orbit inside her body—breathing in through her perineum and lifting the breath up her spinal cord, the back of her neck, and over her crown . . . before exhaling slowly and guiding the energy gently down, over her face, through her throat and her chest, into her stomach and down to the base of her coccyx, where the whole circuit started again with her next inhalation. She launched the orbit over and over, but it only resulted in circulating her confusion and aggravating her anxiety.

Frustrated, she looked up at the leaves shimmering in the late morning sun and suddenly saw an image of her grandmother—the indomitable Mama Betty, the source of her ability to communicate with the Other Side. Mama Betty wore one of her silver wigs, set slightly askew on her large head, as if she had grabbed it off a hat rack on her way out the door. Stolidly built, with the jowls of a bulldog, she wore a mottled mix of pancake and rouge, and her lips were covered with a thick coat of bright red lipstick. Behind her cat-eye glasses, her deep brown eyes smiled at Claire.

"Lookin' mighty blue there, shugah pie," her grandmother said, in her sweet Southern drawl. "Why the long face?"

"I don't know," said Claire.

"Oh yes you do, honey chile."

Claire knew she could never fool her grandmother and said, "Do you remember the time we were driving in your car, and you were mad at Papa, and I asked you if you ever thought about divorcing him?"

"Shore do, sweet cakes. Sunny day, right about noon. Smell of dogwoods in the air. You were driving on Lullwater Road."

Claire recalled the scene like it was yesterday.

Mama Betty continued, "You were wearing one of your pretty little shirts with no bra. My, my, you had a pair of titties! Not that I approved of you being braless. No sir. But you were the baby of the family and been through enough already, losing your momma. What was leaving your bra off gonna do? Turn you into a harlot?"

"I don't know," said Claire. "The sense of freedom was pretty liberating."

"When I was younger, they showed women on the television news *burnin'* their bras. Your Papa said, 'Betty, you burn your bra, we'll have a three-alarm fire!'" Mama Betty threw her head back and laughed.

"How *is* Papa?" Claire asked.

"Oh, he's cookin' away. You know how he is. Chitlins and gravy, sweet potata soo-flay, chicken with giblets, peach cobblah, homemade vanilla ice cream. He feeds twenty people every Sunday, just like always. Finds the strays and fills their bellies." Mama Betty nodded.

"Are there strays in heaven?"

"Oh, there's strays everywhere, shugah pie. Not everyone has a big happy family."

Claire considered her single friends, the people who were estranged from family members, the clients who were closer to their pets than to their adult children. She thought of Wally and said, "I've been thinking a lot about what you said about Papa that day in the car."

"I remember!" Mama Betty said and pointed a finger at the sky. "'Divorce, never. Murder, yes!'"

"Did you really mean it?"

"Oh, yeah—wouldah killed him, given him mouth-to-mouth and killed him again if I could. That man would drive me so crazy, I could plead insanity and *win!*"

"Wally is driving me crazy, too."

"Would have poisoned Papa's food. But he did all the cookin'."

"I don't cook much, either," said Claire, thinking how she would miss Wally's dinners.

"These days, women can leave a marriage just like that." Mama Betty snapped her fingers. "Wasn't like that in my day. No sir, you had to *work* at it. Marriage was for *life.*"

"Well, it shouldn't be a life sentence."

"Fair 'nuff, honey chile. That Wally, he's goin' through his trials no matter *what* you do. Besides, you know what they say. You want to change someone, change *yourself.*"

And with that, Mama Betty blew her a kiss and vanished into the ether.

4

Wally found Bear sitting on his deck overlooking the Connecticut River, a laptop on his knees, a bottle of beer on the armrest of his Adirondack chair. Bob Dylan's "Knockin' on Heaven's Door" played from a small speaker.

"Henrik!" called Bear, using Wally's nickname for looking like the great Swedish golfer, Henrik Stenson. "Been practicing?"

"Yeah. But I didn't hit it like Henrik."

"Who does?" said Bear with a chortle, looking a lot like his namesake—his large head tilted back, his nose raised as if smelling traces of honey. A layer of fat gave the impression that he was soft and cuddly, but Bear was the strongest person Wally knew, capable of lifting the rear end of a golf cart off the ground. He was also capable of hitting prodigious drives of 300 yards, although how they flew and where they landed was completely random. He looked younger than Wally, even though he was two years older. Claire said this was because he had never experienced the stress of parenting. Sure, he had pressures running his successful T-shirt business, but none of them compared to ushering a child through life.

"I brought you a few beers," Wally said, sitting down next to his friend. He opened an IPA and released a deep sigh. Sitting on Bear's deck was always soothing—and he needed soothing after what had happened with Claire. His friend's place was a welcome respite from the world, perched on a slope above the Connecticut River that divided New Hampshire and Vermont. Bear's property covered a few acres on the New Hampshire shore, half of it a rolling field of tall grass where Bear mowed a wide path down to the riverbank. By the water, a stand of white birch glimmered against the surface of the river, and next to the trees, wide stone steps led to a small dock, where Bear moored an old Boston Whaler and two kayaks. The river flowed wide and easy in this stretch, 150 yards to the Vermont shore. On the far bank an old dairy operation had been converted into a horse farm by a wealthy couple. Local riders boarded their thoroughbreds there and rode in equestrian events even in winter, thanks to a large barn covered with solar panels. Split-rail fences lined a portion of the hillside where the horses grazed. A Hilton for horses, Wally called it. Still, what would the area look like without the land trust? Certainly not the picture postcard he admired while sipping his beer. He loved Bear's beautiful backyard and its pristine view. Maybe he would start to feel better here, away from Claire's deep disappointment in him.

"What happened to your face?" said Bear, eyeing Wally's scrape.

"I took a little tumble on the scooter."

Bear shook his head. "This isn't St. Bart's, man. That thing is dangerous."

"I know," said Wally. "But it's fun."

"Not if you get hit by a car."

Wally took a drink of his beer. "What's wrong with having a little fun? Pretty soon, we'll be in some nursing home, drooling on ourselves. Wondering where the time went. If we can remember anything."

"Thank you for stopping by, Doctor Doom."

"We're in the third period, man. What do you want to do before you die?"

Bear turned his laptop screen toward Wally. "Hit my driver like Sam Snead."

Clearly, Bear wasn't in the mood for the big questions. The big questions could be depressing. And a lot of good they had done Wally over the past few years. Now he had no place to live. Would Bear let him stay in the garage apartment? Several guys had taken refuge here over the years, some kicked out by their wives, others between jobs or marriages. Bear had been Wally's friend since grade school, when Wally's dad came to teach English at Hancock College, and Wally didn't know a soul. Chubby and kind, Bear made the effort to befriend him, and their bond grew deeper as they played hockey together from peewees through high school—Bear the stalwart defenseman in front of Wally, the acrobatic goalie. Being a goalie suited Wally's observant nature. He could stand back and watch the flow of play and then react as needed. Not unlike being a writer. And you had to be a little crazy to be a hockey goalie.

Wally finally broke the silence by announcing, "Claire kicked me out."

Bear looked stunned. "What?"

"She says I need to wake up and smell the green tea."

"Shit . . ." Bear rubbed his chin with his meaty fingers. "I didn't see that coming. I thought she was bucking for sainthood."

"Ha ha," said Wally.

"Most wives would have kicked you out a long time ago."

"So I was wondering, any chance I could stay in your garage apartment for a while?"

Bear took a pull on his beer and sat quietly, looking past Wally toward the river.

"If it's bad timing," said Wally, "no worries. I'll find someplace else."

After a long pause, Bear turned to him. "Fine. But you can't hang around here all day, sitting on the deck, staring at your navel. Claire will kill me."

"Kill *you?*"

"Yeah, she's my friend, too. And I'm Josh's *godfather.*" Bear pointed his beer bottle at Wally. "So if you're gonna stay here, you're gonna work. And I don't mean on your golf game."

"No problem," said Wally. "I'm going to work on a novel."

Bear slapped his palm against the arm of his chair with such force Wally thought he might splinter the wood. "A novel?" He threw his head back and snorted, "You think *that's* gonna solve anything?"

"It might."

"Jesus Christ." Bear shook his head.

Wally took a long pull on his beer. If he argued with Bear, he might not be allowed to stay, which would mean being kicked out of two homes in one day. And if he agreed that writing his novel was crazy, he would have no power at all. He needed to take a different tack.

"You're going to be in the book," he told his friend.

Bear eyed him. *Who didn't want to be in a book?*

"I don't have the whole story mapped out yet," said Wally, "but you're definitely going to play a major role."

Bear leaned forward, looking intrigued.

"I mean, look at you—you're a great character. Gruff on the outside, soft on the inside. Thoughtful, yet a man of action, strong as an ox. You're complex without being neurotic. Successful without being arrogant. You've got star power, Bear."

He could see his friend warming to the idea. "And if they make a movie from the book," said Wally, setting the hook, "I could see George Clooney playing your part."

Bear puffed out his already prodigious chest. "So how long is this gonna take, writing your novel?"

"I can write it over the summer, if I don't have anything else to do."

"But you still have a few accounts, don't you?"

"I can do them in my sleep."

"Yeah, that's why your clients are firing you."

"See! Right there! That's what I'm talking about. That's what makes you such a great character! Just when people think you're on my side—*pow!* You kick me right in the nuts."

Bear hoisted his broad body out of the deep confines of his Adirondack chair. "Okay. You can have the summer. But that's it. I don't want to get in the middle of your marital issues. And if you lie around all day, you're coming to work for me."

"Printing T-shirts?"

All of a sudden, moving in with Bear looked worse than getting kicked out by Claire. He couldn't print T-shirts all day. When would he have time to write his novel? He'd be juggling too much, just like in his halcyon advertising days, when he had a roster of a dozen or more clients. Looking back, he wondered how he ever found the time and energy to handle so many accounts. Plus help out with the boys. No wonder he gave up writing novels and burned out on advertising. He'd been out straight for over two decades. What was wrong with taking the time to fulfill a dream before death knocked on the door?

"This isn't a free ride," said Bear, towering over him. "And there *are* ground rules. You get your own food and drink. You keep the apartment clean. If I have company, you stay out of the house. And you don't tell the other guys who comes and goes. They're not always beauty queens. Or single."

"Got it."

"It's not like there's a parade or anything. But discretion is the better part of valor. *Capiche?*"

"Capiche."

"You can thank me when you're rich and famous," said Bear. "And you're back with Claire."

Wally stood up and extended his hand, praying he wouldn't have to print

T-shirts. "Thanks a lot, Bear."

Bear shook his hand with a viselike grip. "Just don't fuck up."

The next afternoon, after his first foray into writing his novel while seated on Bear's deck, Wally stood on the 1st tee at Hancock Country Club with Bear, Danny Bryan and Harry Thrall for their regular Wednesday golf game. He felt a bit groggy because he had fallen asleep in the sun after writing three paragraphs of lifeless prose and feeling stonewalled. He rode his scooter to the club, hoping the fresh air would revive him. Passing the college green teeming with students in various stages of undress—so happy to see the sun!—he told himself to keep his eyes on the road and off the pretty girls. His nap had featured an unsettling dream in which he rode up and down Main Street on his scooter, naked except for his hockey helmet and unable to escape the center of town, while everyone stared at him. Desperate, he turned down a side street, where he ran into a traffic jam due to road construction. Out of nowhere, the lovely coed who had caused his accident climbed on the back of his scooter and wrapped her arms around his bare torso. She ran her hands up and down his chest. His groin stirred. She licked his neck and sucked on his earlobe, her fingers circling his navel as she rubbed her firm breasts against his back. His penis swelled. She explored his navel and pulled out a piece of lint as thick and as wide as he pulled off the dryer filter whenever he washed Claire's flannel massage sheets. The coed shrieked and threw the lint in his face, jumped off the scooter and disappeared. A policewoman directing traffic pointed at him and blew her whistle—his high school German teacher! "Your homework! Where is your homework?" she cried. Wally pulled his scooter onto the sidewalk, frantic to flee, but a young man with five dogs on leashes attached to his belt blocked his way. Wally beeped his high-pitched horn. The dog walker held up a water bottle and sprayed him in the face as the dogs barked and snapped at him. One brown-and-white Jack Russell terrier leapt for his groin, his teeth bared. Just before being dismembered, Wally snapped awake, breathless and sweating. He staggered off the deck into Bear's kitchen and rinsed his face. *What the hell!*

Now he stood on the 1st tee and looked toward the putting green, still feeling discombobulated, and spotted Oscar Bradley Jr., of Bradley

Associates walking toward him. Junior had been a forward on Wally's high school hockey team and his client for the past fourteen years.

"Hey, Wally," called Junior. "You got a second?"

Wally wondered what was up and met Junior at the far end of the tee box.

"Where were you this morning?" asked Junior in a low voice, looking over Wally's shoulder at his playing partners. "Hitting balls?"

"No," said Wally. He had been out on the Connecticut River, soon after Bear left for work, cruising in the Boston Whaler. Hoping to find inspiration for his writing. "I was, ah, working on a new project."

"Well, you missed our annual corporate meeting."

Wally's heart flipped. *Shit!* He was scheduled to present the coming year's advertising plan to the management team. But with everything that had happened with Claire and moving to Bear's, he had completely forgotten.

"Oh, Junior . . . I am *so* sorry!" he said. "I got some unexpected news and I completely spaced it out."

"Dad was *not* happy."

Wally could only imagine. Even in a good mood, Oscar Sr. could be a challenge. When he got angry, he looked like an irate beaver, gnashing his big buck teeth. Junior looked more like Peter Cottontail, a kinder, gentler big-toothed creature, eager to please and always smiling. Together, father and son operated the largest real estate agency in the Lower Valley.

"It's the third meeting you've missed since January," said Junior. "You're not even going through the motions anymore."

What could Wally say?

"Dad wants to hire Nomad. And this time, I can't stop him." Junior's big front teeth dented his bottom lip. "I'm sorry, Wally."

"It's not your fault."

"We appreciate everything you've done. At least I do. It's been a hell of a run."

"Yeah," said Wally, surprised he wasn't more upset to see it end. He would miss the monthly retainer, but on the plus side, he'd have more time for his novel.

"You going to be okay?" asked Junior.

"Yeah, I'll be fine."

Oscar clapped him on the shoulder. "If there's anything I can do, just let me know." He turned and walked back toward the clubhouse. Wally stood next to the tee box feeling the ground beneath him wobble. Or was it his knees?

"What was that all about?" said Bear from the other end of the tee box.

"Oh nothing," said Wally. "Just a little Bradley Associates business."

Bear eyed him skeptically. "Looked pretty serious."

"Real estate is a serious business. Especially when demand exceeds supply."

Wally played so badly on the back nine that on the 16th tee Bear said, "Henrik, come on. Claire hasn't filed for divorce."

Harry and Danny looked at Bear with surprise.

"What are you talking about?" said Harry, shifting on his feet in his bowlegged way.

"Wally moved into the garage apartment last night," said Bear.

"The home of banished husbands," said Danny. "You're an exile!"

"It's not permanent," said Wally, his face suddenly hot.

"It's definitely not permanent," said Bear. "Regardless of what happens."

"I can't believe it," said Harry. "You and Claire . . . you're like peanut butter and jelly."

"I got kicked out by my first wife," said Danny in his deep, smoke-cured baritone, reaching into his golf bag for his one-hitter and a lighter. "Of course, I was kind of fucked up at the time. Weighed about 135 pounds. But hey, that's what happens when you take a lot of black beauties." He laughed, his bushy eyebrows dancing, his tall, lanky body shaking. He patted his well-cultivated wine belly and lit his torpedo pot pipe. A cloud of pungent reefer smoke encircled his head like a halo.

With a sincere look of concern on his face, Harry said, "Did you see this coming, Wally? Any clue at all?"

"We've had some issues, but I didn't think we'd get separated. Not during golf season, anyway. We hardly see each other as it is."

Harry was an ER nurse who had been dumped for a doctor by his wife years ago. Now, at fifty, he was recently remarried and constantly working out to keep up with his younger wife. "Is there another guy?" he asked.

The thought had never occurred to Wally. "I don't think so."

"There's usually another guy," said Harry, "even if they don't say so."

"You don't know that," said Danny.

"I'd be surprised if Claire wants another guy—after living with Doctor

Doom here," said Bear. He stuck his tee in the ground. "Are we playing golf or what?"

Bear addressed his ball and swung like Hercules. It seemed to brush a cloud and fly forever, landing perfectly in the fairway.

"Paging Doctor Drive," said Harry.

"Quite impressive," said Danny. "Nice to see you in bounds for a change."

The others hit their tee shots and marched down the fairway toward their balls. Danny came alongside Wally and said, "The Professor never said anything to me about you and Claire."

"Claire may not have told her yet," said Wally.

"You want me to keep quiet?"

"Tell her whatever you want."

"She's going to take Claire's side," said Danny. "You know that's how it works."

"I know. But it's not like we're done forever." Wally flashed Danny a determined look.

Danny Boy's bushy eyebrows shot up and the corners of his eyes crinkled into a smile. "Okay! Glad to hear it. Just a little summer holiday, eh? I suppose we could all use a little spousal sabbatical now and then. Makes the heart grow fonder."

"Let's hope so," said Wally.

"Of course, I'm a kept man."

At some point in every round, Danny had to find a time to remind the others he had recently retired from his forestry job, largely because the Professor, who was ten years his junior, had been awarded tenure in the drama department at Hancock College.

"She has a job for life," Danny Boy bragged when the news became public back in February. "They can't fire her. It's all about academic freedom. There's really nothing like it, being a tenured professor. Quite a gig."

They reached their balls in the fairway and hit their second shots onto the green. As they began walking again, Danny asked Wally, "So how's business?"

"Couldn't be better," said Wally, his voice laced with sarcasm. *Just lost another account. The only one left now is Hughes Auto.*

"The Professor says there's a job in the development office for a senior writer."

"Thanks, but I've got another plan."

"And what might that be?"

"You'll see."

Danny cocked his head, and then his eyes lit up. "Okay! I get it. You don't want to tell me because you think I'll tell the Professor and the Professor will tell Claire, and then you'll be even more screwed!"

"Claire already knows."

"Whoa! I am *totally* confused." Danny shook his head. "Must be time for another hitter."

He pulled out his torpedo pipe and it made a whistling sound as he lit it. The sweet smell of weed drifted past Wally. Smoking pot was Danny's form of self-medication, ingested in small doses throughout the day. His older brother had been a schizophrenic, and Danny had told Wally he felt lucky to dodge his brother's illness. He waved his whistle at Wally one day and confessed, "Who knows what I'd be like without this stuff." Scared of passing along the schizophrenic family gene, he never wanted to have children. The Professor, to her credit, never pushed him and directed all her nurturing energy into her students, who adored her.

"I'm going to write a novel," Wally told Danny.

"And Claire knows this?"

"Yup."

Danny Boy chuckled. "You *are* crazy." He took a second hit of his whistle, adding another small cloud to the sky.

"No more crazy than sitting in meetings all day at the college. Let's have a meeting to cover what happened in the previous meeting and discuss what we'll do in the next meeting." Wally couldn't do it. Especially the older he got. He could be one doctor's appointment away from potential disaster. Wasn't everyone over the age of fifty-five? Look at his dad. Incredibly fit and active at seventy, playing tennis, riding his bike, when his aorta tore without warning. Emergency surgery saved his life, but it was all downhill after that. Strokes. Wheelchair. Congestive heart failure. Death. Who saw that coming? Fine one day, fucked the next. You know what's crazy? Thinking you'll live forever.

"If you want to put me in your book," said Danny, "by all means, go ahead. Every story needs a stoner." He pulled a packet of peanut M&M's from his golf bag and waved them at Wally.

"No, thanks," said Wally. "I'm good."

Danny Boy sniggered. "Yeah, we'll see about that."

5

Claire didn't answer Roz's texts or calls for two days, as she coped with the aftershocks of Wally's departure. She needed time and space, not Roz in her face. But by the third day, she couldn't ignore Roz's barrage any longer and called her after breakfast.

"Finally!" Roz said, picking up. "I was about to drive out there and see if you were still alive."

"Alive and kicking," said Claire.

"Did you kick Wally out?"

"I was going to, but then he moved out."

"You two. You don't do anything normally."

"Now I feel guilty."

"Oh my god!" said Roz. "Those nuns did *such* a number on you. This is *not* your fault!"

"What will the boys think?"

Claire had been worried about how Josh and Jack would take the separation. She told herself they probably wouldn't be too surprised. Like her, they had seen the change in Wally after his father's death, each commenting on his increasingly obsessive, dreamy behavior. "What's with the scooter, anyway?" Josh had asked during a visit early in the fall. "And the hockey helmet?" In February, Jack had texted her from California, "Is Dad wearing out the carpet, putting all day? Ha ha ha!"

"The boys will understand," said Roz. "They're not idiots, like their father."

"Wally's not an idiot. He's been a great dad."

"Well, he hasn't been setting a very good example lately—lost in never-never land."

"He's always done a lot of cooking. And laundry. And vacuuming and shoveling and—"

"Because he doesn't work!"

"Last week, he told me I looked more beautiful than the day we met."

"Oh, for *Chrissakes!*"

"It was so sweet."

"And you probably let him slip right into your pants."

Claire didn't answer, remembering how she and Wally had wound up on the living room couch, making love in broad daylight like a couple of newlyweds.

"Listen to me," said Roz. "You are in charge of your own destiny. You need to stop worrying about Wally and the boys and start thinking of *yourself.*"

"I don't make enough money to live alone."

"Then have Wally pay some bills."

Claire sighed, wondering how he would ever do that with an overdue business line of credit.

"I can fix you up with a wealthy man," said Roz.

"I don't want a wealthy man! I want my old Wally back."

"And I want world peace. What are you doing later this afternoon?"

"I'm going to tai chi."

"Go tomorrow and come canoeing with me. I'll meet you at the Ledyard Canoe Club at four thirty."

"But I always go to tai chi on Wednesday."

"Well . . . maybe it's time to start mixing things up. Turn over a new leaf."

Claire looked out the studio window at the blooming maple tree, its pale green leaves slowly unfolding in the May sunshine.

"This will be good therapy for you. Meet me at four thirty!" Roz commanded and hung up.

Claire pulled into the parking lot of the canoe club after running late with a client. Stepping out of her car, she could have been mistaken for a runner with her long legs and lean body that was well-toned from her tai chi and massage work. Wally always complimented her on how well she had aged. A few years back, when her hair started turning gray and she talked about dyeing it, he objected.

"It's phony," he said. "Like men who get hair replacements. You're gorgeous just the way you are."

"Flattery will get you everything," she told him.

"I sure hope so. It's been two weeks."

"It has not."

"Okay, nine days, six hours, forty-seven minutes and . . . ," he looked down at his watch, "21 . . . 22 . . . 23."

She spanked him.

"Hey!" He spanked her back and squeezed her butt. "You have a great ass, you know that?"

And off they went, their lustful wrestling match lasting as many rounds as it took for each of them to be declared a winner. The spark when they touched still jolted her. Making love with Wally never got old and neither did hearing him call her a natural beauty.

Now, though, walking toward the canoe club dock, she did not feel beautiful at all. She felt wrung out from her new reality and wondered if Wally would ever wise up to his.

"Claire! Over here!" Roz waved from the dock, standing next to the biggest canoe she had ever seen. A solidly built, bald man with a deep tan knelt beside her, holding the canoe by its gunnel.

"We're taking a war canoe ride!" Roz said.

Was she crazy? A pair of NFL linemen couldn't paddle that monstrosity upstream. It was three times the size of a regular canoe. She and Roz stood no chance. As she continued walking, though, the full dock came into view, revealing a cluster of men and women milling about, organizing paddles and life jackets, coolers and backpacks, and she realized it wouldn't be just her and Roz going for a paddle.

"Come meet everyone!" called Roz, dressed in her own version of canoeing gear—a sleeveless wetsuit top unzipped to her sternum like a Bond girl, her breasts on the verge of spilling out, a pair of linen shorts clinging to her thighs like vellum. Sunglasses rested on the crown of her head, holding her long, brown hair in place. She stepped over and extended a hand, helping Claire onto the dock.

"I was beginning to wonder if you were going to stand me up," Roz said.

Claire leaned in and said in a low voice, "I thought it was just going to be the two of us."

"It *is* the two of us," said Roz. "Plus two other women and some eligible men. Except for Vin Diesel." Roz eyed the tanned, well-built, bald man. "He's mine."

Roz grabbed her arm and marched her over to the group. "Everyone, this is my friend, Claire Scott. She just lost her husband."

"*Roz!*"

"Well, in a manner of speaking. He's not dead. Just exiled. He needs to shape up."

Vin Diesel laughed as if on cue, clearly eager to unzip the rest of Roz's wetsuit. "Been there! Told that!"

"See," said Roz to Claire, "you're not alone. The world is full of troubled relationships. The secret is not to dwell on them."

A man stepped forward to introduce himself.

"Hi, I'm Roger Black. I played hockey with Wally at Hancock High. What a great goalie. Sorry to hear he's in the penalty box." He cackled at his own joke.

"Okay, everybody," called Vin. "Grab a paddle and take a seat. It's war canoe time!"

People began climbing into the canoe. Claire considered climbing back into her car, but Roz had a death grip on her arm. "This will be fun."

"You're impossible."

"And you love me for it." Roz spun her around. "Sit up front, next to Max McClure. The one in the fedora."

Claire looked at a man who was a bit older, with gray hair on his temples, and sharp, patrician features. He had a deep tan and wore clothes more suited for a luncheon at the club than a canoe ride up the river.

"Roz, for the last time, I am *not* interested in another man."

"Oh, don't be silly. I'm going to ask Max for a big donation for Doggone Right. We just need to court him a bit first."

"*We?*"

"He's going to *love* you." Roz patted her on the butt, like a coach sending a player into the game. "Just think of the dogs, honey. And enjoy yourself."

6

———————————

As Claire took her seat alongside Max McClure, she had a flashback to a canoe trip she and Wally had taken nearly thirty years ago here on the Connecticut River. The two of them were engaged at the time and living together in Boston. They came up for Memorial Day weekend to join Bear and Julie and two other couples on a three-day, two-night canoe trip starting in Woodsville, where they put four canoes into the river just below a series of rapids, loaded on coolers of food and beer, tents and sleeping bags, and launched downstream for Hancock. There was no whitewater ahead of them, just the broad, flat expanse of the Connecticut, which ranged from seventy to two hundred yards wide as the river snaked its way south past farms and fields, homes and camps, old settlements and present-day towns. Carried by the current as much as by their paddling, the four young couples enjoyed a leisurely trip, swapping stories and singing songs, jumping into the water to swim and camping at night on the riverbank, where they lit campfires and cigars, drank beer and gazed at the stars. On the final day, they strapped all four canoes together and Bear constructed a makeshift mast and sail, using a tree branch and a tent to catch the steady breeze. Their flotilla of fun sailed downstream, everyone relishing the simple wonder of being alive on the water under sunny skies. *How time flies*, thought Claire. It seemed like another lifetime. Of the four couples, only she and Wally had married. Two other couples split, and seven years later Bear lost Julie to a rare form of cancer and was never quite the same.

"Do you canoe a lot?" asked Max McClure, breaking Claire's reverie as they began paddling upstream.

"Oh, no. I haven't been canoeing in a long time," she said.

"Well, you look like an Olympic paddler. You're in terrific shape."

Claire felt her face flush. "Thank you."

"Your arms look stronger than mine."

She knew her arms were strong from massaging, but were they too big?

"Roz says you give the best massage in the Upper Valley." Max stopped paddling and rubbed the right side of his neck. "I have *the* worst neck pain." He looked at her the way people often did when they heard she was a massage therapist—hoping she might treat him then and there.

Claire did not rise to the bait. "I'm sorry to hear that," she said.

"Perhaps you can give me a quick massage when we reach the picnic area."

"The picnic area?"

"Yes, we're going upriver to eat in a field. Roz didn't tell you?"

"No, she really didn't tell me anything."

"Well, she told us *all* about you. And I must say, she was right. You are a *very* attractive woman."

Claire blushed again.

Max returned to paddling, and Claire watched him out of the corner of her eye. The rhythm and power of his strokes belied his age and elegant attire, not to mention his sore neck. She spotted a tan line above his thin ankles and shuddered for an instant, wondering if he, too, was a golfer.

He turned to her. "I know your banished husband."

"You do?"

"Yes, I used to own several radio stations in the area, and Wally's commercials were always very creative. Better than many of the spots from the big New York ad agencies. Quite a talented fellow."

Claire paddled and said, "He has his strengths."

"And we all have our weaknesses," said Max with a smile. "I love being on the water, don't you? It's so soothing."

He looked back up the river and paddled. Dressed like a dandy, he oozed a life of leisure—clearly, an excellent target for Roz's Doggone Right fundraising campaign. Claire really should pitch in.

"I'll look at your neck up at the picnic area," she said, "I'm also happy to switch sides if you want."

"Thank you," he said. "So far, so good." He removed his fedora, revealing a thick shock of silver hair, and waved it over his head. "Lift your hat into the air if you are happy to meet Claire!"

He turned to her and beamed. "Such a pleasure on this lovely day."

Claire didn't know what to say to this eccentric fellow, so she just smiled and paddled. It was surprisingly hot for early May. She had begun to sweat, and her arms ached from the effort, made more strenuous from having given two massages earlier in the day. How much longer could she keep rubbing bodies? She wasn't getting any younger. What had Roz gotten her into? Despite feeling out of place, she liked being on the river. She always loved looking at the water on her drives back and forth between East Heifer, Vermont, and the college in Hancock, New Hampshire. As she drove along Route 5 on the Vermont shore, the river reflected the seasons—from pewter and snow-covered ice to a shimmering blue ribbon or a slithering green snake. Being down here on the water provided an entirely different perspective, one of weeds and floating logs nestled below the daily din above. She watched a flock of swallows flit and dart just above the surface. A fish jumped, sending a ripple across the water.

"Look!" called Vin Diesel from his seat in the stern. "A hawk." He pointed above the Vermont shore, where a large bird circled over an open field.

The river and its shoreline contained activities all their own, and Claire wondered why she didn't spend more time immersed in its magic. Maybe she would now, as this new chapter of her life unfolded. Maybe she would finally get a kayak and explore the Connecticut River and the lakes and ponds that dotted the region. Being on the water felt so soothing, unlike life with Wally.

Behind her, Roger Black was doing more flirting than paddling, chatting up two women in the row behind him. He opened a large magnum of champagne and started the picnic early, pouring bubbly for the two ladies. In front of Claire, two men argued about Ledyard, a Hancock College graduate and legendary explorer, whose name graced the canoe club.

"He paddled the Connecticut all the way down to its origin at Long Island Sound," said one with thick hair sprouting out of the back of his T-shirt collar.

"That's not the origin, that's the mouth," said the other, a small wiry man with pale skin and a floppy, wide-brimmed hat. "The origin is way up in northern New Hampshire. That's why we're paddling *upstream,* Einstein."

"Don't call me Einstein, you peckerhead."

"Get your facts straight."

"Boys! Boys!" Roz called from her seat in front of Vin. "It's a lovely afternoon. Relax and have some champagne!"

The magnum of bubbly was passed forward with plastic cups, and Claire watched Einstein and Peckerhead fill their glasses. Max had stopped paddling to rub his sore neck, while Claire continued to dig into the water, her arms and shoulders feeling the strain. Was anyone else paddling? She turned around and saw Roz making a token effort in her Bond girl outfit, alternating between paddling and drinking champagne. Meanwhile, Vin Diesel stroked from the stern, his face crimson with the effort.

"Enough!" he cried. "Everyone, finish your champagne and start paddling! I am not an engine. Claire is the only person pulling her weight."

"What about me?" said Roz, holding up her champagne, her pinky extended.

Vin hesitated and then found his tongue. "Well . . . you don't weigh very much, do you?"

Roz beamed and fluffed her hair. "I'll bet you say that to all the girls. I quit eating ice cream because it goes right to my butt!"

"Champagne goes right to my head," said one of the women.

Her girlfriend giggled. "Me too!"

"Everyone paddle!" commanded Vin. "You too, Max. And don't give me that sore neck bullshit. I saw you playing tennis this morning, and you were serving just fine."

Claire looked over at Max, who appeared just as serene and self-assured as ever. So he was a tennis player. Same tan line, different game. He took up his paddle and stroked it through the water with just enough effort to keep the captain quiet.

"All together now," said Vin. "Let's get up to that picnic area!"

Suddenly, the huge canoe began moving briskly upstream as everyone paddled in unison.

Max turned to Claire and raised an eyebrow. "Welcome to the Royal British Navy. We 've had our grog, and now we're feeling the lash. Next comes the buggery!"

Part of Claire was dying to rest, but she couldn't stop paddling now that the whole crew was engaged in the effort. She didn't know these people and wanted to make a good impression. *Why?* Wally didn't worry about making a good impression. But she always wanted to be liked—to be seen as cooperative and helpful, generous and kind—regardless of the situation. Could she help it if she didn't like conflict? She would bend over backwards for other people. Yet avoiding problems wasn't the answer, either. Look at her and Wally. She wished she could be as direct and outspoken as Roz. Or as calm and self-assured as Max. She glanced at him again and wondered if he had ever been married. Did he have any children? He must have made a fortune selling his radio stations.

"Are we there yet?" said Roger Black.

"I didn't know we were on Outward Bound," said the wiry little peckerhead from beneath his floppy white hat.

"Another half mile," Vin Diesel said, "and you can all enjoy a victory drink."

"A *half mile?*" said Max.

"Champagne!" said Roger, hoisting a new magnum.

"We need to keep paddling," said Vin.

"Bugger you!" said Roger and popped the cork. Claire watched it sail through the air, land in the river and bob like a buoy.

"Paddle!" said Vin.

"Or what?" said Roger. "Twenty lashes?"

Roz lifted her rear end off her seat. "I'll take champagne and thirty lashes!" She spanked her vellum-covered butt.

The canoe erupted with laughter.

"I give up!" said Vin Diesel, laying his paddle across his thighs.

"I'll drink to that!" said Max.

The champagne flowed from the new magnum bottle, filling cups for everyone on the big war canoe, and Claire realized they were never going to make it to their elusive destination upstream. They would picnic onboard. And maybe that was fitting. Maybe none of them were destined to reach any destination at all—certainly not her, cast adrift only to land here on a booze cruise. She felt lost among these other souls, newly alone, unsure what she was doing and ready to leave. Why? Why couldn't she just relax like the others? What was wrong with her? She assumed everyone on the canoe was separated, divorced or otherwise disenchanted with their lives. Why else would they be here? Roz had recruited a ship of lonely desperados, and now Claire was one of them.

When Max handed her a cup of champagne, she toyed with the idea of taking a small sip and slyly pouring the rest into the river, but she was so thirsty from paddling that she polished off the champagne in two big gulps. Bubbles exploded in her nose.

Max quickly refilled her glass. "Down the hatch, sailor!"

Claire raised her cup, feeling a buzz behind her eyes. "To the Royal Navy!"

"To mutiny!" said Max, his eyes lighting up.

With no one paddling, the canoe had slowly begun to drift back downstream with the current. Vin continued to steer while everyone broke out picnic fixings—cheese and crackers, smoked mussels, pretzels, sandwiches, spanakopita, even some shrimp with cocktail sauce. Eating, laughing, drinking, the crew soon killed the second magnum bottle of champagne, and then Einstein passed around a large jug filled with margaritas. Claire let Max fill her glass but nursed her drink, while the others drank several as if it were lemonade. Einstein pulled a bottle of tequila from his knapsack and people started taking shots. Claire declined, feeling light-headed already, but Max took a quick belt and passed the bottle on. He leaned in close to her and said, "I would love to get your phone number."

Claire leaned away, hesitating.

"To book a massage," he quickly added, rubbing his neck. "Since we're not making it to the picnic area."

"Oh," said Claire, relieved he didn't want to ask her on a date. "I'll have to check my calendar."

"If we make it later in the day," said Max, "it would be my pleasure to take you for dinner afterward."

So he did want a date. Roz!

Before she could respond, Roz cried out and Claire turned just in time to see her tipsy friend tumble out of the canoe into the river, splashing water everywhere. She surfaced, holding up the bottle of tequila. "Don't worry, I saved the baby!"

Inspired by Roz, Roger stripped off all his clothes, revealing a round hairy belly, and jumped into the river after her. The two ladies in front of him squealed with delight, peeled off their clothes, and the taller one dove in gracefully. Her shorter friend cackled drunkenly, wobbled to her feet and lost her balance. She fell right on top of Max, her groin pressed against his face.

"Get ... off ... me!" Max cried.

"Stop talking to my pussy!" she said.

Einstein lifted the woman off of Max, but she quickly lost her balance and fell overboard, waving her arms as she hit the water.

"Jesus Christ!" said Vin. He grabbed a life preserver from underneath his seat and threw it at her. "Grab that!"

Max collected his fedora from the floor and put it back on, as if trying to restore order. Peckerhead turned to Claire. "Are *you* going skinny dipping?"

"I'd like to see that," said Einstein, slapping his buddy on the back.

Stunned by how quickly things had degenerated, Claire reached under her seat for the life preserver and put it on. She slid to the gunnel, held her nose, and tipped backwards into the river like a scuba diver. When she surfaced, Max called, "Well done!"

"Except for the clothes," said Peckerhead. "You didn't get naked!" He stripped down to his wiry birthday suit and did a tiny cannonball into the water.

Claire began swimming downstream toward the dock.

Peckerhead called after her. "Hey! Where are you going?"

She rolled onto her back and kicked, the water surprisingly cold compared to the warm air. Between her kicking and the current, she quickly distanced herself from the canoe. Voices carried over the water and echoed off the steep riverbank.

"Whooooo! That's cold!"

"My nuts are turning into ovaries!"

What a disaster. Is this what happened when middle-aged people found themselves adrift? She wondered if the sodden swimmers would be able to haul themselves back on board without capsizing the canoe. In the twenty years since she and Wally had moved back to his hometown, three Hancock College students had drowned in the river. Drunk and daring, they had attempted to swim the two hundred yards across the river from New Hampshire to Vermont late at night—fighting the current and their inebriation. They failed. The search and rescue teams never found their bodies. Below the placid surface, the water was dark and murky, the bottom invisible, dense with decomposing tree trunks and other detritus. The dead bodies got caught in this treacherous tangle, never to surface. Wally told the boys there were giant eels in the river that swallowed the students whole— his way of keeping them out of the water. Claire kicked steadily, starting to feel numb from the cold water and the events of the past few days. She had really taken the plunge. Part of her couldn't believe it. She wanted to go home, sink into a hot bath, drink a cup of hot tea and have Wally make her dinner. But he was gone.

Above the rolling green hills to the west, clouds streaked with orange and red reflected the setting sun. To the east, above the New Hampshire pines, Claire spotted the faint silhouette of a half-moon shimmering in the evening sky. As she neared the dock, drunken voices carried downstream.

"Hey!" said Roz. "Where's Claire?"

"She abandoned ship," said Max.

"When?"

"Ten minutes ago," said Vin. "Have another margarita."

"She swam away in a life preserver," said Peckerhead.

"*Seriously?*" said Roz. "She's *crazy!*"

Crazy for listening to you! Claire tossed her life jacket on the dock and headed up the dirt path toward the parking lot, feeling small beneath the towering pines—small and cold and foolish. Not watching where she was going, she stubbed her toe on a pine root.

"*Owwwwwwwww!*"

She dropped to her knees, pain searing through her foot. She threw a handful of pine needles at the root. Why had she listened to Roz? She should have gone to tai chi. Why had she lost her patience with Wally? She got to her feet and hobbled to her car. And that's when she realized the pockets of her shorts were empty, her car keys were in her knapsack, and her knapsack was on the canoe—along with her towel and her sneakers.

Dammit!

Leaning against the car door, she slid to the ground and sat there feeling defeated. Was this an omen of things to come? A foreshadowing of her life as a single woman? Maybe it was all bad karma for wanting Wally out. Instant karma. No line, no waiting—just straight to a good ass kicking because she was such a sensitive, caring, advanced soul. *If only.*

7

Wally sat in the conference room at Hughes Auto, where pictures of the latest model Chevrolets, Toyotas, Volkswagens and BMWs hung on the bright white walls. Joined around the long glass table by Jack Hughes and the managers from service, sales, warranty and accounting, he listened to the young general manager expound about the need to bolster the company's digital marketing presence. To integrate email, social media, web search, online promotion and opt-in messaging with the traditional print, radio, television and direct mail advertising that had been Wally's domain for twenty years.

"We need a company that can do it all," said the GM, his eyes lingering on Wally. A smooth talker with a shaved head and a neatly trimmed black beard, he had the facile, calculating nature of a polished salesman. He sat back in his chair, one leg crossed over the other, his head tilted toward the ceiling like he was a great thinker. Looking down his long nose at Wally, he concluded his speech: "We need total integration."

After the torturous forty-five minutes were over, Wally sat alone in the conference room, pretending to review his notes, which were just a series of intricate doodles, before walking down the hall to Jack Hughes's office. He found the general manager had beaten him there. Jack waved at Wally.

"Come in," he said.

"That's okay," he said, eyeing the GM. "I'll circle back."

"Larry was just leaving," said Jack Hughes. "Weren't you, Larry?"

The slick GM adjusted his necktie. "I'll be back—unlike *some* people."

He smirked at Wally and sauntered off. Wally stepped into Jack's office.

"It's mano a mano!" said Jack Hughes from behind his desk. "The old guard versus the new wave. What's it gonna be, Wally? Embrace mobile devices or hope people still read the newspaper?"

"Both," he said, taking a seat opposite Jack.

Jack leaned back in his chair and swung his feet up onto his desk, the tassels of his loafers dangling like Christmas ornaments. The cuffs of his crisply pressed khakis looked pale next to his tanned ankles. A crisp, yellow Oxford shirt highlighted his ruddy face. He spread his arms wide and declared, "The only thing that's permanent, my friend, is change."

Was Wally about to get fired? Is that what the GM meant? His eyes wandered to the photos on the walls—the photos he'd seen a hundred times—of Jack on renowned golf holes around the world, standing with famous athletes, in exotic locales with his family. In one photo, Jack sat behind the wheel of a vintage 1927 Pontiac, a legacy from his grandfather, who had started the dealership Jack now ran. Next to this picture was a black-and-white shot that Wally couldn't bear to see but could never tear his eyes away from—of Jack scoring the winning goal for Longmont High against Wally and Hancock High in the state finals. For years, Wally didn't know what was worse: Jack scoring that goal against him or Jack stealing Ginger from him in the months afterward. She went to the prom in Jack's shiny new convertible, leaving Wally in the lurch. Seven years later, Jack and Ginger married, eventually had two kids and moved into a big house near Hancock Country Club when Jack inherited the dealership from his father.

Jack swung his feet off his desk and stood up. He grabbed a golf club leaning against the wall and started swinging it. "We need a new way to attack the market," he said. "So we're gonna have a little competition— between Larry's digital agency and you."

A competition?

"Let the cream rise to the top." Jack swung the club and just missed hitting the bookshelf filled with mementos. If only he had shattered the hockey photo.

"I'm not asking you for a digital plan," he continued. "I know that's not your thing. But to keep what you've got, we need a new jingle. Something catchy. An earworm people will sing in the shower or sitting on the can."

Jack swung again and nearly hit his desk.

"Is there a budget for the music demo?" Wally asked.

Jack waved the club at him and smiled. "Larry's agency doesn't want a dime to produce their demo."

Well, they haven't earned you a dime, either, thought Wally. Where was the loyalty? The appreciation? He'd helped Jack make a small fortune over the past two decades, and now he had to make a new business pitch to his own client? At his own expense?

"It's your call," said Jack. "You're either in or you're out."

Wally sighed.

"Winners never quit and quitters never win."

Did he have any choice?

"Nothing ventured, nothing gained," said Jack.

Maybe if his new jingle featured enough clichés, he could keep the account.

"Shall we say the first week of June?" said Jack.

"That's not much time."

Jack swung his club again and nearly knocked over a standing lamp. "You snooze, you lose."

Wally rose from his chair.

"Hope you're still on your game." Jack waggled his club over an imaginary ball and took another heroic swing. "These millennials are mighty creative."

Wally watched the ball drop from the sky onto the fairway, where it bounced twice and rolled to a stop. He took a deep breath and exhaled, purging himself of the meeting with Jack Hughes. Produce a new jingle in two weeks? At his own expense? It reminded him of the old adage: the only downside of advertising was having clients. You were only as good as your last ad, his old mentor used to say in Boston. That was long before the digital age. Now you were only as good as your last tweet. Or your last Instagram post. Or your last Facebook message. An endless stream of digital diarrhea as far as Wally was concerned. 'Look at me! Over here! I'm so clever! I'm so cute! And I'm also better than you, so follow me!' Who had time for all the social media noise? And all those exclamation points! Ridiculous!!!!

Wally struck another 7-iron and thought of Claire, accusing him of avoiding reality by hitting balls. Reality was overrated. What did it get you? Besides heartache and pain? He preferred taking refuge here on the Hancock Country Club practice holes, tucked away from the real world. Very few members used the practice holes. Most preferred the convenience of hitting balls on the driving range near the clubhouse. As a result, Wally often found himself alone here, surrounded by natural beauty. At dawn and twilight, deer ambled from the woods to graze in the rough. In the heat of the day, woodchucks scurried across the fairways from one burrow to another. Crows circled overhead, cawing raucously. The clever birds would swoop down and steal your food, so he always kept his sunflower seeds stored safely in his golf bag. He liked to sprinkle the seeds at the entrances to the woodchuck burrows near the base of the towering pines when he left, but he was never certain if the woodchucks got them before the crows. He just knew they were always gone when he returned the next day and reentered the magical emerald kingdom to hit balls through the air once again. What did Arnold Palmer say? "Watching a golf ball in flight was a form of poetry." Wally agreed. There was magic in striking the ball well and watching it fly through the air—a form of meditation. Except today, he struggled to suspend his thoughts. Why did he ever get into advertising, anyway? From the moment he got in, he wanted to get out. The trouble was, it paid well—far better than the newspaper job he had after college—and he was a natural. Now, he was quickly becoming an advertising dinosaur in the digital age, facing extinction at Hughes Auto. Could he survive without his last account? He pictured himself printing T-shirts for Bear and shuddered.

Trying to clear his mind, he took a drink from his water bottle. Quite miraculously, his next three shots soared through the air and landed in a tight cluster, which boosted his self-esteem. He heard Terry Gross welcoming him to her popular interview program on NPR.

"Wallace Scott, welcome to *Fresh Air.*"

"Thank you, Terry, it's an honor to be here."

"The hero in your novel—or maybe I should say the antihero, ha ha ha—is constantly hitting golf balls, trying to escape his problems, but his mind keeps obsessing on his failures. So I wonder, why doesn't he just quit golf and try something else?"

"You mean like meditation?"

"No, I was thinking more like working. You know, at a real job?"

"His work is interior, Terry. He's a very thoughtful, sensitive person."

"Then let me ask you this. He's been at Bear's for a week already and it's unclear—has he even started his novel?"

"That's a good question. If you mean, has he thought about his story and his characters—yes, he's started his novel. But if you mean, has he written anything yet? Then, no, not really."

"So nothing's changed. He's left Claire and he's still twiddling his thumbs."

"I'm sure you're familiar with the American novelist, Jim Harrison?"

"Of course," said Terry Gross. "Jim Harrison was a great writer, god rest his soul."

"Well, Jim Harrison used to drive around in his pickup truck for months, thinking about his next book, searching for the right voice and plotting his story."

"I think he wrote something like thirty-five or forty books," said Terry Gross. "I'm pretty sure he worked on one project in the morning and *then* drove around thinking about his next project in the afternoon. He didn't dillydally on the golf course."

"No, he dillydallied fly fishing."

"I don't think publishing thirty-five books is dillydallying."

"Well, Wally is pretty close to starting to write. Trust me."

"He seems blocked. Instead of writing, he's hitting golf balls and having imaginary conversations with me."

"F-*bleep* you, Terry!"

And with that, Wally skulled a 7-iron that nearly hit a crow digging for worms in the rough.

8

Claire drove home shivering, blasting the heat even though the dashboard thermometer read 72 degrees. Roz had wrapped her in a big towel when the canoe finally returned to the dock, and asked, "Are you okay?"

"I'm cold."

"I know, that water is a buzzkill! Go home and get a hot bath, and I'll touch base tomorrow." Classic Roz. Crazed one minute, tender the next. She had such a big heart, and not just for rescues. How could Claire stay mad at her?

"I'll call you, too," Max shouted, waving his phone as she walked away. "Roz gave me your number!"

Okay, that was one way she could stay mad at Roz!

Damp and depressed, she drove up Route 5 along the river, the antics on board the canoe being the exact opposite of what she hoped to experience in the absence of Wally. Roz might call her a killjoy, but she had no interest in doing that again. At home, she drew a hot bath and added some essential oils. The soothing scent of lavender rose with the steam. She lay back in the tub, her head against a folded towel and closed her eyes. How long since she had taken a hot bath? Her first winter in Vermont, she took hot baths constantly, a Georgia girl trying to acclimate to the cold. Who imagined she would ever live in northern New England? She and Wally had met in northern Greece on a warm spring evening. She could still see the lights of the taverna strung overhead as they sat outdoors under a rising full moon while bouzouki music played. She hadn't expected to meet Wally, just to have dinner with her college friend who was teaching English at a private Greek college. But her roommate brought Wally along and introduced him as her colleague. Claire could tell immediately that her friend wanted him to be more than that. But as the night unfolded, Wally acted much more interested in Claire. Finally, her friend tossed her napkin on the table and excused herself, saying she had papers to correct. Claire felt guilty and excited at the same time, as Wally raised an eyebrow at her and asked if she might like another glass of wine. They wound up talking until all the other tables were empty and stacked with chairs and the waiter flicked the lights on and off. Wally helped her into a taxi and invited her for lunch the next day at school. From there, the romance blossomed. He helped her get a job in the school's development office, where a woman had just left on maternity leave. There was an empty apartment on campus, and Claire moved in. Her friend forgave her, or said she did. Every weekend, she and Wally explored the northern coast of Halkidiki— sleeping on beaches under the stars, drinking champagne on a hotel balcony overlooking the harbor lights in Kavala, taking the ferry to Thassos to hike among the shepherds. The first time they held hands on a bus ride, an electric shock coursed through Claire, something she had never felt before. Love arrived at such an unexpected time in such an unexpected place! Wally always told her it was love at first sight for him. Being in Greece together, in the ancient romantic light, with the mountains and sea, the beaches and stars, was simply magical. She had always imagined that if there were another person to love, he would be an artist. Wally's ambition to be an author infatuated her. If only she had known what that really meant. She lay in the hot water, wondering where all the time had gone and what the future would hold.

In the morning, she found a text from Roz.

"Hope u r feeling better. Saturday morning at Doggone Right—meeting at 10 for the Labor Day event."

"See u there," Claire replied.

"Can u deliver a dog to Hancock after?"

"Yes."

She sent the text glad to know she would see Roz on neutral territory at Doggone Right, where they had become friends in the first place, and not at some other bizarre outing. Next, she found a voicemail from Max about setting up a massage. She would have to check her calendar and call him back for the sake of Doggone Right. In the meantime, she had her regular clients to attend to, and more of them than she felt she could handle at times. There were moments when she felt burned out on massage. But what else could she do? She had to earn money and it paid well. She would call Max . . . at some point.

In the days that followed, she began to adapt to a house without Wally, to his empty office alcove and his absence everywhere. She found no more of his messes to tidy up in the kitchen, no pools of water on the bathroom floor after his showers. No toothpaste stains in the bathroom sink, no laundry piled up in the living room, waiting to be folded, no empty ice trays, no cartons of milk left with just a splash. She played the music she wanted whenever she wanted as loudly as she wanted. On the third day after the canoe ride, she ate an early dinner and went for a hike up Pinnacle Hill to watch the moonrise—and she didn't leave Wally a note. The next night, she slept with all the windows open and one flannel sheet covering her, not the heavier blanket he preferred, and in the morning she woke feeling refreshed for the first time since his departure. At times she loved being alone. In other moments, her loneliness ached.

Going to tai chi served as her anchor in the storm. For fifteen years, her tai chi practice had helped her cope with the trials and tribulations of life, and it helped to restore her energy after giving massages. Now more than ever, she needed the class community, the shared exercise and the calming meditation. In class, she experienced moments of balance and peace that reassured her all would be well. Somehow. Some way. She just needed to find the way forward. The Way of Claire.

A week after the canoe ride, she entered the dojo one evening as a gentle breeze blew through the open windows, carrying fragrant scents of spring. Soft evening light filled the room with a radiant glow. She slipped off her shoes and walked barefoot across the worn wooden floor to her favorite spot in the corner by the windows. Here, she could look out over trees and fields toward the Connecticut River winding through the heart of the valley. In the winter, the view often consisted of white, silver and gray tones beneath the heavy lid of a pewter sky—a severe, cold scene behind windows misted with condensation from all the body heat. Now, as summer slowly approached and the sun shone in a blue sky and the earth burst with new green growth, the outdoors entered the dojo through the open windows. Claire heard the cacophony of birds and basked in the warm, fresh air, heavy with the thick smell of freshly tilled farmland. She stretched and sighed. The dojo had always been a wonderful refuge, and it felt good to be here in this space she loved, where she had grown from new student to novice, and from novice to accomplished practitioner who sometimes tutored newcomers.

"Hello, Claire," said Joan Marsh, breaking her reverie. At seventy-five, Joan was the oldest member of the class, a spry former schoolteacher with a shock of short white hair, a wiry body and lively blue eyes. Claire thought of her as an overgrown elf. "Lovely evening, isn't it?"

"Gorgeous," said Claire, stretching her torso. "How are you, Joan?"

"Ready to rumble." Joan's joyful expression suddenly turned serious. "Earl wants to buy a motorcycle. The man can barely get out of his chair!"

"Maybe it will motivate him," said Claire. "Make him more active."

"Maybe it will kill him," said Joan. "And then I won't have to."

Claire laughed and thought of Wally's stupid scooter. She toyed with the idea of telling Joan about it—a misery-loves-company confession—but decided against it. The dojo filled with other students. Sifu appeared and circulated through the room, checking in briefly with everyone. When he approached Claire and Joan, he asked how they were on this beautiful evening.

"Very well, thank you," said Claire, placing her hands together in front of her chest and bowing slightly toward their teacher.

Sifu put his hands together and bowed in return.

"I'm ready to kick some ass," said Joan.

Sifu straightened. "Such aggression." He waved a hand toward the window. "On such a lovely evening."

He smiled at Joan, his straight white teeth contrasting handsomely with his dark, trimmed beard. Shorter than Wally, darker skinned and more solidly built—with thick shoulders and sinewy arms—Sifu had intense brown eyes and spoke in a calm, deep voice, a martial arts master sure of himself, who could afford to be gentle and kind because he could tear you apart. During class, his gaze moved intently from one student to another as he made his way around the large room, providing individual instruction and encouragement, but he rarely smiled. He smiled only before or after class, and even then sparingly. Now, he turned to Claire.

"Our friend is off balance," he said.

"I'm not off balance," said Joan. "Earl is off his rocker."

"And this has put *you* off balance," said Sifu.

Joan dropped into a martial stance and raised her hands, ready for battle. "You got a problem with that?" she said, squinting at Sifu.

"No," said Sifu. "The problem is yours. And it is easy to solve."

"Maybe for you. You're not married to an idiot."

"No," said Sifu, suddenly looking forlorn. "I am not."

Joan lowered her hands and came up out of her martial arts stance. "I'm sorry," she said. "I shouldn't have said that."

"It is all right," said Sifu. "Sometimes, we speak before thinking. Sometimes, we meet force with force. But we cannot. We must deflect. And defuse."

"A fuse sounds good," Joan said. "Right up Earl's ass!"

"We must remain calm," Sifu continued, ignoring her joke. "Supple. Fluid. Just as water turns rock into stone, stone into pebbles, pebbles into sand. And then—nothingness."

Sifu bowed at Joan, turned and walked away.

"What an idiot!" said Joan.

"I don't know," said Claire. "I think he's right."

"Not him," said Joan. "Me! I never should have mentioned being married."

Joan touched Claire's forearm and whispered, "He's not wearing his wedding ring." She leaned closer. "I saw Hope at Watson's three weeks ago. Filling her car with gas. She said she was headed to her sister's down in Darien. I don't think she's coming back."

Now that Joan mentioned it, Claire realized she hadn't seen Sifu's wife in class for some time. She had been too absorbed with her own marital problems to notice.

"I had no idea," Claire said. "I'm sorry."

"That's what she gets for stealing another woman's husband. Bit her right in the ass!"

Claire remembered how Hope had superseded Faith, Sifu's previous wife, over a three-year period of flirtation and conquest as intricate and lethal as a martial arts move executed to perfection. Faith never knew what hit her. Now, after some clearly rocky passages, Hope was gone as well.

Joan's face set into an expression of contempt. "I never liked that woman. She had a very dark aura."

Joan's loyalty lay with Sifu. But wasn't he partly to blame, dumping wife number two for bride number three? Or was it wife number three for bride number four? Claire had heard both versions stated as fact.

"How many wives has he had, anyway?" she asked Joan.

"Three. His first wife stayed in Oregon when he moved to Vermont twenty years ago. They were estranged because she wanted kids and he didn't."

"How do you know all this?"

"I have my sources," said Joan, a gleam in her eyes.

Sifu's unsuccessful love life seemed at odds with his masterful in-class persona. Was it bad luck? Or bad choices? Adept deflection? Or simply remaining fluid? Claire wondered if Joan really knew the truth. Three wives? She found it hard to believe he could be so impossible to live with based on what she'd seen in class over the years. But then, who could have predicted she and Wally would become separated?

Claire tried to clear her mind. Class was about to begin. The only certainty was change. In a fluid situation, you need to stay flexible, balanced, aware. She breathed deeply into her belly and slowly exhaled. She closed her eyes and focused her awareness on her body, preparing to delve into the tai chi form.

At one point during class, Sifu spent extra time helping Claire refine her movements in the Sword Form, a series of slow-motion actions that consisted of waving a weighty Japanese sword and required a great deal of skill, balance and strength. Later, he circled back to perform Push Hands with her because her usual Push Hands partner had not appeared and she needed an advanced partner. In many ways, Push Hands was the ultimate tai chi exercise, and Claire relished the challenge of doing it with Sifu. For some practitioners it was a form of combat, for others a dance. Claire preferred the dance viewpoint, with her aim being to neutralize the oncoming force by sensing its arrival and yielding, then deflecting her partner's energy to throw them off balance. At the same time, her opponent was showing Claire where her tension and imbalance lay. For this reason, some called it Sensing Hands for the emphasis on becoming aware of balance, timing and tension—yours and your partner's. Claire loved the challenge of anchoring her feet and turning and twisting in a dance of heightened awareness and fluidity as she sought an opening to throw her partner off balance. How many situations in life called for a similar approach? Sensing the pressure, being fluid under assault, deflecting and then turning the tables? Was this what she and Wally were doing? Revealing to each other their weaknesses? She had yielded to such a degree that she had lost her balance. What would be the end result? Doing Push Hands with Sifu heightened Claire's focus and effort, and in one sequence she even managed to get the better of her master. Or had he simply let her have the upper hand? She could not tell. When they finished, he gently touched her arm and looked at her intently.

"Thank you," he said, and bowed slightly, never taking his eyes off hers. "You will be just fine."

"Thank *you*," she replied, bowing back. As he turned and walked away, she felt a sudden chill race up her spine and goose bumps explode on the back of her neck. Her face flushed. What did he mean: *you will be just fine?* Had he sensed something about her in their Push Hands? Something awry? She thought she had managed his energy skillfully. But she had been with Wally for nearly thirty years, counting their courtship, and the territory ahead was new and unfamiliar. Did she radiate uncertainty?

You will be just fine.

It probably meant nothing, she told herself after class, driving down Radford's compact Main Street between the old brick buildings that faced each other. Sifu could have been referring to her progress with Push Hands. He often spoke in obtuse terms, using New Age speak that could be interpreted multiple ways. She drove past the hardware store and the five-and-dime, the pizza parlor and the general store. Two couples stood in front of the Italian restaurant at the end of Main Street, hugging each other goodbye, one woman clutching a doggie bag. No longer her and Wally, out for dinner with friends.

You will be just fine.

Main Street ended after one hundred yards, and then she crossed the bridge above the falls. The water gushed downhill and soon merged with the broad, smooth flow of the Connecticut. The farmland glowed green on both banks of the river, returning to life after the long, gray winter. Above the mountains to the east, the moon would rise within the hour, nearly full. She planned to commune with it tonight in the labyrinth. She would ask her spirit guides for their support in the days and weeks ahead. Who knew what the summer would bring?

9

Claire took the long way home on the road hugging the river. Soon, her thoughts turned to her friend, Dawn, who had gotten divorced the previous fall. Dawn now lived in the cutest little apartment down in Greenwich, the wealthy Vermont town just across the river from Hancock, where her rent was almost double Claire and Wally's mortgage. But it didn't matter. Dawn had more money than she could ever spend because her husband, Rick, was so eager to get out of their thirty-year marriage that he agreed to terms Dawn's lawyer said were ludicrous. Rick didn't get a lawyer. He told Dawn he did enough deals in the Boston tech world that he could handle the divorce proceedings alone. When Wally heard this, he told Claire: "He's got another woman down in Boston and just wants out." No, she said, he's about to close a big deal and Dawn says he can afford to pay her a king's ransom. To which Wally replied, "Every fifty-five-year-old woman's dream—no more husband bugging her and plenty of cash." Claire said, "Well, her apartment *is* really nice. You should see it. And she seems really happy. It's like she's reborn. And her boys are happy for her, too. Because I guess Rick could be really difficult and depressive when he wasn't on his meds, and life could be just awful for everyone. So it's all for the best." To which Wally said, "Sounds like a trend. The sons side with the mom, the daughters side with the dad. I could be in trouble." And then he looked at her in a way that said, *Now you reply: Oh no, Wally, I would never divorce you.* Claire just said, "The boys would side with both of us. They'd go to soccer games with you and take me to the Four Aces for breakfast."

The thing was, she still loved Wally, even though she didn't really like him. Funny how being infatuated led to falling into love, followed by admiration and respect, then familiarity, then contempt, leading to mild aggravation that became annoyance and sometimes full-blown anger, only to be relieved by a truce for the sake of the kids, during which there were on-again, off-again recurrent feelings from the past—some wonderful, others bothersome—while weariness and fatigue and strong electrical sexual currents (how complicating!) and Wally's complete failure to compromise added up to her love/hate relationship. *Ughhh!*

Raising the boys had taken all their energy. Wally called their early years of child-rearing—the sleep-deprived, learn-as-you-go, exhausting years—'the happiest hell you'll ever know.' Claire looked back and liked the expression, 'The years fly by, but the days last forever.' You put so much time, energy and love into raising your kids, and then suddenly—boom!—you woke up and they were gone. You could look at your spouse and think, *Who* are *you, anyway?* So many couples grew apart while raising their kids, and once that glue vanished, the marriage fell apart. People's hopes and dreams could change. It happened so often, it felt like a cliché.

She drove along the river and told herself to think of something else, something other than her troubles with Wally. *You will be just fine.* Sifu was right, wasn't he?

Suddenly, her grandmother's foggy apparition appeared in the passenger's seat. "You know he's sweet on you, shugah pie!" Mama Betty declared.

Claire nearly jumped out of the sunroof. The car veered and she yanked the wheel just in time to avoid driving into a freshly tilled field "Mama Betty! Are you trying to cause an accident!?"

"And I am *not* talkin' about Wally, either," her grandmother carried on, raising an eyebrow at Claire. She looked like a vaporous vamp, all dolled up in a pair of shiny, red high heels, a yellow sleeveless dress with a snazzy white-and-red geometric pattern, a wavy silver wig and a wide-brimmed red hat with a white lily pinned to it. Her cat-eye glasses were also red, as was her glossy lipstick, applied as thick as butter. Her big arms, worthy of an Atlanta Falcons nose tackle, hung like hammocks, and her short, stout legs dangled off the edge of the seat, like Humpty Dumpty, round and unbound. Who needed a seat belt when you were already dead?

"You look like you've been drinking mint juleps at the Kentucky Derby," Claire said, regaining her composure.

"No, sweet pie," said Mama Betty. "Been out for an early dinner—the blue-hair special. Roast beef, mashed potatoes and green beans. Sticks to your ribs. And I got plenty of ribs!" She laughed heartily and patted her big belly below her mammoth bosom. "As for that Seafood who teaches your class—honey, that boy is *sweet* on you. Whooo weee!"

"It's *Sifu*," said Claire. "*Not* Seafood. You and Wally, I swear."

"Sifu. Seafood. Don't see much difference, honey pie," said Mama Betty. "Though I do enjoy a cup of she-crab soup when I'm in Charleston."

Claire smiled and shook her head. If her grandmother wasn't talking, she was eating and talking with her mouth full.

"That Mister Seafood, he's ready to move from pushing hands to rubbing thighs." She looked at Claire. "But I think you already knew that."

Claire felt herself blush under her grandmother's gaze.

"And while I'm here, I'll tell you something else—it's about Wally, sweet cheeks. That boy is *not* lazy. He just needs to find his voice."

"His voice?"

"That's right. He's a good writer. Just needs to find his voice, is all. And he'll write a *fine* book. Everybody needs a passion, honey chile."

Claire looked at her grandmother's cloudy visage. "You know why I love tai chi?"

"I got my theories."

"I love tai chi because when I'm doing the form and get into the flow, it's like I'm dancing with the universe."

"There you go, honey chile! That's what I'm talkin' about. Creativity at the core of our being." Mama Betty smiled at her. "Same thing going on when Wally plays golf. Chance to recreate himself with every swing."

Claire shuddered at the thought that she and Wally were alike.

"You and Wally, two peas in a pod, shugah pie. Both searching for meaning and ways to express yourself."

And with that Mama Betty's spirit rose out of the seat and vanished through the roof of the car. Claire looked anxiously in the rearview mirror, eager to catch a glimpse of her vapors swirling in her wake, but all she saw was the clear evening sky.

10

Wally was so blocked with his writing that he couldn't even come up with the lyrics for the Hughes Auto jingle. He'd never had trouble writing jingle lyrics before, or any ad copy for that matter, but now the pressure to write his novel had left him paralyzed. After two weeks, he had made no progress, writing a handful of pages that were so poor he couldn't stand to open the document and look at them. Hemingway had said all first drafts were shit. But Wally's output was equivalent to a backed-up sewer system for a city of forty thousand. His anxiety ate at him.

Meantime, Bear bragged to Danny Boy and Harry that Wally was writing a kick-ass novel that would make them all proud and feature the crazy shit Harry saw in the ER and the Zen wisdom of Danny's altered state—along with the escapades of a heroic, handsome stud based on Bear himself.

"We're all gonna be famous," said Bear, standing over his ball on the 13th tee. "Especially Wally."

"I'm in," said Danny Boy in his deep baritone, poised to light his mini-pipe. "As I always say, all we leave behind are our stories."

Harry repeated his previous offer: "Just let me know when you want to sit down, Wally, and I can tell you ER stories for hours. You just have to change the names to protect the guilty."

Wally laughed off their enthusiasm, deflecting the conversation back to golf, knowing he hadn't written a thing and terrified he never would. Not even lyrics for a stupid car dealer jingle. He had negotiated an extension with Jack Hughes by telling him the musicians weren't available to record the demo for another two weeks. Each morning, he brewed a cup of green tea and sat at his laptop, but instead of writing jingle lyrics or his novel, he checked his email and wrote long replies, logged on to his favorite soccer and golf websites to get the latest news and looked at the weather forecast.

Not that the forecast mattered. He played golf no matter what. The season was short, and you couldn't hit balls in the snow. It was now or never. And so much easier to work on his golf game than his novel. Soon, he headed for the practice holes and hit balls for a few hours, but without any joy. Tortured by his stalemate, he returned home to Bear's for lunch, assuring himself he would write after eating a sandwich. But after eating on the deck, with the sun high in the sky, he grew drowsy and closed his eyes. Soon, he fell asleep.

One day, he was jolted awake by a clap on his shoulder. Bear loomed over him, his wide frame blocking the sun.

"Working hard?" said his burly friend. "Or hardly working?"

"Oh, man," said Wally, rubbing his eyes.

"Who knew being a writer was so exhausting!"

"I know. It's crazy."

"So how's my character doing?"

"Really well," said Wally, gathering his wits, sitting up in the Adirondack chair. "Great, actually."

"Shouldn't he be in trouble?" said Bear. "Facing obstacles and struggling to overcome problems?"

"Oh, he's in trouble. Big time. He's being deceived and double-crossed. Lots of bad stuff."

"Excellent!"

"But he's a real hero. Chicks dig him and guys want to be like him."

"I can't wait to read a few chapters."

Wally stiffened. "I don't know about that. It could make me self-conscious. You know, getting feedback too early. It might block me."

"Well, we don't want you blocked." Bear clapped him again with a meaty paw. "We want you in the flow."

Two days later, Bear caught him asleep again. "Sleeping Beauty!" he bellowed.

Wally nearly jumped out of his chair. He had hit balls for two hours that morning, trying to shake off a long, restless night haunted by memories of his father and the feeling that he had let him down. That he had somehow fallen short and failed to earn his father's approval by writing ads. Shouldn't the son of a renowned Faulkner scholar and the author of a best-selling college textbook on writing be able to write books of his own? As Wally watched his father's steady decline from a series of small strokes following his emergency open-heart surgery, he was amazed by his grace and good humor and by his mother's loyal and tender caregiving. He eyed the bookshelves in their living room, wishing they contained just one of his titles. Just one of his close calls. Because when his father died of a final, massive stroke, too soon at seventy-five, Wally lost the chance to see the pride in his father's eyes, and the failure left him crippled.

"I hope you're backing everything up," Bear called from the kitchen.

"Oh, it's all backed up," said Wally. "Believe me."

How would he ever escape this funk?

"Don't get so caught up in the story that you miss our tee time," said Bear.

"Don't worry, I'll be there."

Bear emerged from the kitchen with a sandwich the size of *Great Expectations*. "See you at four, Henrik. Keep pounding it out!"

Wally watched his loyal pal head out the door and took a deep breath. He felt terrible about deceiving him. If only something would kick him into gear. He often prayed to the golf gods. Maybe he should pray to the writing gods. He closed his eyes and uttered an urgent plea for divine intervention, hoping that would do the trick. What did he have to lose?

11

Saturday morning arrived and Claire drove to Doggone Right for the Labor Day fundraiser meeting and then to deliver a rescue dog to a new home in Hancock. She had heard from Wally twice since his departure—once by text, saying he had made the overdue line-of-credit payment, and a second time via voicemail, asking if she wanted him to come mow the lawn. She thanked him for making the line-of-credit payment (figuring he had just received his monthly retainer from Hughes Auto) but declined his offer to mow the lawn. She didn't want to confuse things by having him come around. There were days when she felt vulnerable without him and days when she felt fine on her own. She would mow the lawn by herself, thank you very much. The exercise would be good for her, even if the noise and exhaust fumes were not. But then she mowed the lawn, where Wally had played endless games of soccer and Wiffle ball with the boys, and got teary. He had been such a good dad. Why did he have to behave like an overgrown boy?

Arriving at Doggone Right, she found the gravel lot already filled with cars and parked on the edge of the lawn. The five-acre property in rural Hancock sat on a hillside with panoramic views to the west, toward the Green Mountains in Vermont, and had been left to Doggone Right five years earlier by an elderly woman who loved dogs. Since then, rooms in the rambling old farmhouse had been converted into a veterinary clinic, offices, meeting spaces and training areas where rambunctious dogs were taught to behave in domestic surroundings. In the large barn behind the house, kennels had been built for the rescues, most of them arriving from southern states before being placed in new homes here. Next to the barn was the largest dog run Claire had ever seen, a huge, fenced area of almost two acres, a field where the rescues romped and played, dug in the earth, chased critters and stretched in the sun. The field bordered acres of woods donated to the Valley

Land Trust, filled with miles of trails, where the staff and volunteers took the dogs for walks. Hiking with the dogs was Claire's favorite volunteer activity, although she sometimes helped clean kennels and gave new dogs baths when they first arrived. She often wondered why the rescues would ever want to leave this idyllic canine community, but not all of them got along, and they were expensive to house and feed. Fortunately, people lined up to welcome the dogs into their homes. Doggone Right was a wonderful way station, not a permanent residence.

Claire entered the farmhouse and was struck as always by the strong scent of dog mingling with the potent antiseptic smell of the vet clinic. She walked past the front desk and slipped quietly into the spacious living room, where Roz was already addressing a group of people from a cross-section of the Lower Valley. Squeezed into sofas and armchairs, sitting on wooden chairs and folding chairs and standing around the perimeter of the room leaning against walls and built-in bookshelves were a mixture of elderly retirees, middle-aged trust funders, blue-collar workers, aging hippies, countrified yuppies and a few teenagers. Folks from every walk of life who loved dogs and wanted to help in any way they could. Some sat with dogs at their feet. Others had left their dogs out in their cars, the windows cracked open to the fresh Memorial Day weekend air. Claire settled into a tattered armchair covered with dog hair, while Roz stood in front of the group, summarizing the mission of the Labor Day event—to raise $250,000 in order to add more kennels in the barn, pay for veterinary care, increase staff and rescue more dogs. A murmur spread through the room in reaction to the dollar amount, and Roz said, "I actually think we can surpass our goal. Maybe even double it if everything goes well." A thickset middle-aged man in front of Claire, wearing an orange road crew T-shirt and a trucker's hat, turned to the woman beside him, who looked like she had stepped out of a Talbot's catalog, and said in a thick local accent: "Wouldn't put it past her. She's a wicked dynamo." The woman smiled at him and nodded in agreement. Roz moved on to assigning people to various subcommittees, her executive skills in full bloom. Claire heard Roz place her on a committee overseeing elements of the event itself—in charge of catering, renting a tent, getting a band and lining up a special guest who could help sell tickets and draw a crowd.

"It would be great to get a famous dog lover," Roz suggested. "A celebrity or artist or somebody who can help us raise a lot of money. So everyone, explore your networks. You never know who your friends might know!"

She looked around the room and asked, "Who wants to volunteer to chair the subcommittees?" Claire avoided Roz's gaze. *Not me!* An attractive woman of perhaps seventy, her silver hair pulled back into a tight, neat bun, came to the rescue and raised her hand. She would chair Claire's committee. Roz accepted her offer, and the woman beamed, looking around the room as if she'd just been named the U.S. ambassador to France. Roz assigned the rest of the subcommittee chairs as a clipboard made its way around the room for everyone to provide their contact info, and then Roz made her closing remarks.

"Your chairpersons will be in touch regarding your committee assignments, and we'll all meet here again next month. Meantime, thank you very much for all your help—we're going to have a great event!"

After the crowd dispersed, Claire stood on the front porch with Roz, congratulating her on how well the meeting had gone, when her committee chairwoman appeared and kissed Roz on both cheeks, European style.

"You were wonderful. Roz. Just remarkable!"

"Thank you, Millicent."

The chairwoman looked Claire up and down. "And who do we have here?" She extended her hand with regal flair. "Millicent Fernwater."

"This is Claire Scott," said Roz.

Claire shook Millicent's limp hand. "How do you do?"

"You're on my committee!" said Millicent.

"Yes, I am."

"Well, I can assure you, you'll be working like a dog to help the dogs!" Millicent threw her head back and laughed.

Roz laughed with her and then said, "Millicent is the most active volunteer in the Lower Valley. She helps *every* worthy cause."

"Oh stop it," said Millicent, waving a hand.

"You must be on at least ten volunteer boards and contribute to another *dozen* local charities."

"Well, it's an honor to help," said Millicent, patting her silver bun, "in even the smallest ways." She checked her wristwatch and the diamond-studded band flickered in the sun. "Oh my goodness! I'm late for my next meeting. Lunch with the trustees of Kimball Union Academy. I think they want me to join them. My great-nephew will start there in the fall."

"They'd be lucky to have you," said Roz.

"Yes," said Millicent, "I suppose they would." She smiled and gave Claire a little wave. "Ta-ta! I'll be sending along everyone's assignments on Monday. Strap on your work boots!"

Claire smiled weakly as Millicent got in her car and drove away, wondering what she had gotten into, working under the grande dame of Lower Valley volunteering. Roz began to pace back and forth in an agitated way. She had gotten all gussied up for the meeting in a light summer dress with a floral pattern and a plunging neckline—a bit over the top, but then Roz was running the meeting, not delivering a dog to Hancock, like Claire was about to do in her jeans and T-shirt.

"You look very nice," said Claire, trying to calm Roz down. "And really, you did a great job in there. Everything's going to be just fine, don't worry."

Roz stopped pacing and scowled at her. "I'm not worried about the event. I want to know why you haven't returned Max McClure's calls. He could give us half of what we're trying to raise without blinking."

"I'm going to call him this weekend," said Claire. "I've been really busy."

"He *likes* you. You need to be encouraging. Give him a massage. Play some tennis. Go to dinner. Is that so hard?"

"So, what . . . you want me to be a strumpet for the shelter?"

"Doggone right!" Roz squeezed her hand. "He's a very nice man. With very deep pockets."

Twenty minutes later, Claire emerged from the farmhouse with the dog she would deliver—a springer spaniel, black lab mix named Gus. Gus had a shaggy Rasta look, with the longer black-and-white fur of a springer on his head and torso and a lab's shorter hair covering his legs. Tufts of black-and-white bangs arched over his brown eyes. He stood taller than a springer, with a lab's height and weight, and pulled eagerly on his leash, powerfully enough to jerk Claire along behind him as he stepped out into the fresh air.

"Easy, Gus, hold on," she said, maneuvering her way through the door. Gus stopped and looked up at her, a happy smile on his face.

"Good boy!" she said and reached down to pet him, hearing tires crunch on the gravel. She looked up to see a black Mercedes coupe convertible pull into the lot. When Max McClure climbed out of the car dressed in tennis whites and a blue visor, she caught her breath. *Had Roz set her up again?*

"Claire!" he called. "I didn't expect to see you here."

That makes two of us.

"I'm delivering Gus to his new home in Hancock." She stroked the dog's shaggy black fur.

"And who is the lucky family?"

"The Turnbulls. On Pine Ridge."

"Very nice folks," said Max. "Know them well. He'll love it there." He closed his car door and stepped toward her. Gus barked sharply, and Max stiffened.

"Gus!" said Claire. "Be nice."

"It's okay," said Max. "He's probably been abused."

Claire dropped to a knee and wrapped her arm around the dog's chest. She stroked his sternum. "He seems like a good boy. A bit nervous and high-strung, but who wouldn't be? His owner abandoned him."

"Well, I can assure you, it's difficult to be left out in the cold and completely ignored." Max gave Claire a wry smile.

"I'm sorry I haven't called you back," she said. "I've just been out straight."

Gus gave a sharp yelp, as if accusing her of lying.

"That can happen when you're in transition. I know." Max rubbed his neck. "I would love to book that massage."

"Of course," said Claire, thinking of Roz and the rescues. "We'll find a time."

"Wonderful!" said Max. "In the meantime, I was hoping you might join me for a plane ride."

"A plane ride?" said Claire.

"Yes. I have a seaplane. We'll skim across the water and rise like a hawk. It's really quite spectacular. And landing in a glorious spray of white—it takes your breath away."

How poetic! It sounded divine. But going on a date? How would she avoid the second one? Especially with Roz playing the donation card.

Max rocked back and forth on his spindly tanned legs, waiting for her reply with such an open, vulnerable expression that he looked just like a schoolboy asking a girl out on his first date. Quite endearing, actually.

"The weather looks glorious tomorrow," he said. "If you're free."

Tomorrow?

"Shall we say ten o'clock? We'll take flight and then return for a luncheon on my deck."

She had no plans for tomorrow—and no excuse on the tip of her tongue.

"Okay," said Claire. "Why not?"

"Wonderful!" Max said. "I'll text you my address. We'll take off from my dock by the river."

Claire wondered what she had just done. All she knew was that Roz would be pleased. Where was Roz, anyway? She should be out here to show Max around.

"I think Roz is planning to give you a special tour," she said.

"Won't you be joining us?"

"I'm afraid I have to deliver Gus."

At the mention of his name, Gus barked sharply. And then something caught his eye and he bolted across the gravel parking lot, yanking Claire behind him on the leash so abruptly she staggered behind him, struggling to keep her balance.

"Gus!" she hollered, running in his wake. "Slow down!"

He raced between two cars, dashed around the corner of the farmhouse, and tore off for the large barn.

"Gus! Stop!"

Suddenly, he did—and she almost fell over him. He stood rigidly, ears perked, head lifted, sniffing the air, his tuft of black-and-white hair jiggling on his forehead as he surveyed the grounds. Claire caught her breath and reached down to pat him.

"It's okay." She rubbed his side and pulled a treat from her pocket, given to her by the vet's assistant inside. He licked the treat off her palm with a warm, wet tongue and chomped away, gazing at her with his soft brown eyes. He wagged his tail and barked once.

"You didn't want to take that tour either, did you?"

Gus barked again and set off at a brisk pace, pulling Claire behind him, this time up the hill toward the woods. Reaching a trailhead, he stopped and looked up at her, seeking permission to head into the trees.

"Okay!" she said. "Let's go!"

*   *   *

Thirty minutes later, Claire and Gus returned to the farmhouse. Max's Mercedes coupe was gone. Roz stood on the porch holding a large manila envelope.

"Where have you been?" she said.

"We went for a walk."

Roz shook her head. "First you jump out of the canoe. Then you disappear into the woods. Max can't figure you out."

Claire said, "I can't figure me out right now, either, Roz. Things are a little topsy-turvy."

"Oh, honey," said Roz, pulling her in and giving her a little hug. "Everything's going to be okay. Better than okay!" She handed Claire the envelope. "This is for the Turnbulls. Gus's life story, his immunization records, some helpful suggestions and contact info for the shelter. In case there are any issues."

"I can't imagine there will be any issues," said Claire, patting Gus. "He's a prince."

"Well, the last family couldn't handle him. So you should probably have one of your little animal chitchats to straighten him out. We can only place a dog so many times before we have to . . . ," Roz's voice trailed off.

"Don't talk like that!"

"Then talk to him." Roz pointed at Gus. "He needs to behave. And so do you! Men like Max McClure don't grow on trees."

Claire rubbed behind Gus's ears and asked the question she'd been wondering about for the past week. "If Max is so great, why don't you go after him?"

"*Max?* He's not my type." Roz arched her back and ran her palms down her light summer dress, her cleavage bursting like ripe fruit. "I have plenty of other, younger men in my life. Besides, he's much more interested in you."

"Lord knows why," said Claire.

"You're a very attractive woman. You should be flattered."

Claire tugged gently at Gus's leash.

"Max will be good for your self-esteem," said Roz. "He's a confidence builder."

Claire led Gus to her car. "Goodbye, Roz."

"Have a talk with that dog," called Roz. "And keep me posted on Max. The shelter is counting on you!"

12

The day was clear, blue and blustery. Gusts of wind surged down the river valley, churning the water. Max sat at the controls of his vintage seaplane, the engine roaring as he accelerated into the headwind, the pontoons skipping like stones over the rough water. Jostled in her seat next to him, Claire would have bounced up and hit her head against the ceiling of the cabin if not for the canvas seat belt holding her down. The shoreline raced past in a bouncy blur. She began to wonder if the old plane would ever lift off and looked at Max. The rough conditions didn't seem to bother him at all—unflappable behind his aviator sunglasses, his jaw set, absorbing every shock calmly, his hands steady on the wheel. And then the jarring ride suddenly ended as the pontoons lifted off the water. Max pulled the nose up into the sky, the plane climbing sharply above the river. He made a wide, sweeping turn and looked at Claire.

"Up, up and away!" he called over the sound of the roaring engine. He pointed down at the river, shimmering in all its glory. "A necklace, gleaming in the sun!"

She looked down and swallowed. Braced a hand against the wooden dash as wind buffeted the plane.

"Are you okay?" said Max. "You look a little pale."

"I'm fine," she said, feeling nauseous. "I've just never been in a seaplane."

"Here," he said, handing her an old metal canteen. "Have some water."

She took the canteen, her finger finding a dent in the metal. Was everything in the plane vintage? From the wooden dashboard with its old-fashioned gauges to the handheld radio with its dangling cord to the long bench seat, covered in worn leather. Even the pilot, with his silver hair and lined, sun-creased face, seemed to come from another era. And yet, Max wasn't the one looking a bit out of sorts. He looked vigorous and confident, in complete control. She lifted the old canteen and took a drink, willing her stomach to settle down.

"We'll find a good altitude for smoother sailing," he said, climbing steadily higher and following the river north. "You are an adventurous woman to climb into this old plane."

The things she did for Roz and Doggone Right! She took another sip of water and thought of Gus. She had taken Roz's advice the day before and had driven the dog to her studio for a chat before dropping him at the Turnbulls. She asked Gus what had happened at his previous home, posing her question telepathically while beating gently on a drum to induce a hypnotic state in both of them. Gus lay on his side on the wide pine floor of Claire's studio and looked up at her with one brown eye peeking through a tuft of his long, black Rasta hair.

"Totally dysfunctional family," relayed the dog, blinking once.

"How so?"

"They had a boy and a girl. Both addicted to their screens. Video games. Texting. Social media. It was like watching a slow-motion fat farm. The kids never went outside. Never threw me a ball or took me for a walk. They tried to feed me Cheetos. I don't want cancer."

"What about the parents?"

"If the mom wasn't in front of a mirror, she was at yoga, buying new clothes or going to the hairdresser's. Totally vain. She left me locked up in the house. There was no outside run or electric fence—which I've heard will fry your nuts, by the way."

"That's not true."

"Well, I don't want to find out."

"Was there a dad?"

"Yeah, total workaholic—classic case of avoiding his family. We dogs see that all the time. He'd show up late after work and his wife would bolt, saying it was his turn to have the kids—while she went out with her girlfriends or who knows where. He'd put the kids to bed, pour himself a big Scotch and take me for a walk. *Finally!* Some fresh air! But then he'd dump all his problems on me. Like I'm some frickin' shrink!"

"Sorry to hear that."

"He was buried in debt, his wife didn't like sex, his kids hardly talked, they just stared at their screens. He'd scold them about that and then do the exact same thing! He made more eye contact with his phone than his children."

"That's sad."

"Yeah. They had all the trappings—big house, fancy cars—and their lawn would have looked even better if they let me do my business on it. There's a lot of fertilizer in dog shit, you know. But everyone scoops it up like it's poison and drops it in plastic bags that don't decompose. Humans, I swear."

"So what got you in trouble?"

"I needed to get outside—but they never let me out. So I barked. I pissed. I pooped. They didn't want a dog. They wanted a Christmas card. Happy family in front of the roaring fire with faithful Gus, the imprisoned dog. Fuck that. I'd rather be the main course at a Chinese restaurant."

"Gus! Cancel that!"

"It's true. Give me liberty or give me death."

"I'm sure the Turnbulls will be different."

"If they're not a bunch of wankers."

"Max said they're very nice people."

"Max is a putz. Are you really going to date him?"

Claire let out a deep sigh. "Yes, I am going on a plane ride with Max. For the sake of you and your fellow rescues."

"He wants to get into your pants."

"That's enough."

"I'm just saying," Gus said telepathically, and then he sat up and barked, effectively ending their talk.

Claire looked out the plane window, her stomach starting to settle. Max had found some calmer air and the drink of water had helped.

"Where would you like to go?" he said.

"Wherever you want."

"How about Hancock? We can fly over Heifer Hill on the way."

"Sounds lovely," said Claire, looking down at a captivating panorama that was impossible to absorb all at once. A vast tapestry of green and brown hues that spread as far as she could see, dotted with shimmering lakes and ponds, punctuated by rising hills and mountains, and featuring the occasional signs of civilization—roads, homes, towns. The immense expanse was breathtaking.

"You get a different perspective from up here," called Max over the engine.

"Yes," said Claire, completely enthralled.

"It's humbling."

He flew them over Heifer Hill, and Claire looked down at the elementary school and the academy, where Josh and Jack had gone to school. She spied the white steeple of the Congregational church pointing toward the heavens, where she flew through a clear blue sky. How small and compact everything appeared from up here, as if in a dream! There were no worries or stresses, struggles or sadness from this view, only a paradise bursting with natural beauty and the spotty presence of mankind. Max swung the plane south, and she tried to spot her home, but she was on the wrong side of the plane. Soon, she saw the horse farm down by Route 132, the old quarry adjacent to Route 5 and the broad expanse of water where the Heifer River flowed into the Connecticut.

Max followed the Connecticut down toward Hancock. Claire asked, "How long have you been flying?"

"Since I was eighteen," he answered. "I flew helicopters in Vietnam. I had a bit of a death wish at the time. I was an orphan and didn't think anyone cared about me."

An orphan? He looked like he'd been born with a silver spoon in his mouth.

"But unlike most people," he continued, "Vietnam was the best thing that ever happened to me. I learned how precious life is and how much I wanted to live."

"And after Vietnam?" she said. "Is that when you started working in radio?"

"No, I went to Princeton on the GI Bill. And then I wanted to be an actor, so I went to Hollywood."

He certainly had the looks and the charm, thought Claire.

"But I never quite made it," he said, "and I eventually moved on." He banked to the right, titling the plane so Claire could see out her window. "There's Hancock," he pointed.

Claire looked down at the College Green, bordered by the library and majestic Hancock Hall, the art center and the stately Hancock Inn. Max flew over the business school and the medical school and then he steered the plane over the golf course—shining like an emerald jewel. Claire wondered if Wally was down there playing with Bear and Harry and Danny Boy, his usual Sunday game. Then again, maybe he was at Bear's, writing his great American novel, because Bear had texted her a few days before to say Wally was going great guns, writing every day. "You're my friend, too," he texted Claire. "And I want you guys to get through this." The Professor, Danny Boy's wife, had also written to her to say she was sorry to hear about the separation. "If there's anything I can do, let me know. I am a drama expert, after all—ha ha ha!"

Max turned the plane southeast and soon they flew over the Hancock Medical Center, which looked like a great, white stronghold of the Galactic Empire in a *Star Wars* movie—stretching over acres of land, tucked into a wooden hillside, with gated access points and vast parking lots filled with shining cars. Past the hospital, he circled over the commercial centers of West Longmont, New Hampshire, and Black River, Vermont, and now Claire saw a new patchwork below—of concrete parking lots and big box retailers, old railroad yards and commercial buildings, interstate highways and traffic. Claire was struck by how small and contained the commercial development looked in comparison to the vast, undeveloped land that stretched in every direction. No wonder people loved living in the Lower Valley. They were surrounded by natural beauty, immersed in the sophistication of a college town, on the doorstep of countless recreational opportunities and served by a first-class medical center. If the winters weren't so long and cruel, the area would be ruined by an influx of people. Of course, Wally said it was already ruined, that Claire and the boys should have seen it forty years ago before all the development and people and traffic. The boys teased him that everything used to be so much better, that he was such an old guy, stuck back in the day.

"Maybe so," he said, "But I'm telling you, it *was* better, and you guys have no idea what you're missing."

Max turned north and followed the Connecticut River upstream. As he approached the bridge from Hancock to Greenwich, Vermont, he swooped down so low Claire wondered for a moment if he would try to land on the same stretch of river where they had taken their canoe ride weeks earlier. But the river was busy with people in kayaks and canoes, and upstream Claire could see the college crew teams in their shells, skimming over the water like exotic water bugs. Max pulled the wheel toward his chest and the classic old seaplane climbed into the sky.

She turned to him, eager to resume their earlier conversation.

"So you stopped acting and moved on?"

"Yes. I had done some voiceover work for a radio station and the owner heard I had gone to Princeton. He knew I wasn't making much money as an actor, so he asked if I wanted to come work for him. I became his right-hand man."

"And this was in California?"

"In LA and San Diego. He owned several stations."

"So when did you move to New England?"

"After I got divorced."

So he *had* been married. Claire had wondered about that on the canoe ride. "I'm sorry. Did you have any children?"

Max banked the plane and pointed toward a mountain off to the right, with wide swaths cut into its side. "There's the Hancock Skiway."

Evidently, when he didn't want to talk, he just banked the plane and pointed out a sight below. Was she asking too many questions? Wally had dubbed her Barbara Walters for the way she fired questions at people sometimes. But most people liked to talk about themselves, and she wanted to know more about Max. She tried another tack.

"Wally and I have two boys. They don't even know we're separated yet."

"We couldn't have children," said Max, turning to Claire. "And my wife didn't want to adopt."

Seeing the sadness in his eyes, she suddenly felt awful for interrogating him.

"Turned out I fired blanks," he said. "She found a new husband and had two lovely girls."

Claire didn't know what to say.

Max brightened, but it seemed like an act. "It wasn't all bad. For a while, I made the most of my condition and became quite a lady's man. No chance of getting anyone pregnant. But it got rather lonely. I moved east and built up my own small empire of radio stations, using everything I'd learned in California. Not a very exciting life, but there's still time to make up for it." He smiled at Claire and patted the antique wooden dash. "So how do you like the old bomber?"

"Very nice," she said, relieved to see him brighten. There was more to him than she had thought.

Max flew the plane close to the Hancock Skiway, where trails were cut into the side of Holt's Mountain, and Claire thought again of Jack and Josh growing up skiing there. Soon, she spied the peaks of Smarts, Cube and Moosilauke, all mountains she had climbed with Wally before he became obsessed with golf. Max swung the plane northwest and climbed even higher in the sky. Claire's view shifted from New Hampshire to Vermont, where the

Green Mountains rose in a breathtaking, rolling procession south to north.

"I want to show you something else," said Max over the sound of the engine. He reached a hand down toward the floor and came up holding one of his boat shoes. "Watch this!"

He cut the engine and the only sound was the wind rushing through the drafty cockpit.

Claire's stomach flipped upside down. "What are you DOING!" she cried, seized by panic.

Max casually released the boat shoe. It floated through the air. "Zero gravity!" he said. "Isn't that something?"

Claire nodded, terrified. The plane began to fall.

Max grabbed the shoe out of midair. "Here, you try it."

"No!" said Claire. "We're FALLING!"

Max released the shoe again. Claire watched it float to the ceiling as her stomach rolled more furiously than before. *Was he crazy?* He sat at the wheel, calm as a Hindu cow, smiling, as the plane dropped toward the earth.

"The ENGINE!" yelled Claire. "Turn on the engine!"

Max flicked the ignition and the engine roared to life. He pulled the nose up in a grand loop and leveled the plane. The shoe fell to the floor.

"Oh my GOD!" said Claire, patting her chest.

"I love zero gravity," said Max.

"I like hearing the engine!"

Max laughed. "You look a little pale."

You look a little psycho!

But evidently, he knew what he was doing. He banked the plane south and beamed at her. Could Wally ever fly around like a romantic bush pilot? He was too busy running into cars on his scooter.

"Sorry," said Max. "Most people like to see the shoe float."

"It's okay. I'm fine now."

"Let's go down and get some lunch. We can always come up again another time."

A wave of melancholy flowed over her from a source she couldn't identify. A part of her didn't want the ride to end.

As Max swooped down to land, the wind close to the river was just as strong as when they had taken off. The pontoons hit the water hard, bouncing over the rough surface like washboards—a hundred yards of jarring, stomach-rolling impact that brought all of Claire's earlier nausea roaring back stronger than ever. Before she knew it, her innards erupted, and she threw up all over Max's antique wooden dashboard. Turning to him to apologize, she was seized by a second upsurge that sprayed Max and the steering wheel.

"Oh goodness!" he said, never taking his eyes off the water or his hands off the wheel. "A gusher!" He reached under his seat and handed her a towel streaked with grease stains.

She pushed it back toward him, her other hand over her mouth. "No! You use it. I'm so sorry!"

He wiped down the wheel, cleaned off his hands and handed her the towel as he taxied toward the dock in front of his elegant riverfront home. He looked at her with a kind smile. "I think a little swim is in order. Clean off our clothes and feed the fish. Then, a hot shower, a soft bathrobe, and we'll have lunch on the deck."

But Claire had no appetite for lunch, just an overwhelming urge to flee for home. He could swim, shower and savor lunch on his own.

"Sorry about the rough landing," Max said, as they pulled up to his dock. "I hope you're okay."

She smiled weakly and nodded. *Such a gentleman.* You could tell a lot about a man splattered with your vomit. As she climbed out of the plane, she decided she would have to fit him in for a massage right away.

13

Wally woke up in his Adirondack chair and found Bear sitting next to him.

"Honey, you're home," he said.

"You're printing T-shirts this afternoon," said Bear, glaring at him. "And for as long as you want to stay here."

Wally sat up. "What are you talking about?"

"Your laptop was open. So I thought I'd read about me doing something heroic. But no." Bear chewed on a sandwich with the fury of a grizzly, looking ready to swat Wally with his free paw. "Have you written *anything* since you've been here?"

Wally squirmed in his seat.

"I don't care if you can't write," said Bear. "But don't *lie* to me about it."

"I've done a lot of thinking—a lot of outlining."

"You're printing T-shirts."

Wally leaned forward, radiating anxiety. "If Claire hears I'm printing T-shirts . . . or the boys find out . . . or Hughes Auto—I'm *screwed.*"

Bear ate his sandwich and looked out over the river. The day was cloudy but warm. Wally felt a trickle of sweat run down his temple. After what felt like forever, his friend turned to him and said, "Okay, here's the deal. You can chase down my overdue receivables."

"You want me to be a bill collector?"

"You can collect bills or print shirts," said Bear. "Your call."

That Sunday morning, as Claire flew over Hancock Country Club in Max's seaplane, Wally sat in Bear's office reviewing the list of overdue receivables with his new boss, who wasn't about to let him play golf. Some bills were forty-five days late, a handful closing in on sixty, a couple at ninety days overdue. Bear stabbed a meaty finger at the printout in front of Wally.

"Start with the ones at ninety. After that, move to sixty and focus on the biggest amounts," he said. "Phone calls won't work. I've tried. You gotta show up on their doorstep."

There had to be more than a dozen overdue accounts. Could Wally collect from all of them?

"I don't expect to see you in here every day," Bear said, pacing. "But I do want a daily report by email. Who you saw, when they're gonna pay. I'll cover your gas and give you half of what you collect."

Wally wondered if he could dictate his book while riding around in his pickup. He had squandered the perfect chance to write his novel. What a fool!

"Who knows," said Bear, "maybe this will give you something to write about—other than being a lying phony." He clapped Wally so hard on the back Wally almost fell out of his chair. "Just don't do anything stupid. Claire will never forgive me if someone punches in your pretty face."

Even though Bear said phone calls wouldn't work, the first thing Wally did on Monday morning was make some phone calls. He sat at his friend's kitchen table, drinking a cup of green tea, and tried to channel positive vibes, as Claire would, chanting a mantra, *think positive, be positive, receive positive.* But on his first call to Jerry's Gym in West Longmont, he said he needed to speak to someone about an overdue bill for Bear's Sportswear and was put on hold for ten minutes. He finally hung up and dialed the number again. This time, he was put on hold for five minutes before being disconnected, the dial tone an effective, "Fuck you." Maybe Bear was right. Maybe he would have to visit Jerry in person. But first, he tried calling some other delinquent accounts, starting with Olive's Organic Farm Stand, where he and Claire liked to get fresh produce every summer. Located just a few miles from their home in East Heifer, Olive's was operated by a group of trust fund hippies—kind, gentle folks who must have simply misplaced the bill. He got their answering machine, saying they were in the fields and greenhouses and would call back as soon as they could, so he left his name and number, but this time, learning from his experience with Jerry's Gym, he didn't say why he was calling. Next, he called Boone's Auto, sixty days overdue on an order of embroidered fleece vests. No answer there either, just a male voice with a thick Vermont accent: "Busy workin', maybe on your rig." Nothing about leaving a message. Somehow, Wally didn't expect a return call from Mr. Boone. He dialed the number for Sigma Delta, a Hancock College sorority that was overdue on an order of sweatshirts from Winter Carnival. He got another voicemail: "Hi, it's Lucia, leave me a message, and I'll call you back." This time, Wally said why he was calling, not wanting to be mistaken for some middle-aged stalker, and left his cell number. With strike four, he decided he would have to show up on some doorsteps.

But first, he needed to get into the right frame of mind. On his way to Jerry's Gym he drove to the Hancock Country Club practice holes to get his game face on for being a badass bill collector. He was ten minutes into his routine, striking balls from his favorite spot below the pines on the hill, when he heard the sound of a golf cart approaching.

Who was invading his sanctuary now?

He looked up and spotted a familiar vehicle climbing the hill—a customized golf cart with a BMW logo on the front, a metallic-yellow body and a sky-blue roof. *Shit!* The customized cart crested the hill and zoomed up to Wally, where it skidded to a sideways stop.

"Wally!" said Jack Hughes, Jr., looking as pleased with himself as ever. "How's the jingle coming along?"

"Should have the demo in another week."

Jack propped a foot against the dash and leaned back in his seat. "I thought we agreed on Friday?"

"I know, but I want to give you more than one option."

Jack eyed him suspiciously and ran a hand through his hair. He never wore a golf hat. Maintaining his tan was top priority. "You're not stringing me along, are you? Because I know you're probably distracted." He paused. "Ginger told me the news—about you and Claire."

Wally looked at him.

"Your wife's been a patient lady," Jack said. "And I'm a patient man. But I've got a GM breathing down my neck who wants to sell cars and earn his bonus. And right now, you're slowing things down."

"Next week," said Wally. "I promise."

"You're playing with fire," said Jack. "The digital agency is presenting tomorrow. Some real hotshots, apparently." He smacked his palm against the wheel. "But I guess you're a high-risk, high-reward kinda guy."

Jack stepped on the gas and spun the cart in a tight circle before stopping to share a parting word. "Good luck with Claire—she's a great lady. Hate to see you lose her, too." Then he stomped on the gas and drove away.

Hate to see you lose her, too. Sometimes small-town life could feel so suffocating. All the clichés were true. Everyone knew your business and if they didn't, they made it up. The truth? It was usually subjective. Claire saw their situation one way. He saw it another. And somewhere in between lay the reality.

Jerry clearly liked hitting the weights in his gym. The muscles in his upper body strained against the T-shirt he wore like a second skin, emblazoned with JERRY'S GYM and a barbell logo across the chest. His pecs protruded, his biceps bulged, his neck melted into his shoulders. Below his narrow waist, his thick thighs looked ready to burst out of his tight sweatpants as he balanced on the balls on his feet, rocking slightly to and fro. Wally had never seen such a specimen. Was Jerry even five foot five? He looked like a stunted Arnold Schwarzenegger. Even his ears had muscles. At six two, Wally towered over the diminutive, delinquent payee, but would that matter if Jerry threw a punch?

"We've had some issues," said the wee muscle man, talking out of the side of his mouth like a mini-Mafioso as he cradled a fluffy white lap dog in his arms, stroking its fur. "I need a little more time."

"A little more time?" said Wally.

"Whaddaya, deaf?"

"No. I just wondered how much—"

"Everyone's doin' Pilates and yoga now," Jerry said, nipping Wally's question in the bud. "Flexibility. Stretching. Core." He raised an arm and flexed his bicep. A magnificent muscle popped to life. "Whatever happened to bodybuilding? Powerlifting? Sculpting a beautiful frame?" He put his dog down on the floor and flexed, lifting a heel and posing.

"I don't know," said Wally. "Times change." He looked around the gym. In a far corner, an elderly man did bench presses using tiny weights. The fluffy white dog trotted over to lick his ankles. Otherwise, the place was empty. The mirrors lining the back wall reflected the emptiness, making the gym look even more deserted. Its strip mall location next to a sports bar and pizza place in West Longmont struck Wally as favorable. Plenty of traffic, good visibility. But there was no clientele, and as Wally eyed the glass display case filled with T-shirts and caps, sweatshirts and fleece from Bear's Sportswear, he wondered if he would ever extract a nickel from Jerry.

"The terms were half up front," he said to the little weightlifter. "The balance net twenty. It's over sixty days."

"I know the terms," said Jerry, rising on the balls of his feet, narrowing his eyes. "I'm not an *idiot.*"

"So how much longer do you need?"

Jerry stepped forward and pressed a finger into Wally's solar plexus. "As long as it takes. You got a problem with that?"

Wally bent over under the force of Jerry's finger. He lifted his palms in surrender. "No . . . just take it easy."

"*You* take it easy."

"I'm just doing my job."

"Oh yeah? Well, you can take your job and *shove it!*" Jerry shoved Wally back against a mirror. The fluffy white dog raced over and started barking at him.

"Maybe I'll stop back next week," said Wally, as the little dog nipped at his ankles. Wally wiggled his foot, trying to shoo it away.

"Stop back all you want," said Jerry, grabbing Wally's belt buckle and the front of his pants. He lifted Wally right off the floor like he was doing a curl with a barbell.

"OOOWWWWWWW!" cried Wally.

Jerry did another curl, crushing Wally's nuts in an epic wedgie.

"JEEZZZUS!"

Jerry let go. Wally reeled forward, his hands on his knees, pain surging through his groin. The little dog yelped and nipped at him.

"Fluffernutter!" barked Jerry and scooped the dog up off the floor. "Quiet!"

Wally staggered to the nearest weightlifting station and sat down gingerly on the bench.

The pint-sized Schwarzenegger stepped over beside him, cuddling his little dog, "In a couple-a weeks, I'm goin' down to Foxwoods. We'll see, maybe I can bring your money back then."

Oh, great! A gambler! The odds of collecting just got even worse.

Jerry gently patted Wally on the back. "You know, you really oughta get a membership here—especially if you're gonna go around collecting money."

He gave a high-pitched laugh. "Your arms look like pencils." And then the little bully bounded off on his toes to check in on his lone customer in the back corner, Fluffernutter clutched to his chest like a precious baby.

Wally took a deep breath and slowly got to his feet. Maybe Bear should hire Jerry to collect his bad debts. Jerry could certainly use the work. And with arms like pencils, Wally really should be writing.

June ~ The Strawberry Moon

"The strawberry plant is very delicate,
but the strawberry flavor is strong."

—Anonymous

14

It took Claire nearly a week to fit Max McClure in for a massage after the disastrous end to their plane ride because she was out straight with clients and also busy working on the Doggone Right Labor Day fundraiser. Millicent Fernwater may have been in charge of her committee, but Claire seemed to be the only one doing any work. Evidently, as the committee chairperson, Millicent assigned tasks but didn't actually *do* any of her own. That is, beyond sending Claire a steady stream of emails saying she needed to line up a tent, find a band and get a caterer—oh, and not just any caterer, but one who would wow the crowd of more than two hundred people. And she should also coordinate these efforts, Millicent directed, with the other two members of their committee—a lawyer and a dental hygienist. Claire wanted to write back and suggest that Millicent, as their subcommittee chairperson, should be the one to reach out to the lawyer and hygienist, but instead she bit her tongue. Why was saying no so hard for her? Why did she always bend over backwards for other people? Instead of standing up for herself, Claire promptly emailed the two other volunteers to ask if they wanted to take care of the tent. The lawyer volunteered, but within a matter of days he backed out. He had a big trial coming up and it looked like he might be out of commission for a few weeks—possibly right through Labor Day. So Claire assumed responsibility for the tent and asked the dental hygienist if she would line up the band. But the hygienist said she really didn't know much about music and really didn't feel qualified. "I'd hate to make a mistake!!!" she wrote back. Okay, then how about finding a good caterer, Claire asked. Oh no, the hygienist was on a diet!!! And looking at menus, going to tastings, sampling desserts—it would all be counterproductive. "But I can help you on the night of the event," she wrote back, signing off with a smiley face emoji and her usual three exclamation points.

Would Claire have to do *everything?*

Then Millicent piled on with yet another email. "Don't forget to coordinate lining up the Special Guest! I'll send you a master list of ALL the event volunteers so you can be in touch with every single one and make sure we find a WINNER! Ta-ta for now! Keep up the great work! M."

Seriously? Claire felt her resentment rising into anger, but still couldn't bring herself to write back and say, "You do it, Millicent! Stop being an email bully! We're all meant to be in this together!" She wished she could employ so many exclamation points and stick up for herself. But instead, she proceeded to do everything on her own.

And then she discovered that Labor Day weekend was a popular time during wedding season. *Of course!* Why hadn't Claire remembered? She and Wally had gotten married in the fall. With so many weddings, finding a tent and a dance floor, a hot band and a good caterer would be close to impossible. What vendors would be left at this juncture?

She began to wish she had never agreed to help Roz with the Doggone Right event. But that had been back in the winter, long before her separation from Wally, and she couldn't back out now. She told herself not to bother Roz with her problems working under Millicent Do Nothing—to just keep quiet and do her best—because Roz had a full plate of her own. *Be a help, not a burden.* So Claire spent her evenings researching vendors online, made follow-up phone calls between massage appointments and even skipped a few tai chi classes to visit with potential caterers. All for naught. The first caterer offered a limited repertoire of chicken wings, nachos and meatball sliders, and the second served a sampling of uninspired, overcooked, tasteless food. Even Claire could do better preparing Papa's fried chicken recipe, cornbread and collard greens. She prayed it wouldn't come to that! She soldiered on, sending emails to everyone involved with the event, encouraging them to line up a Special Guest and to keep her posted on their efforts—desperately hoping someone would deliver a hero and save the day. The only thing she felt confident of delivering at this point was plenty of beer and wine. Maybe getting everyone tipsy would do the trick and open up their checkbooks.

All this work and worry began to stress her out. Since Wally's departure, she had added more massages to her schedule to boost her income—because she had no idea what lay ahead. But giving more massages, her body felt the strain. If she had her choice, she would be tapering her schedule, not adding to it. After nearly twenty years of rubbing bodies, her hands and wrists and shoulders were getting worn out. Sometimes her lower back ached. Tai chi helped alleviate her discomfort and ease her pain as it rejuvenated her mind, body and spirit, but it couldn't turn back the clock. No, the clock kept ticking . . . a lot like a time bomb. But what else could she do? Massage paid well, and she wasn't qualified to replace the income doing something else. How did she spell S-T-U-C-K?

Wally had cleared up the overdue business line payment, and to his credit, he had also sent her a text to coordinate paying their bills for June. But what would happen in July? And August? And after that? What would his income be? And how much would she need to earn? If Wally were still at home, his work and income might not be any more certain, but at least he would be able to help her manage Millicent. He was much better about setting boundaries than she was and would put some of the work right back in Millicent's lap, where it belonged, by crafting one of his pointed emails for Claire. Why couldn't she do this for herself? Was she really such a wimpy, Catholic-girl martyr, as Roz always said? Always pleasing everyone else at her own expense?

"You are *such* a Goody Two-shoes," Roz had told her at the Dirt Cowboy back in February. "You want to go to heaven, be my guest. I'm taking a little detour and having some *fun!*"

"I have fun," said Claire.

"Oh really? Letting people walk all over you is fun?"

She really needed Wally to write Millicent that email, but unfortunately— *or was it fortunately?*—he had left.

When Max came for his massage, Claire would not accept his money, not after what had happened in the seaplane.

"It's my pleasure," she said after the session ended. "I feel so badly for . . . about . . . my . . ." She couldn't spit it out.

"Your projectiles?" said Max, lifting an eyebrow, his checkbook open.

Her face flushed.

"It's very kind of you," he said. "But I insist on paying."

Claire shook her head and reached down to close his checkbook.

"Not today."

"Very well, then," said Max. "You'll have to let me take you out for dinner instead. There's a new Italian restaurant in Hancock. Cuccina DiLucia. I've heard it's wonderful."

Claire hesitated.

"You don't like Italian food?"

"Oh, no, I love Italian food."

"Then how about Saturday—seven o'clock?"

Claire looked into his kind, eager eyes. She had been toiling hard, massaging clients and managing her event 'to do' list. Sleeping fitfully, tortured by dreams of a small, tattered tent, a horrendous three-piece band and rows of beef jerky served on plastic trays. A dinner out would be welcome. But she didn't want to lead Max on. He was still just a potential donor for Doggone Right, and that was it, right?

"I don't bite," he said with a smile. He really was a sweet, if older, man.

"Okay," she said, "Saturday at seven."

"Splendid! I'll pick you up at six forty."

"Oh, that's not necessary. We're on opposite sides of the river. I can just meet you there."

Max kept filling her glass of wine. It was very good and very expensive, much better wine than Claire was used to drinking with Wally, and she drank more of it, more quickly than usual, as a result. She had also spent a frustrating day trying to connect with a tent vendor for the event, only to discover their last remaining option was far too small. This experience had left her on edge and even more susceptible to the soothing qualities of the delicious wine. By the time she and Max finished their tasty appetizers, she had already enjoyed two glasses of the exquisite red, and when he lifted the bottle to pour her another, she put her hand over her glass.

"I think I better slow down," she said, feeling a warm, lightheaded glow. "It's lovely wine."

"For a very lovely lady," said Max, smiling at her with a great deal of charm. He cocked his head to one side. "It will go well with your swordfish."

Claire hesitated. "Maybe just a splash."

Max poured a splash that quickly turned into a wave.

"Whoa!" she said, waving for him to stop.

"When in Rome," he said with a smile. He tipped the bottle upside down in the bucket and waved at the waiter. Such a relaxed, confident air. With his expensive clothes, his rich tan and his closely cropped silver hair, Max looked like the aging movie star he had once hoped to be—one who might not have made many films recently but still oozed cachet. The other patrons in the restaurant eyed him, some doing double takes. Who was that handsome older gentleman?

"Roz tells me you've always wanted to go to Italy," he said. "Any place in particular?"

Claire lowered her eyes, not so much demurely as defensively. With the mention of Roz, she wondered where this might be headed.

"I don't know," she said, picturing the white beaches, the blue water and the copper-colored cliffs of the Amalfi Coast, a place she'd always dreamed of visiting. "Pretty much anywhere would be lovely. But I've never been, so I wouldn't really know."

"I've been several times," said Max. "And I have the most wonderful memories. I think you, of all people, Claire, would love it. And I would love to take you there."

A bolt of nervous energy surged through her. *Roz!* Was this part of her fundraising plan? She took a sip of wine. What should she say? Could she stall him? "That's very sweet of you," she said at last. "When were you thinking of going?"

"Whenever it suits you."

"Isn't it really hot in Italy right now? In the summer?"

"It's very nice on the water."

"It's probably crawling with tourists."

"I know some lovely, secluded spots off the beaten track."

"I really can't go anywhere until after the Doggone Right event. I'm out straight with that."

"Italy is *divine* in September," said Max with a smile. The man had an answer for everything! "That will give me plenty of time to arrange everything with Waddell."

"Waddell?"

"My personal assistant."

Of course! Being wealthy, he wouldn't have to do anything for himself. Waddell would make all the arrangements.

"We can spend some time in Rome," he continued. "And then go to Venice—such a romantic city. After that, there's a wonderful villa in Tuscany, with a swimming pool and a tennis court, vineyards, lovely walks. There's a restaurant in the old village nearby that has the *best* beef Bolognese."

It all sounded divine, but what about the Amalfi Coast? She scolded herself: *Claire! That's the wine talking! You can't travel through Italy with Max McClure!* And then she heard Roz in her head, scolding her.

"He'll be putty in your hands! Just go! It's a first-class trip to Italy—are you crazy?"

"No, Roz, I'm not crazy. I'm just not sure about Max."

"You don't have to marry him! Just go on the trip and have some fun. How hard is that?"

Claire didn't have an answer.

"The shelter really needs his money," said Roz, applying the guilt.

"I wish Sifu was inviting me."

"That New Age knucklehead?"

"I find him very alluring."

Max reached a hand across the table and gently tapped her on the wrist. "Hello?" he said. "Anyone home?"

Claire smiled weakly. "I'm sorry. My mind was wandering."

Max lifted his glass. "To Italy."

Claire hesitated.

"And adventure," he coaxed.

Claire wrapped her fingers around the stem of her wineglass, but she couldn't lift it.

"I don't bite," he said, reciting his standard fallback line.

"I know," she said, and heard Roz in her head: *"Some of our rescues bite! Clink his goddamn glass!"*

Max continued to hold his glass up in front of her, his elbow resting on the table. "Shall I wait forever?"

Claire held up her glass. "To Doggone Right," she said.

"And Italy?"

"Italy sounds divine, Max," said Claire, "but I'm really—"

He clinked her glass before she could finish her sentence, like a tennis player poaching at the net. "To a fall trip to Italy!"

He smiled triumphantly as her glass rang. Had she just been tricked into agreeing to go? What if she didn't drink after clinking glasses? Would that void the agreement? She had to do something.

"To Doggone Right," she said, lifting her glass to her lips.

"To Doggone Right *and* Italy," said Max, a glint in his bright blue eyes.

They drank, eyeing each other, Claire terrified she was agreeing to something she wasn't sure about. As she lowered her glass, Claire said, "Roz is very excited about your support of the shelter." Hoping to steer the conversation away from Rome, Venice and Tuscany.

"Roz does a wonderful job," said Max. "Everyone at the shelter does."

"So . . . when do you plan . . . to . . . ah . . . write a check? I think Roz was hoping it would be soon—before Labor Day, so she can use your donation to encourage matching funds." *And maybe that way, I won't have to go to Italy.*

Max held up his wineglass and swirled the deep red nectar. He smiled at Claire. "I thought I'd write the check when we return from the trip." And then he took a good, long drink, looking like the cat who had swallowed the canary.

"I see," said Claire, and blanched. She reached for her wine, her stomach tightening. *Now what?* The waiter brought their meals, and over her superb swordfish with puttanesca sauce, she listened to Max wax poetic about Italy. When he asked if she wanted more wine, she felt so forlorn about her entrapment, she said, "Maybe one more glass."

Max beamed. "You're going to love Italy!"

When it came time for dessert, Claire ordered tiramisu. Why not? She felt totally trapped, like a slut for the shelter, set up by Roz, outfoxed by Max and no longer in control of her own destiny. Why not rub tiramisu on her wounds? The wine could only go so far. Savoring every bite of the sinfully delicious dessert, she told herself that she hadn't really agreed to anything. Not technically. Not legally. Still, the prospects of wrangling her way out of traveling to Italy with Max looked awfully dire, unless she wanted to incur the wrath of Roz and let down all those helpless dogs. She wondered how much Max would donate. She shoveled in another forkful of the moist and fluffy dessert, rolling her eyes in rapture, and decided to ask. What did she have to lose?

"So do you have a figure in mind for the shelter?" she said and licked her fork like a lollipop.

"Isn't that a rather personal question?"

"Yes and no," said Claire, smacking her lips. "Seeing as I am part of the equation."

"So you'd like to estimate your value, is that it?"

Claire piled another bite of tiramisu onto her fork and held it out toward Max. "Wanna bite?"

"No thanks," said Max, patting his trim tummy.

"Roz said you were thinking of fifty thousand," Claire continued, feeling the color rise in her cheeks, astonished at her brazen line of questioning. How much wine had she drunk? What was she doing? She shoved the forkful of dessert into her mouth to shut herself up.

"Yes, I was," said Max. "But I could double that, if things go well."

Claire nearly spit her tiramisu across the table. But she caught herself before splattering her dessert onto Max's tailored linen sport coat. He might give Doggone Right one hundred thousand dollars? Thanks to her? Talk about a high-priced call girl! Her self-esteem swung wildly between the depths of whoredom and the heights of adoration. How had she suddenly become worth one hundred grand at age fifty-one? Max hadn't even seen her naked yet. *Damn.* She had no idea she was so hot. Italy was certainly hot. And Max was pretty hot, too, for a man of seventy. His bank account sizzled. Suddenly, the whole restaurant felt hot. Claire's cheeks and forehead were burning up, her neck and chest scorching.

"Are you all right?" said Max.

"It's a little warm in here, don't you think," she said and reached for her water. Surprised to see Max's face slipping in and out of focus, she knocked over her glass, and when she fainted, her face planted right onto her tasty tiramisu.

Max kindly offered to drive her home, but she declined, wiping her face with a moistened linen napkin.

"I'll be fine," she said. "Really. Just a sugar overload. I should have passed on dessert." *And the last glass of wine.*

"Looks like you're sprouting an egg." He pointed to her forehead.

She reached up and felt a lump.

"Good thing you're not bleeding," said Max. "You shattered the plate. And spilled water all over me."

"I'm *so* sorry."

"It's fine. I like a headstrong woman!" Max laughed at his joke. "Let me fetch you some ice."

As he walked away, Claire's phone buzzed in her purse. She ignored it. Her phone buzzed again and she saw it was Roz. *Not now.* Her phone buzzed a third time. No wonder Roz had sold so much real estate. She was ruthless.

Claire answered. "What *is* your problem?"

"It's not *my* problem," said Roz. "It's *your* problem. You need to get over to the Turnbull's and pick up Gus. *Right now!*"

"Right now?"

"Yes."

"I'm with Max McClure right now."

"In *bed?*"

"No! At Cuccina DiLucia."

"How sweet! I told him you've always wanted to go to Italy." "I know. He told me."

"Well . . . are you going?"

"I don't know."

"You *have* to go! Getting away would be *sooooo* good for you," Roz said, and then she ranted and raved about how Claire needed to go on the trip. Claire held the phone away from her ear. When Roz finally finished, she asked, "So what did Gus do?"

"I don't know. But the Turnbulls want him out right now."

Claire saw Max approaching with a bag of ice and said, "I have to go."

"Tell Max you're going to Italy!"

"Goodbye, Roz."

Max handed her the ice, and Claire pressed the cold plastic against her forehead like a prizefighter between rounds. Now she had to rescue Gus. Who was going to rescue her?

"I'm afraid I have to go," she told Max. "There's an emergency with Gus." "Gus?"

"The rescue dog you met a few weeks ago—at the shelter? Evidently, the Turnbulls are kicking him out."

"Somehow that doesn't surprise me," said Max, sitting back down and putting his napkin in his lap. "He did have a bit of an attitude."

Indeed, thought Claire, *don't we all?* Some attitudes were simply more overt than others. Just look at Roz. Everyone had their view of the world, of right and wrong, happy and sad, smart and stupid. You couldn't get through life without an attitude of some kind. She needed to remember that. And maybe even change her attitude, if such a miracle were possible. Holding the bag of ice against her forehead, she stood and thanked Max for a lovely dinner. He rose like a gentleman, and she let him kiss her on the cheek. She apologized for leaving, even though she was relieved to have the excuse.

"We'll do this again before our trip," said Max, squeezing her hand.

At a loss for how to reply, Claire came up with, "Ciao!" and smiled, delighted to have thought of such a clever, noncommittal, answer. That's the attitude! *Think on your feet, girlfriend!*

She gave Max a coy wave and turned for the door, wondering what on earth Gus had done to be evicted at nine twenty-five on a Saturday night?

15

Claire found Arthur Turnbull waiting in his driveway, holding Gus on a leash. As her headlights swung over him, Arthur held a hand up to his eyes and waved as if he'd just been discovered on a remote desert island. A short, pudgy man in his midfifties, with a mop of disheveled white hair, Arthur was a prominent lawyer in town, known as a brilliant, somewhat eccentric fellow. Wearing a bathrobe and slippers, he looked like a gnome out for a stroll. Gus sat placidly next to him, his head tilted, watching Claire's car, looking as nonplussed and intelligent as ever.

Claire parked and undid her seat belt, but before she could open the door, Arthur Turnbull whisked Gus over to the Prius and ushered him into the back seat. He tossed the leash in after him.

"He's all yours," said Arthur.

"I'm sorry it didn't work out," said Claire. "What happened?"

"Let's just say he lacks manners and leave it at that. Shirley is traumatized. Your shelter does good work, but you need to train these dogs."

"We try."

"Well, you need to try harder!" For a short fellow, Arthur Turnbull slammed the back door with tremendous force. As Claire's car reverberated, he turned for the house, running his fingers through his wild white hair. "Totally inappropriate!" he said.

She looked back at Gus. "What on earth did you do?"

Gus turned away, a Rasta forelock falling over one eye.

"When we get home," said Claire, "we are having a talk!"

But Gus was already dialed into Claire's frequency, and he immediately replied telepathically, their animal communication session off and running: "I didn't do anything the gardener didn't do."

Surprised to hear his response echoing in her head, Claire asked, "And what was that?"

"Stick his nose in Shirley's crotch and hump her like crazy."

"Gus!"

"The woman is insatiable. And her husband has no idea. I was trying to send him a message."

"Well, it clearly backfired."

"Will you please drive? This place gives me the creeps."

Claire put the car in reverse and pulled out of the driveway. Gus hopped into the front seat.

"Did you know, in my last life," he said, perched regally beside her, "I sat on the Swedish throne?"

"Well, in this life," she said, "you're a *dog*."

"I think I'm having an identity crisis."

His pungent dog odor soon filled the car, and as Claire drove past the College Green, Gus eyed pedestrians on the lighted sidewalks with curiosity. His head swiveled, following the students, his little tuft of Rasta hair jiggling above his eyes. He was obviously intelligent, but like some bright adolescents he seemed to get bored easily and find trouble as a result. Claire drove down the hill out of town and soon crossed the bridge to Vermont and headed for home.

"You're not taking me back to the shelter?" Gus said.

"The shelter is closed. I'll bring you in the morning."

Gus eyed her. "You look pretty, all dressed up. Were you on a date?"

"I was."

"Let me guess—Max McClure?"

Claire nodded.

"Then I did you a favor. That's the second time I've saved your ass. Talk about someone who wants to stick his nose in your crotch and hump you."

"Gus! That's enough!"

The dog smiled at her, a string of drool swinging from his gums. He slurped it up with his long tongue.

"You need to stop behaving like such an animal," said Claire.

With that, Gus turned indignant. "*Me?* What about human beings! Dogs don't fight wars. We don't butcher each other by the tens of thousands. Incinerate each other by the millions. We don't drop bombs on civilians. Or unleash poisonous gas on innocent children. And we don't stand by, refusing to stop the carnage. You humans are the lowest form of animal."

Claire looked at him, caught off guard by his outrage. His soulful brown eyes bored into hers.

"You build shelters for dogs," he continued, "but how often do you rescue each other? What about the homeless and the starving? The sick and the suffering?"

"There are lots of people who help others," said Claire.

"Maybe so, but you humans are so arrogant. You think you know everything and rule everything. But you don't know anything and you're destroying the planet. At this rate, you're going to burn it up—if you don't blow it up first."

Claire sighed. "You're depressing me."

"Well, don't call me an *animal*. Because you guys are the problem, not *us*. Dogs are basically just loyal nitwits."

"Except you, apparently."

"I could be loyal to the right person." Gus blinked at her. "You have nice legs, you know that?"

"Oh please."

"Life is short. You can't spend all your time alone."

"I can't adopt you right now, Gus. Things are too uncertain."

"I'm good company. Stimulating, thought-provoking, devilishly handsome in a PC, biracial way."

Claire shook her head. "I can't do it."

"You know how to work a can opener, don't you? Fill a bowl with water? It's not rocket science taking care of a dog."

Claire sighed. Her head ached. Through the windshield, she could see the moon above the trees on the opposite shore of the river, casting a luminous glow over the water.

"I love the moon," Gus said. "Never saw it from the Turnbulls. They hardly took me outside."

Claire's heart went out to him, but she couldn't get sucked in. *You don't know what you're doing with your own life, how can you be responsible for his?*

The next morning, she returned him to Doggone Right. The manager reassured her that they would give it one more shot and try to place Gus into a new home. When a volunteer led Gus back to the kennels, Claire leaned over the counter and said to the manager, "Please, don't do anything to him without letting me know."

"Don't worry," said the woman. "We won't."

"I can deliver him to his new home, if that helps."

"Thanks, Claire, we'll keep you posted."

Driving away, fighting back tears, she couldn't shake the feeling that life without Wally was more derailed than life with him. What was wrong with her? Too much wine and sugar? A suitor she didn't really want? An eagerness to please Roz and the dogs? An inability to confront Millicent? Who knew she would develop a crush on a rebellious canine philosopher? Maybe she was just exhausted from her added client load and the Doggone Right to-do list. But whatever it was, being alone after so many years had left her feeling adrift. She missed Wally, and for better or worse, wanted him to come home.

16

Wally heard someone call, "FORE!" and ducked, but as fate would have it, ducking put his head directly in line with the errant shot. He felt a sharp blow above his right ear and stumbled forward. His world spun wildly out of focus, and then everything went black.

Out of the darkness, the ghostly image of an elderly woman's face appeared to him. With jowls like Jabba the Hutt and makeup that could have been caked on with a putty knife, she looked stern and imposing. A thick layer of ruby-red lipstick covered her lips and a nest of wavy silver hair topped her head. She stared at Wally from behind a pair of blue cat-eye glasses this time and declared, "Lawdy me, look what the cat dragged in!"

He recognized that deep Southern accent. It belonged to Mama Betty, Claire's beloved grandmother. No wonder her gray hair looked so tidy—Mama Betty always wore a wig.

"Am I dead?" said Wally.

"Not yet, honey chile," she said. "But if you keep lyin' to yourself, you might be. In a spiritual fashion."

"I know. It's terrible. I've got writer's block. "

"Not anymore, you don't! I'm here to help."

"You?"

"That's right, sweet cheeks. You did say a prayer, didn't you? To the writin' gods?"

Wally thought back to the plea he had issued on Bear's deck a few weeks earlier and to the subsequent prayers he had made, seeking inspiration for his writing. "Yeah, but I expected a different—"

"More famous writer?"

"Yeah. Kinda."

"Well, you got me. Fitzgerald is drunk and Hemingway is shootin' ducks."

"What about Jim Harrison?"

"Gone fishin'. And he is catchin' some whoppers, too!"

Wally's head throbbed. A warm trickle flowed into his ear.

"I reckon you're gonna need some stitches when you come to."

"So I'm really not dead?"

"Not your time, honey chile. Not even in the waitin' room. You just took a good shot—and who knows, mighta just knocked some sense into you!"

Mama Betty straightened her cat-eye glasses on her thick pug nose.

"I'll see *you* tomorrow mornin'," she said. "Six o'clock sharp—at the keyboard!" And with that she vanished in a puff of smoke.

Wally heard another voice call to him.

"Wally? *Wally?* You still with us?" It was Harry. His golf buddy, the ER nurse.

Wally opened his eyes and saw Harry leaning over him.

"Hey," said Harry. "Welcome back."

Wally's head throbbed and his right ear rang. Harry pressed a towel against his temple.

"What happened?" said Wally.

"You got hit by a golf ball."

"Shit." He tried to prop himself up on his elbows.

"Easy," said Harry. "There's no rush."

Wally looked up and saw Bear standing next to Harry. "You were out," said Bear. "For like a minute. It was scary."

"Traveling among the ether, I would imagine," said Danny Boy, peering over Harry's shoulder. "Off in another dimension."

"I've seen people fall into a coma," said Harry. "We didn't want that."

Wally didn't remember anything. He was only conscious of opening his eyes and seeing Harry come slowly into focus, staring down at him with a look of grave concern.

"Do you know where you are?" Harry asked.

"Hancock Country Club."

"Can you tell me your birthday?"

"June twenty-fifth."

"And where do you live?"

"At Bear's. You know that."

"Yes, I do," said Harry. "Let's make sure you don't have any other issues. You fell pretty hard."

Harry put Wally through a series of tests, asking him to wiggle his fingers and then his toes, to follow Harry's finger with his eyes—side to side, up and down. He tested Wally's neck, lifted one knee and then the other, making sure Wally's spinal column was functioning properly. As Harry checked him out, Bear held the towel against the side of his head. It felt like he'd been whacked by a splitting maul. A crowd had gathered behind Danny, a semicircle of other golfers eager to see if Wally was okay. He spotted Jack Hughes among them.

"How y'all doin'?" he called to the crowd, surprised to hear himself speak with a Southern twang.

Terry said, "We're all doin' just fine," mimicking his Southern drawl. "It's you we're concerned about, Henrik."

"No need to fret yourselves," said Wally, sounding more like Bobby Jones than Henrik Stenson. "I feel more chipper than a jaybird." *What was with this Southern accent, anyway?* He noticed Bear and Harry eyeing each other, probably wondering the same thing.

"It looks like everything's working," Harry said, finishing his exam. He helped Wally sit up. "Let's look at that wound."

Bear pulled the towel away. Wally felt a warm trickle flow over his ear.

"I think you're going to need some stitches," said Harry.

"Can't you sew me up?" Wally asked, his voice laced with Southern charm. "With that little med kit of yours?"

"Nope. You'll have to go to the ER."

Wally took the towel from Bear and pressed it against his wound.

Jack Hughes came over and knelt down next to him. "I'm really sorry, Wally," he said. "That shot got away from me. I never pull the ball like that. *Never.*"

Jack Hughes had hit him?

"I yelled fore, but you moved right into the path of the ball."

Seriously? *Jack Hughes?*

"I got hit once down in Florida," Jack continued. "Right between the shoulder blades. You play enough golf, at some point, you're gonna get hit. Are you okay?"

Wally looked at Jack and said, "Don't you worry your pretty little face, Jackie boy. Nothin' wrong your lawyah can't fix—with a little million-dollah settlement."

Jack gave out a nervous laugh.

"Or maybe you'd prefer a separate business arrangement, whereby I maintain my status as your *ex*-clusive advertisin' agent? With all the radio comin' my way, togethah with the print and *di*-rect mail. Seein' how I've made you a small fortune by providin' all that—with some real *cre*-ative flair, I might add—for the past twenty-so years."

Jack opened his mouth to speak, but for once no words came out. Not a single tried-and-true cliché.

"What's the mattah, Jackie-boy? Cat gotcha tongue?" Wally's Southern accent was so entrenched he wondered who was talking, anyway—him or another being?

Jack Hughes nervously ran his hand through his hair, squirming, searching for a solution.

"I already gave you an extension on the jingle," he said. "Against the wishes of my GM."

"Your GM is nothin' but a vipah in our little Garden of Eden," said Wally. "If it ain't broke, don't fix it! Ain't nothin' broke in your advertisin', Jack. Y'all mintin' money!"

"We need a digital presence," said Jack.

"Then y'all *get* a digital presence! Shouldn't affect the general advertisin'."

Jack scratched his head, looking unsure.

Wally pulled the towel from his head. A crimson circle stained the fibers. He turned to Bear. "I think we bettah get a few photos. Just for the record."

Bear pulled out his cell phone and started taking pictures of Wally's head wound.

Jack Hughes put a hand in front of Bear's phone. "That won't be necessary, fellahs! We don't need photos. You can have all the radio, Wally."

"And all the print and *di*-rect mail."

"And all the print and direct mail."

"And a five-thousand-dollah monthly retainah."

"Now wait a minute . . ."

"Been five years since I had a raise, Mistah Jack," Wally said in his new Southern twang. "Bear, I believe blood is flowing ovah my ear."

Bear lifted his phone and took a photo.

Jack Hughes threw up his hands. "Fine! Five thousand a month."

"Bettah make it six," said Wally, letting the blood drip from his ear onto his shirt. "Shake on that?"

Wally extended his hand and Jack shook it lamely.

"Got us plenty of witnesses," said Wally, looking at his friends. "Each one a Bible-swearin', church-goin', Lord-lovin' man of his word. So you'll be keeping yours." He looked at Jack Hughes.

"Yeah, yeah," said Jack, waving a hand at Wally. "Of course. Just stop talking in that stupid Southern accent!"

"Lawdy, wish I could," said Wally. "But it sho''nough is liberatin'!"

Jack slunk off with his playing partners, and the crowd dispersed.

Bear helped Wally to his feet. "That, my friend, was *awesome!*"

"Performance of a lifetime," said Danny Boy. "Quite clever, throwing the Southern accent at him like that. Never seen Jack Hughes tongue-tied before."

"Me neither," said Harry.

"Worked like a charm, I reckon!" Wally said.

"You can let it go now," said Bear.

"Wish I could," said Wally, stuck deep in the north Georgia mountains. "But this way a talkin' appears to be a *di*-rect *ree*-sult of gettin' hit by that onion!"

"You gotta be kidding me," said Bear.

"I don't think he is," said Danny Boy, reaching into his bag for his one hitter. "I think he's our very own Southern gentleman."

"Amen!" said Wally.

"There *is* a syndrome," said Harry, eyeing Wally warily, "that happens sometimes with organ transplants. The recipient takes on the characteristics of the donor."

"He didn't have a fucking brain transplant," said Bear. "He got hit on the head by a golf ball!"

"There's another possibility," said Danny Boy. "If you're open to it."

"What's that?" said Bear.

"Another entity could have entered his body."

"Another entity?" scoffed Bear. "Have another hit."

"There are souls in the ether," said Danny Boy, "looking for a vessel to carry them. When Wally was out, another being could have slipped in."

"You are *so* stoned," said Bear.

"It could be a post-traumatic effect," said Harry. "Head injuries are unpredictable. It could pass. We'll just have to see."

"If y'all just wrap up my head," said Wally, "we can finish our round and *en*-joy the back nine."

"I think you need to go to the ER and get stitches," said Harry. "Maybe even an x-ray or CAT scan."

"Nonsense!" said Wally. "Just wrap me up."

Harry shook his head. "I don't advise it, but if that's what you want, we'll give it a try." He took a thick piece of gauze from his portable med kit and placed it over Wally's wound. Then Harry wrapped an ACE bandage around Wally's head that made him look like a wounded soldier coming off the battlefield.

"Rhett Butler lives," said Danny Boy, a cloud of smoke drifting above his head.

"I do believe I had the honor," said Wally. He climbed to his feet and teed up his ball. Took his stance and told himself to concentrate. But at the top of his backswing, his ball got blurry, the ground tilted up at him and suddenly everything went black again.

17

As usual, Wally showed up late, and when he finally walked into Hopper's Bar & Grill wearing his hockey helmet and his high school letterman's jacket, Claire's heart sank. Had nothing changed? She scolded herself for thinking anything would be different after six weeks apart. Silly woman! The idea of having lunch with Wally, delayed for a week by some stupid golf accident, suddenly felt like a bad idea. She had acted impulsively, feeling lonely and confused. Why hadn't she just checked in with Bear? Or talked to the Professor, who would have the latest news on Wally from Danny Boy? A little recon would have gone a long way.

Wally gave her a peck on the cheek and took a seat across the booth. "Well, bless your heart, honey chile, it is *mighty* fine to lay eyes on you," he said in a thick Southern accent. "You're lookin' pretty as a peach!"

"Thank you," said Claire, wondering what he was up to with a Southern accent.

"Sorry I was *dee*-layed. Finishin' a chapter and lost *all* track of time!"

"Wallace!" she snapped. "What's with the Southern accent?"

"Long story, honey chile. But the short version: I am channelin' your grandmothah! Mama Betty is in the house!"

"Ha ha. Very funny."

"She is one *helluva* writah."

Claire said, "If this is your idea of a joke . . ."

"Don't get your knickers in a knot, sweet pea! I'll tell you all about it ovah lunch. I am *stahvin'*!"

Claire looked around, embarrassed by Wally's loud Southern voice, aware of people looking over at their table because of his booming proclamations. She leaned forward and said, "Can you please keep it down?"

"Sho' 'nough, shugah plum!" he said in a near shout.

"And can you take that helmet off?"

"No, ma'am! Doctor's orders! Can't risk another head injury for a year. Or I might turn into a vegetable patch."

"Will you stop talking like that!"

Wally leaned forward and took her hands in his. "Sweet cheeks, I am *rollin'* down the track. Thousand words a day. Pilin' up the pages like fresh-picked cotton. Pure and fine! Never seen a' thing like it, *no sir.*"

Clutched in his palms, her hands felt as sticky and humid as a July day in Georgia. She pulled them away.

"I think I need a drink," she said.

"Reckon I'll join you. Little glass of blackberry wine."

"Blackberry wine?" said Claire. She leaned back in the booth. "You *are* channeling Mama Betty."

"True enough, honey chile! Woman's changed my life. I'm tellin' you, this book is gonna be *somethin'!*" Wally picked up the menu. "What looks good? I could eat a horse!"

Claire stared at him, dumbfounded. What had happened to her husband? The short version appeared pretty clear. But what was the long story? Beyond the fact that Mama Betty had been a formidable presence in her day, the secretary to Governor Sanders of Georgia who wrote his speeches and organized his political calendar—in addition to giving him sage political advice. If Wally was channeling her grandmother, watch out. Mama Betty could not only write, she could also run the state of Georgia from behind the scenes, long before women even held office.

The waitress arrived and Claire ordered a Bloody Mary. When Wally asked for blackberry wine in his Southern accent and his hockey helmet, the waitress smiled at him gently, like he was a lunatic, and said, sorry, but they didn't have any blackberry wine.

"No blackberry wine? Then bring me a Southern Comfort, darlin'," he said and winked at her.

When the young lady left, Claire leaned across the table and said, "You can't wink at the waitress like that and call her darlin'. This isn't Atlanta in 1966!"

"All right, Miss Claire," said Wally, in his rich Southern tone. "Calm down. Ain't nobody cryin' foul."

Claire couldn't believe what she was seeing. "So how did Mama Betty . . . you know . . . slip inside you?"

Wally knocked his hockey helmet with his knuckles. "Appears to be when I got hit by a golf ball."

"That turned you into my grandmother?"

"Evidently, honey chile. Because when I came to, Mama Betty started talkin' through me. Danny Boy says it can happen. Dead people lookin' for a vessel to express themselves. And Harry says some people who have transplants, they start actin' like their donors. Mama Betty, she comes and goes. When I sit down to write, watch out! She blows in like a hurricane, and I just try to get it all down. After I'm done writin', she tends to linger for a spell—or until she eats somethin'! Then I'm back to bein' regular ol' Wally."

Claire shook her head, dumbfounded, and muttered, "My grandmother is your muse." The realization both astonished and pained her. Why couldn't Claire be Wally's muse? She was the one who had stayed loyal and supportive through all the years of close calls and rejections. The one who believed in him enough to support his decision to leave the ad agency. Now Mama Betty was getting all the credit for him writing this novel? *Totally unfair!*

The waitress brought their drinks and Claire ordered a Caesar salad. Wally ordered a bowl of tomato bisque, a house salad, a basket of chicken wings, a hamburger, a hot dog, onion rings, a side of mac and cheese and a coffee milkshake.

"Eating for two, are we?" said Claire.

"Might as well be pregnant," he said, patting his tummy. "Givin' birth to the great American novel! All that writin' burns up the calories."

"Mama Betty always had a good appetite."

"Can't blame her, with Papa's cookin'. That man *loved* his kitchen. Brisket. Grits. Black-eyed peas. Coleslaw. Key lime pie. Makes a mouth water just talkin' about it."

Claire asked if Mama Betty was helping Wally with Hughes Auto as well. Or was she strictly a fiction writer?

"Oh no, " said Wally, with a bright smile. "She writes some mighty fine ad copy. Wrote us a jingle just the other day. And got me a raise!"

"Jack Hughes gave you a raise?" Claire couldn't believe it. Wally had tried to get a raise from Hughes Auto for five years—with no luck.

"That's right. Jack hit me with the golf ball. While I was lyin' there, bleedin' like a stuck pig, Mama Betty put the screws right to him. Doubled my retainah! I'll cover all the bills from now on, sweet cheeks. You don't need to worry 'bout a thing."

Was he serious? She didn't have to massage anyone? She found it hard to believe. "Are you kidding me, Wally? Because if this is a—"

"Six thousand a month," said Wally. "Doubled up on old Jackie boy. No joke."

Claire didn't know what to say. Mama Betty always was a fierce negotiator. "I can't believe it, Wally."

"I'll tell you what else," he said. "I am shootin' *lights out*, now that my writer's block is ovah. Breakin' 80 every round!"

Claire smiled weakly and sipped her drink, pained to see him doing so well. Why wasn't he pining away for her? Feeling lonesome and confused, his life upside down, like hers?

"That scarf looks *mighty* fine wrapped 'round your pretty little head," said Wally.

Claire's fingers touched her forehead beneath the silk. "Oh, thanks . . . I bumped my head last week, too. But I didn't turn into Mama Betty." *And run into a string of absurd good luck!*

"I think she wants to help me win you back, honey chile."

Claire swirled her stick of celery in her drink. *Mama Betty was trying to save her marriage?* She had told Claire, *Wally's a good writer. Just needs to find his voice, is all.* Had she really jumped in to help?

"If you really want to win me back," said Claire, taking the leap, "why don't you come do it back at home?"

Wally looked into her eyes and hesitated, intertwining the fingers of his two hands in front of him as if in prayer, lifting his fingers up and down in a manner eerily reminiscent of Mama Betty. "Oh lawd, honey chile. I don't know. I am pilin' up the pages."

"You can write at home—with Mama Betty's help."

Wally fidgeted in his seat and looked apologetically at Claire. "Oh, I don't know, darlin', she just *loves* bein' at Bear's. Sittin' on that deck, lookin' at the river. Watchin' the birds dart through the early mornin' mist. Seein' the sunset and later on, the moonlight reflectin' like quicksilver on the water. Yes ma'am, lotta inspiration livin' at Bear's."

Claire felt her stomach tighten. "Is this Mama Betty talking? Or you?"

A crimson tide rolled up Wally's face, giving her the answer before he even opened his mouth. "Slap my head and call me silly, but I am in the flow, shugah plum. If I break the rhythm now, I don't know *what* will happen. Might lose all my momentum. And then I could lose you *forever.*"

Why was she so weak and stupid? Asking him to come home!

"Can't have that," said Wally. "I'd be naked as a jaybird without you."

What infuriating logic! Staying at Bear's so he wouldn't lose her? He was crazier than ever. Why did this hurt so much? Was he just trying to get even?

The waitress appeared and delivered their food. Wally's prodigious order barely fit on their table.

"And your milkshake," said the waitress, squeezing the tall glass into the last open space.

"Why, thank you, sweetheart," said Wally, oozing Southern charm. "Oh, and darlin', I'll take a piece of your *pee*-can pie for dessert when the time comes."

The waitress rolled her eyes at Claire and left for another table.

Wally picked up an onion ring and said, "I do expect the book oughta be completed by Labor Day. And then I can move back home."

So he wanted her to spend the whole summer alone? Could he be any more selfish? She watched him chew the onion ring with his mouth open just like her grandmother used to do. "By Labor Day," she said, stung by his decision, "you could weigh two hundred and fifty pounds and have jowls bigger than Mama Betty. Stop eating with your mouth open!"

"That's your grandmother, honey chile. Not me."

"Well, it's gross. And take that hockey helmet off!"

"I reckon it's safe in here," said Wally and carefully removed his helmet.

He reached for his milkshake and sucked on his straw so long and so hard he came up gasping for air. Then he pulled a chicken wing through his front teeth, skinning off the meat. "Nothin' personal, sweet pea" he said with his mouth full, giving her a good glimpse of chicken. "But stayin' at Bear's, we're gonna have us a bestsellah!"

Claire stood up. "Do what you want," she said, a tremble in her voice. "You always do." And with that, she walked out, wondering why she ever thought she missed him or wished he were home.

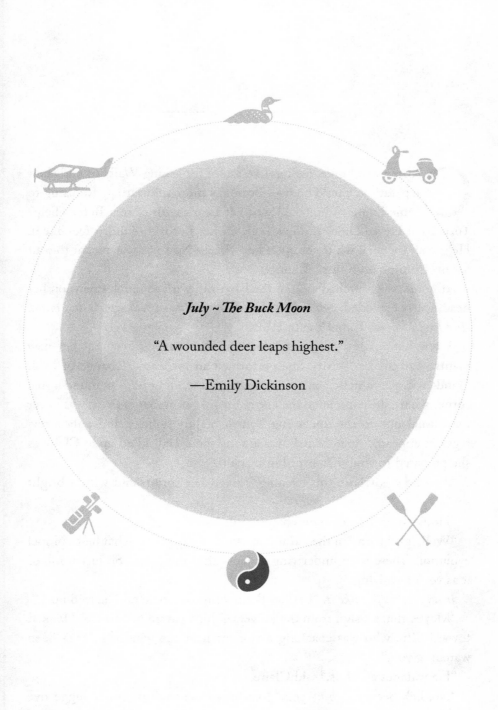

July ~ The Buck Moon

"A wounded deer leaps highest."

—Emily Dickinson

18

Claire drove home, feeling like a fool for asking Wally to end their separation. Could he have been any more infuriating? Refusing to come home so he could write at Bear's with Mama Betty's help? Turncoats! He said he was doing it all for her, but it sure didn't feel like it. He got all the luck while she spun her wheels. Now she was meant to wait for his triumphant return? Enough!

At home, she marched around the labyrinth with so much intention her head nearly exploded. *I am aligned with the divine in body, spirit and mind. And I will thrive.* To heck with Wally.

A few hours later, she went to tai chi class, eager to cement her new mantra and lift her spirits. She performed an intricate exchange of Push Hands with an athletic young man half her age, and then she found a free corner where she completed the entire Sword Form. Attendance was lower than usual due to the upcoming Fourth of July holiday, and only a few regulars appeared. Joan Marsh was among them and sidled up to Claire as she prepared to wrap her sword in its cloth case.

"And how is Claire this evening?" asked her spry friend with a bright smile.

"Honestly, things are a bit chaotic right now."

"Well," said Joan, "in the natural world, chaos theory is what helps propel evolution. There is an underlying order within the chaos. So just think of it as you're evolving."

It sure didn't feel like it. "I asked Wally to move home and he said no."

"Maybe that's a sign from the universe." Joan patted her arm and looked toward Sifu, who was coaching a student near the windows. "He's been watching you."

"He watches all of us," said Claire.

"No, he's been *watching* you." Joan lifted her eyebrows in a suggestive way. "Trust me. You know what they say. When one door closes, another one opens." She smiled and walked away.

Claire finished wrapping her sword in its cloth cover and lingered as she often did after class. Her Push Hands combatant had a question for Sifu about the practice—perhaps because Claire had gotten the better of him in their contest. The young student listened to Sifu's answer, thanked him and walked out, leaving Claire alone in the dojo facing her teacher in the center of the floor. This was nothing new, but now, with Joan's words ringing in her ears, she felt a nervous excitement. She asked him about a section of the Sword Form, and he answered with his usual patience, fetching a sword and demonstrating a subtle improvement for her to make. Claire unwrapped her sword and shadowed his movements in a graceful duet, as they smoothly waved the weapons unison, stepping and sliding fluidly together across the dojo floor.

When they finished, she thanked him, and he gave her a warm look in return. Their conversation drifted to the lovely evening outside the open windows, and Claire surprised herself by asking if he would like to go for a walk. "Yes," he said, "a walk would be nice."

They strolled down Main Street and meandered past Town Hall, before heading downhill toward the riverbank. The warm summer air smelled of the fertile earth as dusk fell. They reached the water and sat on two large rocks, watching the river flow. Claire peppered Sifu with questions about Qi Gong, sticking to their common ground, letting him talk and enjoying the sound of his voice, even though she didn't understand everything he said. Soon, the bugs found them. Or, more accurately, they found her—hovering over her bare arms, her neck and her face, landing, biting, distracting and annoying her. She waved them away as best she could while she listened to him, and soon realized the bugs were not bothering Sifu at all. Not a single one. He sat three feet away as if encased in a protective shield, a no-fly zone for the irritating insects that plagued her. After five minutes of flailing her arms at the black pests, she finally blurted, "The bugs aren't bothering you at all!"

Sifu smiled in his benevolent way and said, "They are attracted to your energy."

"Well, I don't want that." A bug flew in her ear. She squished it with her pinky.

"Your electrical field is a magnet, drawing the bugs to you."

"And yours isn't?"

"My field resonates at a higher frequency," he said. "They are pulled toward your lower vibration."

Another bug flew into her eye. She felt a sting and blinked, then rubbed her eye and pulled her eyelid, trying to get the bug out.

Sifu slid closer. "Here, let me help." He moistened the tip of his little finger with his tongue, leaned in and gently touched his moist finger against the base of her eyeball. 'There!" He held up his pinky and showed her the black spot.

"Oh, that stings!" She rubbed her eye and it gushed moisture, reacting to the vanquished invader. "Thank you."

Sifu held out an arm next to hers, where a squadron of bugs landed and took off as if she was an aircraft carrier. Side by side, his arm looked like an empty runway.

"That's amazing," said Claire. "And really annoying."

He laughed and pulled his arm away, and then he settled back on his rock, sitting serenely with his legs crossed, just like the Buddha. "With peace comes tranquility. With tranquility, stillness. With stillness, quiet." He smiled at her. "With quiet, calm."

She smiled back at him and waved her hand at a dive-bomber near her forehead. "If you say so."

"If you remain calm, distractions fall away. Bugs are merely a distraction."

"You're telling me!" She stood up. "Shall we go?"

Sifu rose from his seat on the rock. "Yes, it is time."

They walked back up the hill, past the Town Hall, back down Main Street and reached their cars outside the dojo. Sifu pressed his hands together in front of his chest and latched his deep brown eyes onto Claire's. He bowed slightly from the waist.

"Thank you," he said. "I enjoyed our walk. And our talk."

Claire returned his bow, pressing her hands together as she held his gaze.

"Thank *you*, Sifu. Sorry the bugs got the best of me. What a nuisance."

"A nuisance is a lesson."

Claire nodded, her hands still pressed together.

"A lesson is a gift."

"I'll try to see it that way." She rubbed her eye where the bug had lodged earlier.

"A gift is precious. Goodnight, Claire-san."

Driving home, she stewed on his pronouncements, trying to determine what, exactly, they all meant. But she fell short. Were they some kind of riddle only an enlightened being could decipher? Perhaps she needed to meditate on their meaning and stop pushing so hard. To relax and let answers come to her. Easier said than done.

A few days later, she found a chemical-free odorless bug repellent at the natural foods store in Black River and brought it to tai chi class in her bag. After class ended, she made her usual visit to the bathroom, where she rubbed the repellent on her arms, neck and face just in case she and Sifu went for another walk. She wanted to be able to sit with him by the river and exude peace and tranquility, stillness and calm. He would marvel at her progress— in just a matter of days!—and congratulate her on raising her vibration closer to that of the Great Spirit, the All Knowing, the Universe, God. But Sifu didn't invite her on another walk. And she didn't want to appear too eager by asking him again. So she waited. And waited. And soon she began to wonder if Joan was mistaken about his interest in her. And if she had gotten excited for no good reason and was just being foolish again.

19

An explosion of productivity followed the fireworks of July 4th, as Wally piled up the pages and collected bad debts for Bear. He wrote every morning from six until nine, at which point he fed his muse a hearty breakfast of eggs and pancakes, sausage and bacon, toast and muffins, grits and granola and washed it all down with OJ and green tea. Waddling a bit as he put on weight, he felt good about the progress of his novel and confident in his next steps. The story seemed to be writing itself now. Ideas came to him throughout the day and night, demanding to be scribbled down in small notebooks he kept stashed all over—on his bedside table, at the kitchen counter, in his golf bag and his truck. Sometimes, he had to pull over to the side of the road to write down what came streaming into his head because he knew that if he didn't capture the idea then and there, it could vanish forever.

One morning, as he devoured a four-egg omelet with onions, mushrooms and cheddar, a side of bacon, a bowl of grits, an English muffin, a blueberry muffin and a slice of cantaloupe, a woman appeared at the foot of the stairs, looking a bit disheveled and embarrassed.

"Looks like I overslept," she said, and gave Wally an expression of *Oooops!* "Please. Don't let me disturb you." She pointed to his notepad and the pen in his hand. He'd been making notes between bites.

He stood. "It's no problem." Except that the Bear's rule was not to come into the house when he had a lady friend over. *How could he have known?* "Would you like a cup of tea? Or something to eat?"

"Oh no—thank you. I really should be going." She turned for the front door, which Wally never used. He always came into the house through the slider off the deck.

He called, "Have a good day!" and watched her go. An attractive woman of perhaps forty-five, dressed in business attire, a handsome handbag over her shoulder. He saw no sign of a wedding ring. Had Bear met her at a bar last night? Perhaps down at the Sheraton? She must have been from out of town and here on business because local women didn't dress like that in the evening, especially in the summer. But who knew? Bear was active on Match. com, and she might have driven up from Concord or Manchester after work for drinks and dinner.

It might not have been their first rendezvous, either. It was none of Wally's business. He just hoped Bear wouldn't find out she had seen him on her way out. Rules were rules.

After eating his big breakfast every day, he hit the road on his collection duties. For longer treks, he always drove his pickup. On shorter trips, he took the scooter. Since channeling Mama Betty, he had learned to show up at the tougher cases as quickly as possible after eating, in the hour or two before she vacated his being, so he could take advantage of her quicker wit, stronger personality and better negotiating skills. Employing her attributes for several weeks, he had collected many of the outstanding bills Bear had assigned him—much to his boss's delight. Bear no longer scowled at him but smiled, pleased with his results. He clapped Wally on the back and called him "Hector the Collector!" Not likely a tribute to Homer and the Trojan hero of *The Iliad*, since Bear wasn't a big reader, but who cared? Wally liked being viewed as a hero for a change, and he looked forward to the day when Claire would view him as one as well.

Meanwhile, three debts gnawed at him. One was Jerry's Gym, where he had returned twice, only to be angrily rebuffed by the tiny Terminator—even with Mama Betty in his corner. On his last visit, he ran for the door when the mini muscleman stepped out from behind the counter, wielding a barbell like a baseball bat. When he thought about Jerry's epic wedgie, his nuts ached. He racked his brain, trying to think of ways to coerce the angry little Arnold into paying, but he came up short. So he shifted his focus to Boone's Auto Repair and the Hancock sorority, the other two accounts where he continued to strike out. In Boone's parking lot just off the state highway up in a remote part of Vershire, a burly dog strained against a heavy chain and bared its teeth so ferociously that the first time Wally made the thirty-mile drive out there, he didn't even dare get out of his truck, let alone try to walk through the door into Boone's garage. The dog could keep the money!

But today, he armed himself with some special treats, including brisket inspired by Mama Betty and Papa, a heaping helping of grits in a big metal bowl and a big steak bone from a dinner he'd cooked for Bear the night before. Pulling into the parking lot at Boone's, he tossed the steak bone out the window at the dog straining against the chain, madly barking, pawing up a cloud of dust—and nearly hit the killer in the snout. The dog lunged for the bone, snatching it with ease, and settled into the dirt to gnaw on it. He eyed Wally as he chewed.

"Good boy," said Wally, climbing slowly out of his truck. "Finish that and then feast on *this.*" He tossed the brisket toward the dog. The beast immediately dropped the bone and rose to grab the brisket out of the air with a powerful leap and snap of its jaw, making the catch just before being yanked backward by the chain. Wally shivered at the thought of what those teeth could do to his body. He looked at the big metal bowl containing the grits. How would he deliver them? He couldn't put the bowl inside the range of the chain without putting himself in danger. Not to worry. For now, the dog had plenty to eat. Wally stepped into the garage.

Inside, his eyes strained to adjust to the dim light, while the smell of oil and lingering exhaust engulfed him. Why didn't Boone work with the garage doors open? It was mid-July. He soon realized he was standing in a three-bay garage jam-packed with old tires, boxes overflowing with spare parts, two lifts, large oil drums, racks of tools, air compressors—an assemblage of auto repair equipment and paraphernalia that appeared to have accumulated over decades, found its place and never moved. How did the mechanics move through all the grease-covered, grimy stuff in the shop? And where were they? It was hard to see anyone in the warren of parts and poor light.

"Need somethin'?" said a voice behind him.

Wally turned around and faced what looked like a scarecrow—a tall, reed-thin man of perhaps sixty-five or seventy, with a gray-flecked stubble, penetrating eyes and an Adam's apple the size of a large marble. His long-sleeved green shirt and pair of green pants, stained with grease, hung loosely on his skinny frame. His hat said, "BOONE'S GARAGE" and looked as if its owner wore it to bed.

"I was hoping to speak to Mr. Boone," said Wally.

"'Bout what?"

"Well, about an order he placed for some fleece vests—back in the winter."

The thin man's eyes narrowed. "There a problem?"

Wally shuffled his feet. "Well, actually, yes—there's still a balance due. The deposit only covered half." Wally had discovered that some people didn't understand this, and sometimes collecting a bill was as simple as making it clear. *You still owe the other half.*

"Always pay my bills," said the man, evidently Mr. Boone.

"I'm sure you do," said Wally. "Maybe there was an issue with the mail. I don't know. But the check hasn't arrived."

Mr. Boone pulled a pair of rectangular wire frame glasses out of his shirt pocket and perched them on in his long, narrow nose. "Let's have a look." He stepped around a stack of tires to where a standing desk piled with papers rested against the wall. He opened a drawer and pulled out a check register. Business sized, a multiple-ring binder—just like Wally used for his ad business before everything went electronic. Mr. Boone opened the register.

"What month did you say?"

Wally pulled the invoice from his pocket and unfolded it. "The order was placed in February. And the balance was due in March."

Mr. Boone flipped through the register. "There's the deposit," he said. He kept flipping forward. "And there's the balance—paid on March 17."

St. Patrick's Day, thought Wally, looking at the entry where the mechanic's finger pointed. $579.65. "And the check cleared?"

Mr. Boone reached back into the drawer and pulled out an envelope stuffed with bank statements. "Here's March," he said, clearing a space on his cluttered desktop. He laid out the statement and ran his long finger down the list of transactions. "Yup. Right there."

Again, Wally looked and saw the cleared transaction for $579.65.

"May I see the check?"

Mr. Boone found the check and handed it to Wally. He flipped it over.

The endorsement wasn't Bear's usual stamp but a signature that wasn't Bear's handwriting, either.

"You're right," said Wally, "you paid the bill, and the check was cashed. But it wasn't cashed by us."

Mr. Boone took the check from Wally's hand and looked at the signature on the back. He shook his head and sighed. "Goddamn Everett." He took off his well-worn hat as if removing a part of his skull and rubbed a hand across the thin strands of hair covering his crown. His eyes looked sad and distant.

"Ever known a drug addict?" he said.

Wally shook his head. He didn't think so.

"Gave my nephew a job in the shop. After my wife died last fall, I needed the company. Nephew needed the work. Lasted until May, then told him you're done. Never showed up anyway. Left his angry dog out there for me to feed." Mr. Boone shook his head and swallowed, his large Adam's apple rising and falling like the ball in Times Square on New Year's Eve. "No idea where he is now. Could be dead. Damn opioids."

"I'm sorry," said Wally.

"Everett's idea to order all them vests. We only needed a couple for us. But he said they'd be good promotion. Build up business. Give 'em to customers."

"That can work," said Wally, looking around the old garage, "if your business is big enough."

"Just wanted to skim the money. Buy his drugs."

Well, thought Wally, *it looked like he had a helluva time on St. Patrick's Day.* He looked at Mr. Boone. "You're all set. We don't need another check."

"Oh, no!" said Mr. Boone, flipping his check register back to the current date, where fresh checks awaited his entry and signature. He picked up a pen.

"I pay my bills."

"You did," said Wally, putting his hand gently but firmly over Mr. Boone's pen. "It's all good."

Mr. Boone looked at him. "Missus always said I was too nice to Everett. We never had kids. Just this shop." He lifted his chin toward the second bay, where a lift stood empty. "She was the better mechanic." He shook his head. "I was the better fool."

"It's not your fault," said Wally. "All kinds of people get addicted. Rich, poor, smart, stupid. It's awful. Everybody's vulnerable. You can't control what Everett does."

Mr. Boone gazed at his wife's lift. "Know anyone who wants an angry dog?"

Wally thought about it for a moment. *Could Doggone Right take a chained beast and make it homeworthy?* "Can I let you know?"

"'Course," said Mr. Boone. "Ain't going nowhere."

"Thanks for your help," said Wally.

"Thanks for yours." Mr. Boone extended his hand, the fingernails filled with auto grime, and gave Wally a firm shake.

Outside, the scary dog lay in the dirt that encircled the tree anchoring its chain and chewed happily on the steak bone. Seeing Wally, it didn't leap up and start barking. It just looked at him and returned to chewing. Wally grabbed the bowl of grits off his front seat and walked tentatively toward the dog. Maybe he would just splash them onto the ground. Play it safe. But the grits wouldn't taste as good mixed with dirt and the dog looked so placid that he kept walking slowly closer to the edge of the worn circle. When he leaned over the perimeter and placed the bowl just inside the boundary of the chain, his heart raced. The dog stirred but never stood and didn't bark. It just kept chewing. Maybe the killer was just hungry.

"Good boy," said Wally. "Good boy!"

He climbed into his truck and headed back to Bear's, owing him a new stainless steel mixing bowl and a good excuse for why he had failed again to collect from Boone's Auto—and how he never would.

The next morning around ten, he rode his scooter to Sigma Delta, dressed in his best parental preppy clothing. He left his hockey helmet hanging from the handlebars and climbed the broad stone steps to the front door of the stately brick house. He looked for a doorbell but didn't see one, so he knocked instead. No answer. He knocked again and peered through one of the narrow horizontal windows that bordered the door.

"Can I help you?"

He turned around and saw a tall Asian American student standing by his scooter, wearing a knapsack, her hands on her hips. He felt the color rise in his cheeks, feeling like a busted Peeping Tom.

"Yes . . . ah . . . thank you," he said. "I'm looking for Lucia."

The student gave him a wry smile. "You and every other guy on campus." She cocked her head. "Aren't you a little old for her?"

Wally's face felt hot. He tried to chuckle, but his throat tightened and his small laugh came out as a gasp. Finally he said, "I just wanted to ask her about a bill for some T-shirts you guys ordered for the Winter Carnival."

She shook her head. "We are not *guys*. We are women. And we will make our own mark in the world as *women*, not *guys.*"

Wally blanched. "Of course. I'm sure you will. My apologies. Guys is just a euphemism—you know, for *people.*"

"No, *guys* is a subtle but toxic form of domination. And some *guys* don't get it," she said.

"I'm sorry. I'm not one of them," said Wally. He took one step down toward her. "Please forgive me. I'm all for women's rights. I think women are probably the answer to the problems of the world."

The girl looked skeptical.

"Men have done enough damage with our wars and greed and poor communication skills and lack of empathy and pretty much being obsessed with our alpha-ness."

"You really think so?"

"Yes. I really do. *Honestly.*"

She strode up the front path and climbed the steps, marching right past Wally. He was surprised to find she was almost as tall as he was and wondered if perhaps she was a basketball player. Or maybe a southern California volleyball star recruited to Hancock College to leap up and spike the ball. *Except she probably came from Portland, Maine—you stereotyping knucklehead guy!* The lanky student stood with her hand on the doorknob, almost eye to eye with Wally, a look of mild disgust on her lovely face.

"Would you like a cup of tea?" she asked and smiled at him for the first time.

Had he won her over? "Ahhh, okay."

She pointed up the street. "Then you should go up to the Dirt Cowboy. Those *guys* have a great selection of teas from around the world." And with that, she pressed the code into the keypad, opened the door and disappeared inside the sorority house.

Stung, he made his way down the steps to his scooter and swung his leg over the seat. As he strapped on his hockey helmet, he saw her. The girl who had caused his accident back in May—turning into the walkway of the sorority house and headed right toward him, swinging her hips in a short skirt as her dark hair flowed over her shoulders.

"So," she said, stopping in front of him, a look of amusement on her beautiful face. "We meet again."

Tongue-tied by her beauty, Wally said, "Unh huh."

"Excuse me?"

"Yes!" he said, way too loudly. "Yes. We meet again."

She smiled, a flirtatious look in her eyes. "Where are your golf clubs?"

"They're at home," he said, his heart racing. Had he ever seen such a stunning female in the flesh?

She ran her fingers through her hair and looked him up and down. "I'm glad to see there was no permanent damage."

He sucked in his newly developed belly, not wanting to look like a middle-aged chubster, and thought of Claire kicking him out—*of him leaving before she could kick him out!*—and replied, "It's too soon to tell."

She gave him a quizzical look.

"About the permanent damage. The verdict is still out."

"Oh." She flipped her hair from one side of her head to the other in a captivating cascade. "Well, I hope everything's okay in the end."

"Me too," said Wally. He pointed to the sorority house. "Do you live here?"

"Why?" she said, a look of uncertainty flashing across her face.

"Don't worry," he said. "I'm not a *stalker*. I'm just looking for someone. Regarding a business matter. Do you by any chance know Lucia Bonaventura?"

She lifted her chin slightly. "May I ask who's asking?"

"Oh, I'm Wally—ah, *Wallace*. Wallace Scott." He extended his hand.

She shook it. Her skin was soft and warm. "Nice to meet you, *Wallace.*"

"And you are?"

"Lucia Bonaventura." She smiled the most gorgeous smile and let go of his hand.

Oh shit! Collect a debt from *her?* That would be mission impossible. He fiddled with his hockey helmet, trying to think of what to say.

"I didn't realize we had a business relationship," Lucia said.

"Yes, you gu—you ga—you *sisters* bought some T-shirts for the Winter Carnival from my friend—Bear's Sportswear? And part of the bill is still outstanding."

"So you're, like, a *bill* collector?"

"Actually," he said, sucking his gut in further and unsnapping the chinstrap of his hockey helmet, "I'm, like, a writer. I'm just doing Bear a favor. He's really busy in his shop."

"Oh." She looked remarkably saucy *and* skeptical.

"I'm writing a novel," he blurted.

"Is that right? My dad's a writer."

"Really?"

"He writes screenplays in Hollywood."

Maybe her mom was an actress and that's where she got her looks. "Very cool," he said. But actually it was totally uncool—being relegated to a father figure.

"I'm not in charge of paying the bills anymore," said Lucia. "I used to be the treasurer, but now I'm the rush chair."

It was certainly a rush standing next to her.

"But if you give me your number," she continued, "I'll look into it and give you a call."

"Thanks," said Wally. "It's not a lot of money, but it does add up." He took out his phone and she pressed hers against his, capturing his number.

"Now we know where to find each other." She gave him a sultry smile and turned to go.

Wally watched her sashay up the walkway in her short skirt. At the door, she looked back over her shoulder and gave him a little wave. Oh, what he would give to be twenty again.

20

While Claire waited for Sifu to ask her to walk by the river after class some evening, Max kept texting and calling, asking her to play tennis, have lunch, take a hike, see a movie, go for a swim. She deflected all his invitations like an adept tai chi master, not wanting to offend him but not wanting to encourage him, either. She liked Max and wanted to help the rescues, but she was infatuated with Sifu and eager to have another outing with him. What was taking so long? Finally, one evening after class, she found herself alone with him discussing the difference between the Yang and Chen styles of tai chi, when he suggested they continue their chat over a pizza at the Italian restaurant on Main Street. Claire's heart leapt. At last, her big chance!

"That sounds divine," she said, her butterflies fluttering.

"The divine is everywhere," said Sifu. "Within *and* without."

"Well, I'm pretty sure we can sit outside on the deck at Café Colatina." She laughed, giddy as a schoolgirl, but he didn't seem to get her joke. She excused herself to use the bathroom, not being dressed for a date in her tai chi T-shirt and lightweight pants, and eager to spruce herself up. As she washed her face and applied a little makeup, she took a deep breath and looked at herself in the mirror. *Relax, girlfriend, this is what you've been hoping for. Enjoy!* When she met Sifu at the dojo door, he held it open for her.

"Why, thank you," said Claire, waltzing past him.

When was the last time Wally had held a door open for her? Probably the refrigerator door when he wanted something to eat. Last fall, she had been making dinner when he appeared in the kitchen after golf, clutching a towel around his waist following a shower, his smelly golf clothes in his arms. As he held the refrigerator door open with his foot, he asked if she would mind reaching down to grab him a cold beer. Just as she looked up to hand him the beer, his towel came off.

"Oh, sorry!" he'd said, feigning surprise, his package at her eye level. "Do you see any sausage down there?"

"Very funny, Wallace." She pressed the can of cold beer against his balls.

"OH! SHIT!"

She kept pressing.

"JEEEZUS, CLAIRE!"

He staggered back and dropped his laundry. "That's not funny!" he'd said, cradling his sack.

"That all depends," she'd said.

Seated at the restaurant in Radford, she faced Sifu on the deck and ordered a beer, while he asked for a glass of red wine. As the waitress got their drinks, she began to regret suggesting that they sit outside—because down below, off to her right, lay the 9-hole Radford Golf Club, its fairways and greens spread across an old cow pasture above the river. Was there no escape from golf and Wally's haunting presence? Why did she have to be reminded of him now, when she was finally alone with Sifu? When her beer arrived, she took such a long first drink that Sifu lifted an eyebrow in alarm.

"You are thirsty!"

"I'm always thirsty after class," she said, wiping the back of her hand across her mouth. *And when I get nervous.* "Push Hands is such a great workout. I just love it." She took another drink of her beer and told herself to calm down.

Sifu calmly sipped his wine and looked at her. "What is wrong, Claire-san?"

Claire felt his dark brown eyes boring into hers, as if reading her mind, her heart, her spirit. Maybe that's what Sifu meant—a person who could see inside you, who could intuit what you were thinking and feeling and wanting and hoping and trying to put out of your mind. *And it's not Seafood either, Wallace!* She looked away, trying to shake Wally's presence.

"You know," said Sifu, "tai chi and Qi Gong can bring up emotions that need to be released."

Her stomach tightened.

"Sometimes, it can be hard to let them go," he said with a compassionate look.

She took another drink, eager to settle down, but when she came up for air, she blurted: "Wally and I are separated!" And sprayed beer across the table.

Sifu recoiled under the impact of her spittle and reached for his napkin.

"Oh, I'm so sorry!" she said.

He wiped his face. "Of course," he said. "You are off balance."

But Claire suddenly felt lighter, relieved by her confession. "I don't know if it will be permanent, but it could be."

Sifu said, "What is permanent but longing?"

"Sorry?"

"What is longing but desire?"

Claire shook her head, uncertain of the answer. His riddles could be so confounding.

"What is desire but a failure to accept? What is failure but disappointment? And what is disappointment but longing."

There he went, full circle again. He looked so sincere and sympathetic, sharing these abstractions. And he looked so good in his black T-shirt that hugged his pectorals and biceps. Good enough to eat.

"Are you hungry?" she asked, feeling the beer on top of her emotional release. "I'd love to get a pizza."

"It is the circle of life," said Sifu.

"A pizza? I mean, it's a circle, but I'm not sure—"

"No!" he said. "It is the yin and the yang. The circle of opposites. The nature of being. Balance, Claire-san. If we lose our balance, we can fall. We don't want you to fall."

She sighed and looked away. Spotted a couple down on the 9-hole course, standing in the fairway, the woman lining up her shot, the man hovering, watching her too closely. Sifu reached across the table and took her hands in his, his palms radiating heat. He had some serious chi!

"The end is the beginning. Do not fear the future. Do not relive the past. There is only today to Push Hands with the universe." He squeezed her hands in his. "You are very lovely, Claire-san—just the way you are."

She felt her cheeks burn as he looked into her eyes. *What poetry!* His touch was exhilarating. Not as intense as Wally's spark, but a deep, penetrating current that radiated peace. Isn't that what she needed? A sense of peace and belonging?

The waitress brought their pizza and they ate slowly, Claire enjoying how he looked at her and the sound of his voice as they talked about tai chi philosophy. When they finished eating, Sifu shared more wisdom.

"Separation is distance. Distance is space. Space is freedom. Freedom is separation."

She nodded, trying to absorb his message.

"You are free, Claire-san. Not all of us can say that."

What did he mean—*not all of us?* After holding her hands and looking into her eyes and telling her she was beautiful, was he saying he wasn't free and available?

When the bill came, they split it, Claire telling herself: if you try to pay, he might think you want to get into his snug-fitting, all-natural, soft-cotton, butt-hugging tai chi pants. And now, it sounds like that may never happen.

They walked to their cars in silence, and when Sifu put his hands together, bowed and said goodnight, Claire bowed back. Disappointed he did not kiss her, even on the cheek, as she could have imagined earlier when he held her hands in his and looked deeply into her eyes. Would they even have another date? How had things gone so suddenly wrong? What good was being free if she couldn't explore her fascination with this handsome, captivating man? She wondered what could be holding him back.

21

As the sun set over the practice holes, Wally hoped Lucia would call him back with an update on the Sigma Delta sorority payment. It had been four days and still no word. Had the little siren simply charmed him on the front walk? Played him for an old fool? He had begun to wonder. On the ad front, his new jingle had helped Hughes Auto sell more cars than any previous summer. Whenever he saw Jack Hughes at the golf course, his client gave him a stinging high five that made Wally think he was still underpaid. Not that it would matter for long. In another six weeks, his novel would be done and his life would change forever. He hit a 5-iron so purely it felt like he'd struck butter.

"Wallace Scott, welcome back to *Fresh Air.*"

"Thank you, Terry, it's great to be with you again."

"There's a rumor your book is being optioned for a television show—a seven-figure deal. Can you tell us about that?"

"I'm sorry, Terry, I can't. Those negotiations are ongoing and highly confidential. What I can tell you is that Brad Pitt is interested in playing yours truly, and I'm pretty sure if that happens Claire will be eager to get back with Brad. Ah, I mean, with me. Ha ha ha."

"I can only imagine."

"I like Brad. I'm not sure how good a golfer he is. But he can audition."

"A while ago, you refused to move back home," Terry Gross said. "Do you really think Claire is going to wait around for you? Or welcome you back later?"

"When I publish my book, she'll see me differently. She'll respect me again. See, Terry, part of the problem is that after a certain age, women don't really need men anymore. We become obsolete on a biological, day-to-day basis. We've provided our sperm, helped raise the kids, and now what? We annoy with our maleness. After a certain age, money is far more useful to women than any man is. Why are you looking at me like that, Terry?"

"Because Claire just walked into the studio, and she's ready to swing a golf club at your headphones. Claire, would you like to pull up a microphone?"

"Thank you, Terry," said Claire. "And f—*bleep* you, *Wallace!* It's not just about money. I don't care about money more than you do. But you're right, after a certain age men *can* seem pretty useless—especially when they revert to acting like *boys!* And what about trying new things? A lot of men just aren't very open to that. So don't tell me that women just care about money. We like money, but what we really want is someone to grow with and explore with—someone to love."

"Oh my god," said Wally. "I think I'm going to cry."

"You think you're so funny," said Claire.

"Isn't this all about patterns?" said Terry Gross. "What the psychologists call our habitual behavior? It seems like that's what you two are talking about."

"No question we are all compelled by forces we don't always understand and struggle to control," said Wally. "We know we shouldn't eat ice cream every night, but we eat ice cream every night. We know we should exercise more often, but we sit around and watch TV. We should be nice to others, but we cut off the driver next to us. We hate our jobs, but we don't quit. I think we're scared, Terry. A lot of people are just plain scared. We buy self-help books, study with gurus, see a shrink, drink Scotch, smoke pot, and where does it get us? The chance to forget how weak and undisciplined we are. But guess what? We're human! We're not perfect. We're flawed. We follow our same old patterns over and over, like DNA, until we die or something drastic happens. We'll change for a while, only to revert back to our old ways. We don't want to think about death. But if that realization is strong enough, we have a shot at launching a new beginning."

"It seems like you broke a pattern by getting hit in the head by a golf ball," said Terry.

"That was shit luck!" said Claire. "And Mama Betty is a traitor!"

"Luck, will and circumstances," said Wally, "they can change your life."

"I can't believe this," said Claire.

"I'm not a marriage counselor," said Terry Gross. "I'm a renowned NPR host with arguably the best female voice in radio history and an uncanny

knack for getting famous people to admit things they might later regret—
but I think there may be a solution to your problem."

"Really?" said Wally. "What's that?"

"Get a divorce. The kids are gone. No trauma there."

"And end the story here?" said Wally. "It's only page 129. We haven't even
reached the last act. There's a lot more action coming, Terry, don't quit on us
now."

"Yeah," said Claire, suddenly siding with her husband, not wanting to be
axed yet. "There are some big surprises ahead."

"You mean, like those adulterous escapades?" said Terry.

"Hey, don't give everything away!"

"Yeah," said Wally. "And getting a divorce—that never even crossed my
mind."

A heavy silence fell over the studio.

"Claire?" said Wally.

"No comment."

"Well, ha ha, there you have it," said Terry Gross. "My guest has been
Wallace Scott, the surprise bestselling author of a book that's not finished
yet—and his estranged wife, Claire, who crashed the party and kind of stole
the show. I'm Terry Gross, and this is *Fresh Air*!"

22

Claire missed the next two tai chi classes—one to give a massage to a client who had an emergency with her lower back and the other to meet with a caterer. With the Doggone Right event now just five weeks away, she was starting to panic. Millicent was no help, busy with all of her other volunteer activities, and informed Claire via email that she would be spending the first two weeks of August down on Martha's Vineyard. "I won't be much use from there, I'm afraid!" *As if she'd been of any use from here!* The lawyer continued to be tied up with his big court case, and the dental hygienist apologized that she was no help between her work and her kids, who were out of school for the summer. As a team of one, Claire felt overwhelmed. All she had lined up so far was the tent, lights, chairs and tables. Still no band and still no food, which had begun to trigger anxiety dreams in which she struggled to feed two hundred people all by herself. In one nightmare, she toiled in front of a giant oven the size of her kitchen, trying to prepare endless racks of lamb for well-heeled donors. The massive enterprise got away from her as the lamb fat burst into flames and smoke poured from the oven, stinging her eyes. A large Greek man with a thick black mustache played loud bouzouki music as a crowd swelled onto a dance floor and launched into a traditional Greek line dance. Out of nowhere, Wally appeared and took her hand, pulling her into the line. They danced joyously until the smoke from her burned lamb grew so thick that sirens sounded and fire trucks arrived and everyone fled, leaving her standing alone on the empty dance floor, suddenly naked. Shrieking, trying unsuccessfully to cover herself, she dashed past the firefighters racing in to douse the flames—and woke up gasping for air. *Good night!* What had Roz gotten her into? No more skipping tai chi to visit caterers. She needed to get back to the dojo.

And so, nearly two weeks after her pizza outing with Sifu, she returned to class late on a Thursday afternoon eager to cultivate, as he would say, her balance and a sense of peace. She spent ninety minutes doing tai chi and the Sword Form and felt much better. As the class dispersed, Sifu ambled over to where she stood chatting with Joan Marsh. He bowed and asked Claire if she would like to join him for an iced tea at the café up the street.

"What am I?" said Joan, thrusting out a hip. "Chopped liver?"

"No!" he said. "You are a beautiful lotus flower! Please, Joan, join us as well."

"That's okay, I need to get home to Earl. He's grilling eggplant parmesan for dinner."

"Grilling?" said Claire, having a flashback to her smoke-filled nightmare.

"He grills everything in the summer," said Joan. "I hardly cook at all. It's wonderful." She winked at Claire. "You two have fun." Then she bowed to Sifu. "Maybe next time, handsome."

Sitting over their iced teas, chatting about the recent run of good weather and the intricacies of the Sword Form, Claire tried not to appear too eager or excited to be with him again—especially if he wasn't free. But then he looked up at her and said, "You have been absent. I began to wonder if you would ever come back to class. The dojo has felt empty without you."

She felt her face flush and sipped her tea.

When he asked what her plans were for the weekend, her heart leapt. She breathed deeply into her abdomen and told herself, *Be calm, be mindful . . . calm . . . mindful.*

"I'll probably do some planning for an event I'm helping organize," she said, trying to look nonplussed. "Maybe work in the labyrinth. I might go up to Lake Glory for a swim at some point."

"Then you must stop by my house," he said, looking excited. "And we can go for a swim together."

"You have a house on Lake Glory?" Funny how little she knew about him.

"Yes. At the south end. Please, come for a swim and then join me for dinner. Can you do that—on Saturday?"

Caught off guard, she hesitated for a moment. *Dinner on the lake? With Sifu?* Her skin tingled. "Thank you, that sounds wonderful. What can I bring?"

"Just your radiant presence."

"Let me bring something, Sifu."

He smiled and sipped his peppermint iced tea. "Why don't you surprise me?"

Claire spent the next two days trying to think of something that would surprise him. She had just been given a bottle of Dom Perignon from her grateful client with the back pain emergency. But would champagne *surprise* him? It could also appear too romantic. She couldn't bring flowers, and a plant was boring. Hardly a surprise. Maybe she would bring a pie. Blueberries were in season. She could buy a blueberry pie at the farmers market on Saturday morning. But then he would ask if she had baked it, and she would have to say, "No." How about a book? On tai chi or the martial arts? Oriental philosophy or Asian history? He probably had a library filled with such titles. What could she bring that felt appropriate and original?

She decided to call someone with more dating experience.

"I was just thinking about you!" Roz bellowed, picking up Claire's call. "Oh my god! That is *so* amazing that you called RIGHT when I was thinking about you! MOVE OVER, ASSHOLE!"

Claire heard a horn blast. "Where *are* you?"

"Leaving Boston. I had lunch with an old real estate friend. This traffic is RIDICULOUS! Look at this idiot. GET OUT OF THE WAY!"

"I'll call you back, Roz."

"NO! This is fine. What's up?"

"I need your advice. I'm going to a friend's tomorrow and I need to bring him a surprise."

"Is it Max?"

"No, it's not Max."

"You told me you were going to call him."

"I've been busy, Roz."

"He is SO eager to see you! You HAVE to call him!"

"Okay, okay . . . I'll call him this weekend."

"Promise?"

Claire crossed her fingers. "Promise."

"So who's your friend?"

Claire hesitated. "My tai chi teacher."

"You told me he's been married THREE times!"

"He's a very attractive and intriguing man. And I need to surprise him with something when I go up to his lake house. Any ideas?"

"He has a LAKE house?"

"I was thinking of bringing him a bottle of Dom Perignon."

"Gay guys who own lake houses love champagne."

"He's not gay, Roz."

"He's been married *three times*! Trust me, he's either gay or he's impotent. And believe me, you do NOT want an erection that lasts four hours. I've been there and it is NOT pretty."

Claire sighed. "Thanks for the help."

"Move over, CHOWDERHEAD!"

"Goodbye, Roz."

"Do NOT hang up on me!"

Claire gave her the dial tone.

She decided to bring the blueberry pie. So what if she hadn't baked it? The homemade pies from the farmers market were mouthwatering masterpieces and, with a few scoops of Ben & Jerry's vanilla ice cream, would be the perfect treat after swimming in the lake. She drove to Sifu's and found his driveway with her GPS. A quick check of her face in the rearview mirror, another application of lip balm and she fluffed her hair before putting on her wide straw hat with the red, purple and white dried flowers on the brim.

She stepped out of her car into the glorious July day, the sun high in an azure sky. What a gorgeous property! Sifu's handsome, two-story shingle-style home rested on a slight rise overlooking the water, and the grounds were impeccable—neatly trimmed bushes, colorful flower beds and a broad green lawn that sloped down to a small, private beach. She spotted a powerboat moored to a dock, and floating twenty yards offshore, a small raft. How could he afford such a magnificent lakefront home by teaching tai chi?

Just then, he appeared from around a corner of the house, looking fresh from a swim. A towel draped around his neck, his dark hair glistening, his lean, muscular torso shimmering with moisture. His powerful legs gleamed as well—just below a snug fitting Speedo with a tiger-stripe design. Claire caught her breath seeing him nearly naked, oozing sexual vitality. He smiled at her and said, "Welcome, Claire."

A German shepherd bounded up next to him, dripping water from its fur. The dog leapt over to Claire and rubbed its wet body against her legs, dampening her sundress.

"Yin!" called Sifu. "No! Come here!" He clapped his hands and the dog rushed to his side, where it shook from head to tail, spraying its master with water. "Forgive me," he said, holding the dog's collar. "Yin can forget his manners—especially around such a pretty woman."

Claire blushed, appreciating the compliment, if not her wet sundress. She held out the pie and ice cream. "A little something for later. I hope you like blueberry pie."

His eyes lit up. "I love blueberry pie! What a *wonderful* surprise!" His teeth gleamed in the sun, contrasted sharply by his closely cropped black beard and tanned handsome face. "And Ben & Jerry's. Thank you!"

"My pleasure."

He smiled and excused himself to put the ice cream in the freezer and the pie in the kitchen. As she watched him walk away, the tiger-print Speedo hugged his firm cheeks even more deliciously than his thin cotton tai chi pants had. *Now there's a gluteus maximus!*

He returned with the towel still draped around his neck, carrying a bottle of sparkling mineral water and two glasses. She noticed his belly protruded slightly over his small swimsuit, but unlike Wally, there was not an ounce of jiggle in his stomach, just firm, round muscle—the site of his well-cultivated chi. There, behind his navel, in his dan tien, he stored the potent energy force that he used to easily defeat his pupils in the dojo. And just below his firm belly, she couldn't help noticing what looked like a long curling banana, arching downward inside the tiny tiger-print Speedo. Goodness! So *that's* why her boys called it a banana hammock.

Five years earlier, Josh and Jack had presented Wally with a Speedo as a joke on his fiftieth birthday. But when he put it on, there was no sign of a banana. Not like Sifu's. And Wally's belly, hanging over his suit, hardly glowed with the firm, solid power of her tai chi master's stomach. Wally cupped his soft belly in his hands as he modeled the suit and declared with a silly grin, "All bought and paid for!" The boys laughed. Claire's own dan tien was a hybrid of Sifu's and Wally's—one half firm, cultivated chi, the other half soft, indulgent weakness (damn Reese's peanut butter cups!).

She pushed the memory aside and snapped back to the lawn by the lake, back to Sifu approaching her, and realized she was staring—right at his crotch. She quickly tore her eyes away. Perhaps Sifu's wives couldn't handle his firepower. Maybe riding a tiger could do a girl in.

He led her across the lawn to a pair of zero-gravity chairs by the edge of the lake and poured her a glass of mineral water. Claire settled into her chair and flipped off her sandals. Gazing across the glimmering water, she eagerly soaked up the warm rays of sunshine.

"This is gorgeous," she said.

"Thank you," he said, "I feel most fortunate."

Cozy in their lawn chairs, sipping mineral water, they watched powerboats crisscross the lake, some pulling water-skiers, others towing kids on inflatable tubes that skipped across the lake like stones. Claire enjoyed watching the action and sitting next to Sifu. But she had skipped lunch because she didn't want to look tubby in her one-piece suit, and now the lack of food and the hot sun left her feeling a little lightheaded.

"I think I better cool off," she said, rising from her chair and removing her wide straw hat.

"By all means," said Sifu, waving a hand at the water, remaining seated.

Claire slipped off her sundress and stepped into the lake in her one-piece suit. Yin stood like a sentry, his ears perked, watching her wade through the cool water, held back by Sifu's order to "Stay!" Thigh-deep in the lake, she dove in. The refreshing water did the trick. She floated for a few minutes and emerged feeling much better. Walking back to her chair, she felt Sifu's eyes on her and hoped he approved, but she didn't dare to look at him. She dried herself with a towel and sat back down.

Sifu filled her water and she asked, "How long have you had this lovely home?" This was the first of a series of questions she posed as they sat by the lake. She learned that he had inherited the house from his father, who inherited the place from his father, a brilliant Wall Street tycoon. Sifu's father tried finance but didn't like it, so he became a diplomat who served in Asia and took his family with him on tours of duty to Japan, Korea and Vietnam. Later, they were stationed in India and Ladakh. Sifu studied with martial arts masters in different countries, learning tai chi, Qi Gong and Kung Fu. His longest stay was in Ladakh, on the edge of the Himalaya, where he apprenticed with a Chinese master who had fled Mao and, according to Sifu, had a wealth of knowledge about the esoteric arts, including the darker ones.

When Claire probed about this, he grew silent. She asked about his family, and he poured himself another glass of sparkling water and then topped off her glass, finishing the bottle. His mother, father and younger sister all died in a plane crash in the mountains of Ladakh, he said. He had stayed behind to study with his master. He was nineteen.

"I'm so sorry," she said, knowing how hard it had been to lose her mother when she was seven. She couldn't imagine the shock and pain of losing both parents and your only sibling in an instant.

Sifu looked across the lake. "Time for some exercise," he said. "If you will excuse me."

He swam smoothly out to the raft twenty yards away, climbed up the ladder and stood on the planks, surveying the lake. Then he picked up what appeared to be a wooden sword and began to perform the Sword Form. Claire marveled at the way he maintained his balance as the raft swayed beneath his feet. At times, the wake of motorboats rocked the raft, and yet he continued to move gracefully, perfectly balanced, sometimes standing on one leg while gently moving his arms, before stepping into the next pose of the Form, looking as solid as a well-rooted tree in a heavy wind. Alone at nineteen? Did he have any other family? Aunts, uncles, cousins? What did he do next? Where did he go? How did he wind up in Oregon? Did he go to college? Had he ever done anything outside the world of martial arts?

She closed her eyes and turned her face toward the afternoon sun. The distant hum of a motorboat carried across the water. There was so much to learn about this captivating man with the tragic past. A warm breeze caressed her skin. Her eyelids felt heavy, and soon, she fell asleep.

23

As Claire snoozed by the lake, Wally struggled on the golf course. Not with his golf game, which had never been better, but with his client, who had never been more manipulative. Jack Hughes was in rare form, playing against Wally and Bear in the HCC member-member tournament with his partner, Hans Jarmann. Jack kept trying to throw Wally and Bear off their games, coughing on their backswings, moving in their line of sight and not conceding a single putt. On the final hole of their match, he walked over to Wally as they approached their tee shots in the fairway.

"You're playing great, big fella," said Jack.

"Thanks," said Wally, waiting for the punchline.

"I wonder if you really want to beat the only client you still have." He clapped Wally on the back and strode off. By the time they reached the green, Bear and Hans were both out of the hole after making a series of errors, and it was down to Wally and Jack.

"Mano a mano!" said his client. "For all the marbles!"

Wally had a putt for par from ten feet above the hole. Far enough away so missing it would look legitimate. Jack was on the green in two and stroked a long birdie putt that stopped two feet from the cup. He looked at Wally as he dug in his pocket for his ball marker, fishing forever, waiting for Wally to give him the putt for par.

"Quit stalling," said Bear, "and mark it."

Jack looked at Wally and marked his ball.

Wally walked around the green, sizing up his putt from every angle, wrestling with himself, even though he didn't really have a choice. *Throw the match. Win the match. Throw the match. Win the match.* He knew the putt broke to the right. All he had to do was pull it slightly, and he would miss. Understandable, given the pressure. Bear would never know he had done it on purpose. But when he stood over his ball and drew his putter back, for some reason—maybe nerves, maybe luck or maybe because he really didn't want to be a slimeball—he didn't pull the putt. He sent it on the perfect line down the hill. It curled right, headed straight for the hole and dropped into the bottom of the cup. Bear jumped up and hollered, "BOOM SHAKALAKA!"

Wally froze. *What had he done?*

Bear gave him a walloping high five that stung like a swarm of bees. "PARTNER!" he roared. Was this the end of Hughes Auto? One putt and down the drain?

"Didn't see *that* coming," said Jack Hughes, glaring at Wally.

Me neither, thought Wally. And then he said, "Your putt's good, Jack."

"What!" said Bear.

"Pick it up," said Wally, desperate to keep his client happy.

"No way!" said Bear. "That's for the match. He needs to putt that."

"It's eighteen inches."

"It's two feet!"

"It's for a tie," said Wally.

"Actually," said Hans, "if we tie you guys, we win the flight."

"Then he's definitely putting!" said Bear.

Wally said nothing. He looked up at the sky, powerless to affect the result now. Every golfer knew you couldn't give a two-foot putt to win a tournament. Under that pressure, people missed. Would Jack? Wally couldn't watch and closed his eyes. When he heard Jack's ball drop into the hole and Hans holler, "Well *done!*" he looked over and saw his opponents locked in an embrace. His six grand a month was safe. Or so he hoped.

Bear stepped over to Wally. "I can't believe you wanted to give him that putt."

"I thought it was for a tie."

"You wanted your client to win."

"No, I didn't."

"Bullshit."

Hans and Jack shook hands with Bear and Wally. "A lot closer than last year," said Jack, clapping Bear on the shoulder.

Bear looked ready to send him tumbling across the green with a mighty swipe of his paw.

"Why don't you boys come over to the house tonight?" said Jack. "Ginger and I are throwing a little member-member party. "

"Thanks," said Bear. "I've got plans."

"Wally?"

He couldn't accept with Bear eyeing him. "I'll have to see."

"Well, we know you won't be out with Claire." Jack chortled.

"Let us buy you a beer," said Hans.

Bear scowled and picked up his bag. "I'm not thirsty," he said, and lumbered off to the parking lot.

Feeling as if he had no choice, Wally joined his opponents for a beer on the clubhouse deck, crowded with the other tournament participants. At one point, Jack pulled out a cigar and lit up.

"Close, but no cigar!" He laughed and punched Wally's arm. And then he turned serious. "I can't believe you made that putt."

"Dumb luck," said Wally.

"Dumb *decision*," said Jack. He puffed on his cigar and blew a stream of smoke at Wally's face.

Wally took a pull on his beer, wishing it would wash away his shame. How could he try to throw a match with Bear as his partner? It was one thing to do it while playing alone. But Bear had been his loyal friend, taking him in, encouraging his writing, giving him work. He felt lower than a snake's belly, as Mama Betty would say.

He finished his beer and got up to leave.

"Look forward to seeing you at the party," said Jack, as if issuing a command. "Can't cry in your beer all night, mister *adman*!"

24

When she awoke, Claire found herself covered in a warm fleece blanket. Across the lake, the sun was dropping behind a hill on the opposite shore. The mirrorlike water reflected the early evening sky—streaks of orange and red melting into rich shades of blue. How long had she slept? She was wearier than she realized from event planning and massaging, Wally and her life. She heard soft music coming from the house and turned to see a string of colored Chinese lanterns glowing the length of the screened porch. A table had been covered in white linen and set with two chairs, crystal glasses and silverware that glowed under the light of two candles. Her host had clearly been busy, after thoughtfully covering her with a warm blanket. She saw his silhouette bent over a counter in the kitchen, working at a cutting board. The whole scene looked like a fairy tale with Prince Charming as the chef.

As she entered the kitchen, Sifu looked up and smiled. He wore a traditional martial arts outfit, with black silk pants and a red silk top with inlaid black and silver trim. A very striking costume for a very handsome man. He held her eyes as he bowed slightly, hands in front of his chest.. "Did you sleep well, Claire-san?"

"I did. Thank you for the blanket."

"Of course." He opened the refrigerator and took out a bottle of Moët & Chandon. "May I offer you a glass of champagne?"

She loved champagne! "Thank you, that sounds lovely."

He popped the cork and filled a flute for each of them. They clinked glasses and she took a drink. "Oh, my, that is *divine!*"

He smiled and waved an arm down the hall. "Please, help yourself to a hot shower. The bathroom is on the right. And take your champagne. There's a shelf inside."

Wally drank beer in the shower. Now, thanks to Sifu, she would drink champagne.

"I'll get my things," she said, and went out to the car to fetch the bag with her dinner clothes. She had packed two outfits in a canvas bag to give herself a choice, and then she had thrown in a light-pink silk nightshirt—just in case. In the bathroom, she took off her sundress and her bathing suit and hung them on a brass hook next to Sifu's tiger-skin Speedo. A large glass bowl of fruit rested on the counter by the sink, with fresh apples, oranges, pears and a banana. Hungry and wanting something in her empty stomach to help absorb the champagne, she peeled the banana and took a bite. She stepped into the shower and relaxed under the hot water, feeling the warm glow of the wine. What a delight! A girl could get used to champagne in the shower.

She chose the pastel floral sleeveless dress and a pair of low-heeled sandals that accentuated her legs, in an effort to match Sifu's arresting costume, and applied a touch of makeup after combing her wet hair. When she returned to the kitchen, he refilled her glass and said, "You look beautiful."

She demurely lifted her glass. "And you look very handsome."

"Come, let me show you around." He led her into a large living room that overlooked the water and featured a magnificent stone fireplace. There were two large stuffed chairs, a long leather couch, reading lights, a hand-carved coffee table, a round wooden table and chairs. He escorted her into the study, with its shelves of books, a rocking chair and standing desk . . . through the laundry room . . . past a spacious mudroom . . . into a guest bedroom adjacent to the bathroom where she had showered . . . and then he led her upstairs to a master bedroom that overlooked the lake. She admired the bedspread, an ornate yin and yang design in crimson and gold, a stunning piece of embroidered art. Two other bedrooms, including a spacious bunkroom, and a full bath with Jacuzzi completed the second floor. He ushered her back downstairs and opened a door leading to the cellar. He flipped a light switch, and she followed him down. Below, racks of wine lined one wall of the stone cellar, organized by type, vintage and country.

"I have some very fine port for after dinner," Sifu said. "If you like port."

"Only if you have a cigar to go with it."

He laughed and extended a hand back upstairs. "Please," he said, "after you." As she neared the top of the stairs, the pale blue eyes of a large

Siamese cat gleamed at her from the doorway. She reached out her hand. "Hello, kitty."

The Siamese darted away. "That is Yang," said Sifu from behind her.

Yin, the dog, Yang, the cat. Opposite forces, contained beneath one roof. How Sifu of him.

When they sat down to eat, Claire felt warm all over, happy to be at such a lovely home on the lake, enjoying the delicious champagne and the company of her teacher. Under the soft, romantic light of the screened porch, he served her four exquisite courses—lobster bisque, Caesar salad, grilled tuna with roasted yellow peppers and red potatoes, and for dessert, her blueberry pie à la mode.

"I love your crust," Sifu said, as he savored the pie. "What's your secret?"

"The farmers market," she said.

He laughed. "We should go there together sometime."

After dessert, they sat at the table, sipping the last of the champagne, gazing over the placid water as darkness fell and lights blinked on around the lake. It was a balmy night, calm and still, and voices carried over the water. A campfire flickered on the far shore. Claire watched a three-quarter moon rise and climb toward tissuelike clouds. Stars emerged like pin holes through a dark blanket.

"Magical," said Claire.

"Yes," said Sifu. "I am very lucky. And so happy you could join me." His eyes smiled at her as he rose from his chair.

Claire leapt up. "Let me do the dishes!" she said. "You cooked such a wonderful meal."

"The dishes can wait," said Sifu. "Please excuse me for a moment."

Claire cleared the table while he went to the bathroom. Coming into the kitchen, she caught her reflection in the windows and was surprised to see how happy she looked. How content and peaceful. It had been so long. Stacking dishes in the sink, she heard the sound of music coming from the living room. Was that Pink Martini?

"Claire!" Sifu called. "No dishes! Come join me."

She found him standing by a row of open windows facing the lake, silhouetted in the moonlight. He stepped over and took her in his arms.

"We can watch the lake as we dance."

Holding her lightly, leading her expertly, he swung her around the floor, a marvelous dancer, twirling her in and out to the lively tune. Spinning together in sheer delight, Claire found herself breaking into laughter. The moon glimmered off the lake, shining like her heart. When the song ended, he bowed and in return, she curtsied. The next song began, a slow, romantic ballad and when Sifu pulled her close she melted against him. She felt the sinew in his back, the strength of his chest, the power of his thighs, and rested her head against his shoulder, taking in his intoxicating scent. His lips gently brushed her crown. She looked up, and he kissed her softly, tenderly. He tasted of champagne and blueberries, and as they kissed, he grew hungrier, kissing her more deeply as his thigh pressed against her mound, sending a quiver through her loins.

"Oh, *Sifu*," she said, "this is—"

He put a finger to her lips before she could say, "more incredible than I ever imagined." He stepped back. "Claire, before we go any further, there is something I must tell you."

She looked into his eyes.

"This is not easy for me," he said, suddenly looking distraught. "I don't want to hurt or disappoint you."

She gave him a coy look, remembering his Speedo. "Don't worry. I think I can handle whatever it is."

25

Wally felt obliged to attend Jack's party and figured he would stay just long enough to say hello to Ginger and take some razzing from his client. Easy enough for $6,000 a month. Bear knew where he was going but didn't say anything but "I'm having company tonight, so when you get home, stay out of the kitchen."

Stars were emerging in the evening sky as Wally parked his scooter next to the carriage house of Jack and Ginger's stately home near Hancock Country Club. Inside, the party was in full flow. Music and voices poured out the windows over the wide front lawn. Wally skirted the front door to avoid the bustling crowd and circled around back, where a broad lawn contained a cabana and a swimming pool. He grabbed a beer from a cooler and looked around. Across the lawn, beneath a string of white lights, he spotted Harry Thrall and Danny Boy with their wives. Harry caught his eye and lifted his beer, waving him over. Ever since getting remarried, Harry loved accepting party invitations and smiled broadly standing next to his attractive young wife, Barb.

"Wally!" he said. "Where have you been?"

"You didn't see my interview on the Golf Channel?"

"We heard you lost on eighteen," said Danny Boy in his deep baritone.

"Actually, we tied our match but lost the flight," said Wally. "How did you guys do?"

"We won our flight," said Harry. He wrapped his arm around Barb and gave her a squeeze—as if she were the trophy.

"Harry sunk a few of his usual bombs," said Danny Boy, his bushy eyebrows dancing in delight. "And I chipped in twice. Most demoralizing for our opponents."

"Congratulations," said Wally and clinked their drinks.

Danny Boy's wife, the Professor, said, "Ginger's been looking for you.

She was worried you wouldn't come without Claire. How are you doing?"

"I'm fine."

"You don't look fine."

"He lost on matching cards," said Harry, trying to lighten the conversation. "He'll be better after a few beers."

"Or some tequila," said Danny Boy, raising his glass. "I highly recommend the margaritas."

"Sounds good," said Wally. "If you'll excuse me . . ."

He slipped away before the Professor could say anything else, knowing she was right. Of course he didn't look fine. He didn't feel fine. He hadn't been to a party without Claire in decades. Seeing Harry excited to be with Barb and Danny Boy with the Professor, two well-matched eccentric souls, left him wondering what he had done, telling Claire he didn't want to come home when she had asked him. Did he say no just to get even? Maybe he had put too much weight on Bear's advice to return home as a conquering literary hero. Of course, there was also the issue of Mama Betty's mojo, the use he could not afford to lose, and staying at Bear's he had remained extremely productive. But all this left him here at the party alone, feeling awkward and uncomfortable. He told the bartender to add an extra shot of tequila to his margarita. That might take the sting out of being solo. He carried his drink out to a quiet spot at the far end of the pool and gazed into the glowing blue water, lit from below. After a minute, Ginger Hughes sauntered up to him and softly touched his forearm. She kissed him on the cheek.

"Wally, it's good to see you. I didn't think you'd make it."

"I wouldn't miss it," he said, and took a drink. "You look terrific."

"You're so sweet."

"You're so sweeter."

Ginger laughed. "Where's Bear?"

"He had other plans. But he told me to say hello and give you a big hug. For old time's sake."

Ginger smiled flirtatiously and opened her arms. "Please—go right ahead."

Wally gave her a hug, soaking in her alluring scent. He still carried a torch for his old high school girlfriend, partly because she was the one who dumped him and broke his heart. He saw Ginger around the club and at the occasional holiday party, where after a few eggnogs, they would lapse back into their old intimacy, sharing a special bond based on that long-lost teenage love. They still had a connection. He knew she was happy and better off with Jack than with him. She could never have handled his roller-coaster freelance lifestyle. She lived a much more stable, comfortable life with Jack and circulated in the wealthier social circle of Hancock, a group Wally and Claire overlapped with a few times a year—at a big holiday party or a gathering of golfers like the one tonight. Ginger had aged extremely well, thanks to her natural good looks and living a stress-free life—filled with spa treatments and a personal trainer, winter getaways to the Caribbean and summer vacations on Nantucket. She went to yoga class, played tennis and golf, skied and kept herself as svelte as a starlet and just as richly tanned. In her linen skirt and sleeveless blouse, gold necklace and matching gold hoop earrings, she exuded an elegant appeal. And her pretty smile could still melt his heart. He hugged her close, careful not to spill his drink on her blouse.

When their embrace ended, Ginger said, "Tell Bear thank you," and patted him on the chest, smiling up at him.

"I will," said Wally.

She ran her hand down to his paunch. "You're looking more his size these days."

Wally spread his arms. "Eat to win. And more to love."

Ginger's eyes twinkled.

"Where's your husband?" he asked.

"Off with Hans. I'm second fiddle tonight. You golfers." Ginger shook her head.

"We are men of passion."

"You're overgrown boys."

"You sound just like Claire."

Ginger stood silently for a moment. "I heard about that, Wally. I'm really sorry."

"Yeah, me too."

"How long has she been seeing him?"

Seeing him? Wally looked at her, stunned.

"Her tai chi teacher. Have they been dating for a while?"

Wally couldn't breathe, sucker punched by the news. *Claire was seeing Seafood?* "Who told you that?" he said.

"I thought you knew. Everybody knows."

"*Everybody?*" Wally's mind reeled. Did the Professor know? Danny Boy?

What about Harry? And Bear? After taking the sucker punch, did he have any corner men? Or had they all seen it coming and clammed up, afraid to tell him?

"Why is the spouse always the last to know?" said Ginger, shaking her head in sympathy. "I'm sorry, Wally, I shouldn't have said anything."

"No. It's okay. I'd rather know." But part of him wished he didn't know. Why hadn't his friends told him? What did 'seeing him' mean?

"How long has this been going on?" he asked.

"I don't know. But Ellen Barnes told me she saw Claire this afternoon. Swimming up at his house on Lake Glory."

Wally lifted his glass and finished his drink.

"Ellen has a place just down the road. Nothing like his. Evidently, his home is *gorgeous.*"

Part of him couldn't believe it. While the other part screamed: *Of course! She's worshipped him for fifteen years—now they're together!*

Ginger placed a warm hand on Wally's forearm. "I'm sorry, Wally."

"Yeah." He gave out a short, sad laugh.

"What's so funny?"

"Here I am, being told that my wife is seeing another guy by the girl who dumped me forty years ago."

"I'm so sorry, Wally. I hope everything works out." Ginger gave him a sympathetic look. "I really should mingle. I *am* the hostess."

Wally gave her a weak smile and watched her go. He needed another drink. Inside, by the bar, he cornered Harry and asked if he knew about Claire and her tai chi teacher. Harry shifted his feet and lowered his eyes. "Wally, I didn't—"

"What about Danny? Does he know?"

Harry nodded.

"And Bear?"

"None of us wanted to upset you," said Harry. "Bear says you've been writing up a storm."

"Fuck Bear."

"He's just watching out for you, Wally. We all are."

"Don't do me any favors," he said, and took his fresh drink back out to the pool.

26

Over the next few hours Wally got drunker than he'd been in years. He turned down Harry's offer of a ride home with Barb as their designated driver, saying he'd get an Uber. But he never called an Uber. Instead, he accepted a ride from Jill Vanderhausen, who had joined him by the pool, accompanied by a pitcher of margaritas, a hearty laugh and a pair of long, tanned legs that caught his sodden eye. By the time they left together, he didn't care who saw him climbing into her black Mercedes, because Claire was with Sifu, for fuck's sake. And what the hell was that all about, anyway? The yin, the yang and the wang!

"I thought you might like a little nightcap," Jill said, pulling into her driveway on The Ridge, just down the road from Kyle and Ginger's, a quarter mile from the club.

"A nigh-gap," said Wally, sauced and slurring. "Gud idea."

Ten years younger than Wally and divorced from a neurosurgeon for nearly three years, Jill had never had kids and never remarried after securing the big house and enough alimony to fund her taste for the high life. Since becoming single again, she had earned a reputation for welcoming to her bed a string of men—married, separated, divorced, she was indiscriminate— and every guy in Hancock knew it. Rumor had it that she also threw wild parties for the future titans of American business (and some of their more decadent professors) in the MBA program at the Buck School of Business. Wally had seen Jill more than once in the Canoe Club bar, where she cast a mesmerizing spell on graduate students fifteen years younger, thanks to her sensuous good looks, her perfectly tailored clothing and her ability to cover the tab. Her reputation as a racy, attractive single woman in a town with few of them left her with few female friends. But Wally knew she and Ginger had been close for a long time, based on their mutual interest in yoga classes, spa treatments, trips overseas and, he suspected, the vicarious thrills Ginger got whenever Jill shared the details of her postdivorce liaisons. Especially the ones with the Buck Business school boys in their late twenties and early thirties who could go all night.

"Next yeur," slurred Wally, as Jill parked her car, "Bur and I are gonna *win* the mumbur-mumbur!"

Jill gave him a sultry look. "I'll take care of your member, *member.*" And with that she leaned over, caressed his face and kissed him deeply with a soft, deft tongue. When their kiss ended, Wally blurted, "I'm *murried!*"

Jill feigned surprise. "I had no idea!" She ran a hand up his bare thigh and underneath his baggy shorts. "I thought you were a lonely single man. Whose wife is up on Lake Glory, getting her twat tickled by her tai chi teacher." She pulled her hand out of his shorts and unbuckled his belt. "Tickle me, Wally."

"I dun't knuw," he said.

"Oh yes, you do," she said, as her fingers deftly opened his shorts. She licked his ear and kissed his neck. "Oh yes," she whispered, "you know." She slid her hand inside his underpants and began stroking him, making him hard, as she licked his neck. She ducked down and took him into her mouth. Whatever reservations he had in his drunken big head vanished as she expertly sucked his little head. *Tit for tat, Claire. Tit for tat.* Oh, could she swallow a sword!

But she stopped short of sucking him off all the way, expertly building his tension right to the edge of climax before pulling her lips away. She squeezed the base of his hard-on, backing him off the cliff, probably knowing that at his age, in his condition, he would be one and done—snoring in the front leather seat of her sleek sedan in 11.9 seconds, while she lay alone in the house, restlessly turning in bed with no action of her own. She clearly had other ideas. She led him inside by the hand as he staggered behind her, holding his shorts up, his hard-on pointing like an Irish Setter in the dark, rigidly aimed at the next stop in the hunt.

She kissed him by the kitchen counter and then lay back onto it, her long legs wrapped around his waist. Wally pushed up her skirt and discovered she wasn't wearing panties. He leaned over and helped himself to a midnight snack, inspired by her oral teasing to return the favor and lick her with gusto. Her fingers tugged at the hair on the side of his head.

"Oh, Wally! Oh, yes!" she moaned. There was no need to back her off the cliff. She would not be one and done. Wally lapped her like the dog he was, drunk and disorderly, and she climaxed with a prolonged cry of delight.

Finally going limp, she cooed, "Mop me up and ring me out!"

Wally stood and rolled his neck, trying to work out the kinks. But the kinks, he soon discovered, had only just begun. Jill's orgasm had set her off. She slid off the counter and led him out of the kitchen.

"Follow me, you naughty boy," she said, taking his hand.

She marched him down the main hall of the stately home, past original artwork on the walls—an eclectic collection of watercolors and large oils, galloping horses and ships at sea, portraits and abstract expressionist works—and into the main foyer by the front door, where a six-foot tall replica of Michelangelo's sculpture of David greeted visitors. She patted David's penis and smiled at Wally. Then she turned and led him up a grand curving stairway to the second floor. The thick runner of Oriental carpet felt cushy underfoot, and Wally clung to the ornate, hand-carved banister to steady himself as he climbed. They passed more artwork in the upper hallway. A large, ornately painted ceramic bowl rested on a side table, and another sculpture, this one of a naked woman, stood by a daybed tucked into an alcove by a small round window. At the end of the hall, Jill ushered Wally into a large master bedroom that exuded a warm, regal feel. Gold-and-crimson-patterned wallpaper lined the walls. An elegant makeup table stood in one corner, a large stuffed chair with an ottoman in the other. A wide mirror with a rich mahogany frame hung opposite the bed, just above a low-lying dresser. Windows lined the exterior wall, their shades open to a stand of ancient pine trees. Was that a large walk-in closet around the corner? Or the master bath? He didn't have time to make a determination as Jill led him to the king-sized bed, pushed him down onto a soft silk comforter and proceeded to be the master of her master bedroom.

Over the next hour, Wally followed one command after another, as she guided him through a series of sexual escapades both exciting and alarming. She mixed him a black Russian from a wet bar in the bathroom suite (complete with a Jacuzzi, a sauna, two tiled shower stalls, a long counter with two sunken sinks, a series of broad, open shelves stacked with fluffy towels, a toilet and a douche spray toilet for cleaning your undercarriage)—and the potent mixture of caffeine and alcohol revived him.

"Hit me with the graphite fly rod!" she commanded, relishing the lash and sting on her tight, tanned ass.

"Spank me with the paddleball racket!" she barked. Wally wasn't too sure and hit a gentle forehand. "You call that a spanking?" He hit a harder cross-court shot, rolling his wrist at the end.

"Ohhhh! Ahhhh!" she cried. "Again!"

She ordered him to fetch the whipped cream from the bathroom fridge. "Spray it on my boobs and lick it off!" *If you insist.* When he finished, she said, "Now, it's my turn," and sprayed whipped cream on his balls and licked them clean.

"Do me from behind and bark like a dog!" He embraced the dog style, but not the barking. "Bark!" she commanded. He let out a small yelp. "What are you, a toy poodle? Bark like a Doberman!" He gave it his best shot.

"Stand up!" she ordered. "I want to watch in the mirror!"

Oh no, not that. Please. Wally didn't want to watch himself in the mirror with his receding hairline and recently added girth. He didn't need the mirror to see her perfect body, never stretched by childbirth, sculpted by a personal trainer and toned by yoga. Then he realized: *she wants to watch herself!* Sometimes, he could be a little slow.

Throughout, remarkably enough, Wally stayed hard. After she had sucked him in the car and he had pleased her in the kitchen, he had been erect for fifteen minutes without spilling his seed, the first step in reaching a state where his erection could last for a while. The second step was having all that tequila. Tonight, there had also been a third step—a lubricant that Jill rubbed on his shaft soon after pushing him down on the soft comforter, a cool, thick gel that made all his slipping and sliding, pleasing and pounding a lot easier, with less friction and stimulation. He wondered if there might also be numbing agent in the gel—a silent assistant to serve her seemingly unquenchable lust. Because he soon became the little engine that Could. Not. Come. He seemed suspended in amateur porn-star status, and the longer he lasted, the louder she yelled, barking orders like a drill sergeant who didn't want the drill to end.

"Get the neckties in the drawer! Tie me up!"

He wrapped the silk ties around her wrists and secured them to the bedposts.

"Tie my feet!"

He wrapped two more expensive ties around her ankles—nicer ties than he'd ever worn, from Hermes—and knotted them at the lower posts.

"Spank me! Bruise me! Just like *Fifty Shades of Grey*!"

"That's okay. I'm good."

"No, Wally! Make it hurt—so it feels *good*!"

"I'm not really into that." He knelt over her spread-eagled on the bed. Reached for his Black Russian and took a sip. "Did you really like that book?"

She gave him a frightening look, transforming into the Sigourney Weaver of *Ghostbusters* who channeled the evil entity—her eyes wide and crazy, her hair seeming to stand on end. "Use the NIPPLE CLAMPS!" she commanded. "In the DRAWER!"

Nipple clamps? He found the nipple clamps and attached one, wincing as he did.

"AGHHHH!" She writhed in pain. "YEESSSS!"

That's it. She was making him sober now.

"Do the OTHER!" she screamed at him, practically levitating, eyes bugging out of her head,

"That's okay."

"DO IT!"

All right, all right . . . take it easy. He secured the other nipple clamp.

"AGHHHH! YESSSSS! Yes, yes, YEESSSS!"

Wally shuddered. He may have been Johnny Wadd Holmes for a while, but he was no Marquis de Sade.

"Bite me, Wally!"

"I'm not a two-year-old."

"No! You're like a twenty-two year old! Why would Claire ever leave you?"

Claire. Not what he needed to hear on top of Jill's screams from the nipple clamps. He patted her firm, flat tummy, just above her tightly trimmed mound. "Relax for a second. I'll be right back."

He went into the bathroom, feeling light-headed and alarmed, and closed the door. Leaning against the wall, covered in a sheen of sweat, he closed his eyes. His heart hammered his ribs. *Oh, Wally, Wally, Wally.* What are you doing here? He opened his eyes and faced his reflection in the mirror, his stiff dick pointing at him like an accusing finger. What the hell are you doing with this insatiable beast? He looked down at his numb dick and shook his head. *Hey, wait a minute.* If he hadn't come yet, maybe he could pull a Bill Clinton and say he never had sex with that woman. There would be no sperm stains on her sheets. *You should have blown your load two hours ago, instead of holding off and unleashing the tequila muscle. You would still be asleep in the front*

seat of her car. You can rationalize the blowjob as a moment of weakness. But two
hours of sex in the Cougar Corral—what kind of weakness is that?

He needed Tylenol. And toothpaste. And a gallon of Gatorade. He opened a cabinet and found a bottle of Aleve and downed two tablets, drinking from a crystal glass. He brushed his teeth with an ergonomic toothbrush and organic peppermint toothpaste. What would he tell Jill on his way out? You're a fucking psycho, thanks for a lovely evening? Or, I'm just headed downstairs for a bite to eat. I'll untie you when I get back? Or maybe, I really appreciate you keeping those clamps away from my scrotum. Oh, and for the record, I didn't come, so we never had sex. Gotta go. Toodle-oo!

He returned to the bed, where Jill lay gnawing on her lower lip, her hips writhing. Beads of sweat dotted her forehead in a fever of excitement. Leaving her alone, tied up like a goose, appeared to have calmed her down and turned her on at the same time.

"Come to bed, Wally," she moaned, the spirit of Sigourney Weaver vanquished. She lay stretched before him in all her stunning glory. He felt his loins stir as she moved her hips. And for a moment he hesitated. Did he really have to leave? She lay spread-eagled, his for the taking and deliciously tempting. He walked around to all four corners of the bed, making sure her bonds were secure. He couldn't risk her getting loose and chasing him downstairs, a return of the Sigourney Weaver evil spirit, to wave a knife at him in the kitchen simply because he wanted to go home. And not to Bear's but to East Heifer. Home to his bed, to his own wife and his former life. Where he would try to forget that this had ever happened. But Claire might not even be there, sleeping with Sifu at Lake Glory. *Goddammit!* What was she doing? First, she invited him back. Then, she ran to Sifu! He pulled on his shirt and buttoned it.

"What are you doing?" asked Jill.

"I'm just a little chilly."

She gave a throaty chuckle. "I'm hotter than Hades in July."

He pulled on his shorts.

"Wally?" She tugged her wrists against the ties. "Are you leaving?"

"No."

She gave him a coy look. "Are you *teasing* me?"

"Yes," he said, amazed by the effect bondage had on her. "Yes! I'm teasing you."

"You are *such* a *devil!*"

He leaned down and stroked one of her ankles with a finger. Then he traced a line up her leg and over her hip, past her mound and across her stomach. When he reached her breasts, he removed one nipple clamp and then the other, and then he returned to trace his finger up her long neck to her jaw and her moist temple. He stroked her hair, and she closed her eyes and bit her lip, her hips slowly writhing.

"Ohhhhh Wally. *Ohhhhh yes.*"

If he ever told his golf buddies that he walked out right then, none of them would have believed him. But that's what he did. On his way down the stairs, he heard her call:

"I'm going to burn up!"

"Just try to relax."

"Who's going to untie me?"

"I'll be back. Just get some rest."

At the bottom of the stairs, he heard her call again.

"Wally?"

He stopped by the statue of David. "What?"

"I won't tell Claire. Or Ginger. Or *anyone.*"

I sure hope not, he said to himself. "Thanks, I appreciate that."

"And Wally?"

"Yeah?"

"Don't worry. There's a young Buckie coming over for brunch at eleven. He can untie me, and then we'll eat." She paused. "And then we can have our brunch." She laughed a deep, dirty laugh. He had to hand it to her. At least she was honest, and true to herself, unlike him.

27

Claire had an adventurous night of her own after Sifu pulled down his handsome silk trousers in the living room.

"Jiminy Cricket!" she shrieked.

"I want you to know now," he said. "Before we go any further."

His penis was no larger than a wine cork. Just as rigid and just as small. Her head spun and her heart tumbled. "What about your Speedo?"

"A banana."

Claire thought back to the banana she had gobbled in the bathroom, where his tiger-print suit hung to dry, and realized she must have eaten him already. "Were you *born* this way?"

"No." Sifu retreated a step, pulled his pants up and tied the black cord at his waist. "I was cursed."

"*Cursed?* " said Claire, feeling as if she had been, too. "How?"

"It is a long story."

"I'm not going anywhere," she said, confounded by what was unfolding.

He led her to the couch and sat down next to her. "After I lost my family," he began, "I stayed in Ladakh, studying with my master. He helped me face my grief and welcomed me into his family. He treated me like a son. But living there, I soon fell in love with his daughter. She was a year older and studied with her father, too. She was a very gifted martial artist. And very kind, thoughtful and pretty. We tried to keep our feelings for each other a secret, but my master quickly saw the truth. He acted happy for us. One day, he took me aside and taught me an esoteric exercise to bolster my manhood. For virility and making healthy children, I thought. Over several weeks, I followed his directions, but instead of growing stronger, my penis grew smaller. The harder I tried, the smaller it got. Finally, I went to my master, ashamed to have failed. 'No,' he said, 'you have succeeded!' I did not understand. 'My daughter will never marry you. You are a foreigner, and I will never approve.' "

Sifu hung his head. Claire had never seen him look so fragile. "Oh my god," she said. "That's horrible. What an awful man."

"But before shrinking my manhood, I had already made my true love pregnant. When she finally began to show months later, she feared for my life. But before we could run away together, her father banished her to a secret place. I had no choice but to flee Ladakh before he killed me."

Sifu looked out across the dark lake, where a few lights still twinkled on the far shore. He looked tortured, slouched on the couch next to her, his normally erect posture collapsed into the sorrow of a haunted, broken man.

"I have never seen my child. There is a void I cannot fill."

Seeing his anguish, Claire knew what he needed to do. And it had nothing to do with her—or with them. He had to overcome the wreckage of his past. Of course he wasn't free! What a terrible burden to carry for so many years.

"You need to reverse the curse!" she said and urged him to return to Ladakh—to find his true love and finally see the child he had left within her. He needed to resolve the conflict with his old master—to seek revenge or find redemption, whichever did the trick. "Otherwise," she said, feeling their roles reverse, "you will never have balance."

"Balance," he said, gazing blankly at the water. "Balance is peace. Peace is power. Power is life. And life is death."

"And death lasts a long time!" she said, taking his hand in hers. "You have so much life still to live. You need to get on a plane and resolve this—or you'll never have peace."

"You are right. I have reached the end of the line, Claire. Too many wives left stranded and unhappy. While my own joy remains just beyond reach."

He sighed and stood. Clapped his hands together and asked if she would like a cup of chamomile tea.

"Do you have any bourbon?" She needed something stronger to cope with the unexpected turn of events.

"Do you like Angel's Envy?" he asked.

"I love Angel's Envy," she said, thinking, *How Sifu of him to have an Angel in the house right when I needed one.* "Thank you."

He fetched her a large tumbler of the brown water on ice and went to make himself a cup of tea. She took her bourbon out onto the porch and plopped down in one of the rocking chairs facing the lake. *Good night! Who saw that coming?* The haunting cry of a loon echoed over the water. Was the bird speaking for her? *They were so close! And yet, so far away.* She took a long pull on her bourbon, feeling its warm rush, and shook her head with rueful smile. *Just her luck—a wine cork and a broken heart.* Rocking in her chair, looking at the dark water and the lights twinkling on the far shoreline, she felt suspended in limbo. In no-woman's-land. The kettle whistled, and soon Sifu joined her with his tea. He took the rocker next to hers and looked so haunted and vulnerable that her heart sank again—for both of them. They sat in silence for a minute until the loon's call echoed once more.

"The voice of the universe," said Sifu mournfully. "So full and yet so empty. So lost and yet found."

And what had she found? Disappointment and a drink to wash it down.

They sat watching the lake for a while, each savoring their drinks, and then Claire sighed. It had been a long night.

"It is late," said Sifu. "You should not be driving alone at this hour. There is a guest bedroom upstairs overlooking the lake. It is lovely in the moonlight. You should sleep there."

He was right. It wasn't ideal to be alone on the road at two in the morning. And after drinking champagne and the big tumbler of bourbon, she shouldn't get behind the wheel, anyway.

"Thank you," she said, "that sounds divine."

And then, quite divinely, Sifu came to her in the night. She heard him enter her room and opened her eyes to see him silhouetted by the moonlight streaming through the window—the outline of his curly hair, his lean muscular torso, his strong arms and powerful legs. A warm breeze floated through the open window, carrying a slight scent of pine with it, as he stood facing her with a slightly open stance, a golden aura surrounding his body. She could not see his eyes with the moonlight shining behind him. But she thought she saw his chakras glowing like embers beneath his skin. Was she hallucinating? Small, fiery circles seemed to radiate from his crown, his third eye, his neck and his heart, down to his solar plexus and his sacrum, and, lowest of all, his perineum, the root chakra that connected him to the earth. He stood there glowing like a being from another world, an unbelievable sight.

He walked toward the bed as if floating and slid in beside her, his warmth embracing her before he even touched her. A magnetic presence set off a tingle in her body like an electric current. He did not speak but communicated by telepathy. *I am here now, let us merge together in the Universal Truth.* She replied with her own thought, *Sounds good, chakra boy!*—and felt his hand gently stroke her cheek. He kissed her neck and tenderly caressed one of her breasts, his fingers and palm pulsing with energy. *What potent chi he had! So powerful, he could turn his hand into a human vibrator!* She cooed like a dove while his hands roamed over her skin, vibrating, stimulating, pleasing and teasing. Somehow, he had become Shiva with multiple arms and hands—one squeezing her butt, another stroking her thigh, a third tweaking her nipple, a fourth kneading her spine and one hand marvelously massaging her mound with a perfect pulsing pressure. His hands stimulated every erogenous zone in her body, pressing all of her buttons at all at once. *Oh, Sifu! Oh, yes! Play me like a piano!*

She reached down to touch him and felt a slick fabric covering his groin. Ran her hands back over his buttocks and realized he was wearing his bathing suit. Keeping his little cork dork stashed in his Speedo! She supposed it made sense. He could never enter her with his mini member. But who cared? His magnificent, humming hands were all over her, driving her crazy with their pulsing—a master of her libido in a Speedo. She grabbed his wrist and pulled his hand down to her moistness. *Enough teasing! Put those vibrating fingers to work!*

He obliged her. Strumming her softly, moving gently around her best button of all, he led her slowly but surely into the ether of ecstasy. *Who needed his dinky dong!* He had other tools in his belt—tantalizing tools from another dimension, divine gifts that made her shudder and writhe and moan like a maiden in blessed distress. *Oh my god! I'm going to explode!*

But he pulled his vibrating fingers away at the last second and watched her hover on the edge of ecstasy, smiling down at her. She arched her back and lifted her hips. And then he crouched down and licked her, savoring her like a delicious piece of candy. She felt sweeter than honey and hotter than Hades. His tongue sent sparks flying, igniting her inner fire. And then, suddenly, miraculously, his tongue swelled into the size of a penis! A giant, hot tongue penis moving inside her, making short strokes, then longer, deeper strokes, all while bopping her button and building to a glorious crescendo. *How was this possible? Oh . . . my . . . god!* She had never been a screamer, but she couldn't help it—when his tongue finally launched her over the edge, she exploded like a comet, and screamed from the depths of her being.

"ARRGGGHHHHHHHAAAAAAAAAAA!"

And then screamed again. And again, calling his name. A primal beast unleashed. Uncorked. Undone. Unreal!

She felt a hand on her shoulder. Shaking her.

"Claire? Claire! Are you all right?"

She opened her eyes and found Sifu sitting on the side of her bed. Wearing a pair of red silk pajamas with ornate golden trim—ever the martial artist.

"You cried out," he said. "Screaming. Several times."

She rubbed her eyes. "I must have been dreaming."

"Not a nightmare, I hope." He smiled.

Claire shook her head. "Anything but."

"You called my name."

She smiled weakly, disappointment in her eyes.

"You do know," he said . . . and hesitated. "You must know . . . that I do love you, Claire—as a very dear and trusted friend."

Claire nodded. "I know."

"And I appreciate all you did for me earlier tonight. Because you are right. I must go to Ladakh and find my true love and reverse the curse."

"Yes," she said, "that will be good for you." *But holy mother of god, those Shiva humming hands, vibrating all over my body . . . and that tongue dick trick of yours . . . that was good for me—absolutely amazing!*

He stood up. "I will see you in the morning. Sweet dreams."

Couldn't be any sweeter, dreamboat.

In the morning, Claire helped Sifu book a flight online—an open ticket from Boston to Ladakh because who knew how long it might take to succeed on his mission. It might take a week. Or it could take months. She assured him that closing the dojo for a while would not be a problem. It was summer and people had plenty to do in the nice weather.

"No," he said. "I have a better idea. You will run the dojo while I am gone."

"I can't do that!"

"Yes, Claire, you can. You have helped me teach many new students. Now you will be the master."

"But I'm not ready to—"

"Please!" He pressed a finger to her lips. "Silence. You are ready even if you are not."

"Excuse me?"

"By teaching, you learn. By learning, you grow. By growing, you know. By knowing, you teach."

There he went again on his circular route. "If you say so."

"Good," he said and smiled for the first time since the night before when he had launched into his sad story. "You will be an excellent master."

Her spirits lifted with his faith in her. A faith she didn't have in herself. "I am honored. I won't be nearly as good as you, but I will do my best."

"Your best will be more than enough."

She bowed at him. "Thank you, Sifu."

"No, thank *you*, Claire-san. I have needed to do this for many years. You are right. Now is the moment."

"Comes the moment, comes the man!" she said. But as soon as the words escaped her lips, she regretted saying them. Even though they triggered a tingling sensation from her dream.

But Sifu was not riled by her comment. Instead, he repeated her mantra from the night before: "Reverse the curse!"

"Reverse the curse," she echoed, hoping he could overcome his sorrow and pain. He deserved to be free of his past—to be with his true love and know his child. But what if his old love had moved on? What if she had a mate and good marriage and did not harbor the same old longings as Sifu? Might Claire replace her then? She quickly pushed the thought aside. *Don't be selfish! What are the odds of that?*

Driving home, she wrestled with her heart and her head. *A future with Sifu? No, don't go there. But maybe it's possible. He was pretty magnificent in that dream. No, stop it!* Her phone buzzed, interrupting her argument, and she saw it was Roz. *Not while I'm driving.* Roz called again. And again. Like a dog after a bone. Finally, Claire pulled over.

"Where the HELL have you been?"

"Good morning to you, too, Roz."

"I've been trying to reach you for twenty-four HOURS!"

"I've been out of cell range."

"Rubbish! You've been BANGING your tai chi teacher! And while you were SCREAMING for more, we had to bring Gus back to the shelter—for a *third time!*"

Claire's heart sank. *Oh, no!* "What happened this time?"

"It's a long story," said Roz, "but the bottom line is, that dog is impossible to place."

"I don't believe that."

"We can't keep housing and feeding him when he doesn't cooperate. I'm afraid we're going have to put—"

"I'll take him."

Roz paused. "I thought you didn't want a dog right now."

"I don't. But I can't let him be put down."

"You really think you can handle him?"

"I handle you, don't I?"

"By turning off your STUPID phone!"

Claire thought of turning it off again. Instead, she said as calmly as possible, "I'm going up to the shelter right now."

"I'll meet you there. I want to hear ALL about your WILD night!'

"There's nothing to tell."

"Oh, you're *telling* me! I'm bringing coffee and chocolate croissants and you're sharing the WHOLE story. Every last, delicious detail!"

"Goodbye, Roz."

When Claire stopped to get gas, more bad news arrived from the Professor, who texted to say she wanted Claire to hear it 'before any rumors reach you.' She wrote that Wally had left the member-member party the night before 'Drunk with Jill Vanderhausen—that cougar!!!' Claire suddenly felt sick to her stomach. How could Wally do such a thing? She went limp in her seat. Jill Vanderhausen? *Really?* A driver honked behind her. She turned and saw a grizzled man stick his fat head out the window of his huge pickup truck.

"You gonna pump gas? Or stare at your phone all day?"

Hold your horses! I'm trying to process here! Just because she might have been ready to ride Sifu's tiger—until she found out it was a Tinkertoy—didn't give Wally the right to go home with Jill Vanderhausen! It took years for her to reach that point with Sifu—studying with him, getting to know him, admiring his mastery and his muscles, welcoming his glances and recent advances. It was not the same thing as Wally sleeping with some sexy divorcée ten years younger, who dressed like a high-class call girl, with a shapely figure and sultry eyes and enough money to keep him for as long she liked. *Wally, how could you! I'm no prude, but you said you wanted to come home after you finished your book!*

"Come on, lady!"

Men! If they didn't have a small penis, they had no compass! Claire threw open her door and stepped out of her car. Faced the pickup and clenched her fists. "Keep your pants on, pal!"

"Pump your gas, girlie!"

She dropped into a martial arts stance and raised her hands like Bruce Lee. "You want a piece of me?"

The fat-headed driver looked unsure.

"Come on, *big guy*," said Claire. "A little kick in the *nuts* might do you some good!"

The driver sat back in his seat and took his hands off the wheel.

"Do *not* FUCK with me!" she barked, channeling her inner Roz. The driver looked at her like she was crazy.

"You SIT and you WAIT!" Claire stared him down. The big bad dude backed up and squealed out of the station, flipping her off.

Claire reached for the gas pump, her hand shaking with adrenaline. *What had she just done?* She didn't know Kung Fu—just tai chi. The burly man could have broken her in half. *But damn!* That felt *good!* She should stick up for herself more often. Stop bending over backwards for everyone else, trying to please other people all the time. What about *her?* And to hell with Wally! He should have kept his dick in his pants and kept her from getting so damn angry in the first place! *Wallace! How could you!*

28

A few hours later, Claire pulled into her driveway with Gus in the front seat beside her and saw Wally's scooter parked by the garage. "What the hell is *he* doing here?" she snapped out loud.

Gus looked taken aback. "And I thought *I* was in trouble," he relayed.

"I don't need *two* impossible males in my life." She got out and slammed the door, feeling her blood pressure rise like it had back at the gas station. She let Gus out, her hand trembling as she opened his door in anticipation of seeing Wally.

"You stay here!" she ordered Gus.

She marched into the house, her heart pounding, but found no sign of Wally. Back outside, she spotted Gus lying in the overgrown grass. She hadn't mowed in a few weeks, a result of seeing more of Sifu. Hearing a humming sound out near the studio, she walked over to find Wally in the labyrinth armed with the electric Weedwacker, trimming with his hockey helmet on. *Did he think a branch would fall on his head?* He didn't hear or see her until she stood five feet away, hands on her hips, glaring at him. He shut off the Weedwacker.

"You have some nerve showing up here," said Claire.

"Just cleaning up a bit," said Wally. "It looks like you haven't mowed in a while,"

"I thought you didn't *want* to come home."

"I changed my mind."

"Is that right, *party boy?*"

Wally's face went ashen.

"You and Jill *Vanderhausen?*"

"Claire, I—"

"I don't want to hear it!" She held up a hand.

"What's going on with you and Sifu?'

"We're friends."

"Are you living with him?"

"No, I'm not *living* with him. Who told you that?"

"Are you sleeping with him?"

"That's none of your business."

"I have a right to know. Everyone else does."

"Nobody knows *anything*. Least of all *you!*"

He looked stricken. Exhausted and lost. Fine by her. He deserved to suffer.

"Obviously, you can do whatever you want," he said, looking defeated. "I just want to know."

"There's nothing to know," she said, her jaw set. "He's a *friend*. And he has problems—just like the rest of us."

Wally hung his head.

She pointed to the Weedwacker. "If you're going to use that, you really should wear safety goggles." She turned and stomped back to her car, collected her beach towel and her overnight bag and climbed the steps into the house.

Half an hour later, after taking a shower and sitting for several minutes in her favorite stuffed chair performing the microcosmic orbit in an effort to calm down, she got up and looked out the window, hoping to see Wally's scooter gone. Instead, he was kneeling in the overgrown grass, scratching Gus behind the ears. So much for feeling calmer. She snapped back to full alert and strode to the door in her bathrobe, her hair wrapped in a towel. Stepping onto the deck, she said, "Why are you still here?"

Wally looked up at her. "I thought we could get something to eat."

"You don't look like you need anything more to eat."

Wally looked down at his belly and patted his paunch. "It's Mama Betty's fault."

"Stop blaming everyone else for your problems. You make excuses for everything."

Wally stood up. "The book is going really well, Claire."

"That should give Jill a thrill."

"Claire, come on. Can't we talk?"

"There's nothing to talk about. I want you to go back to Bear's. *Now.*"

Wally bent down and tore a handful of grass from the lawn and tossed it in frustration. "I'm *really* sorry, Claire."

"That makes two of us."

"I love you."

Claire put a hand on her hip and thrust out her jaw. "Well, you should have thought of that before you whipped it out!" And with that, she whirled back inside, letting the screen door slam behind her.

At midnight, unable to sleep, Claire sat with Gus on the front deck, gazing at the starry sky.

"I think you're being unfair to Wally," the dog conveyed.

"That's because he scratched behind your ears."

"No, it's because you're being a hypocrite. Roz said you had a big night, too."

"I didn't sleep with Sifu."

"But you would have. If he weren't handicapped."

Fair enough. If Sifu's teeny little weenie had been even half the size of the banana he used as a decoy, yes—she probably would have slept with him. As it was, her dream came darn close.

"You're no better than Wally," Gus relayed.

Claire sighed. "Maybe not. But Sifu is no Jill Vanderhausen. She's a homewrecker!"

"Excuse me, but I think your home was already fractured."

Claire gazed at the moonlight shimmering off the leaves of a sugar maple, and thought of her uncle's toast at her wedding: *I have three words for you—tenacity, tenacity, tenacity.* Had she used hers all up? "I think every marriage has its cracks after twenty-five years," she said.

"Twenty-five years," said Gus. "You should be proud. You know what that is in dog years? A hundred and seventy-five!"

"Right now, that's what it feels like."

"No one ever said marriage was easy," the dog transmitted. "You have to find a way to stay friends."

"Easy for you to say. Try raising kids, working, paying the bills—having a life of your own and still keeping the romance alive. It's hard."

"Some people do it."

"Yeah, but seeing the same person day after day, year after year—there's a difference between stability and stagnation."

"That's why there's wine, silly girl. And date nights. And weekends away from the kids. To keep things fresh."

"We did that, silly dog. But then things changed. Wally changed."

"From what I've seen in other homes lately, you guys are lucky."

"Oh *please* . . ."

"You're both upset because you love each other. And that's a beautiful thing."

Claire looked at him, speechless.

"What's the matter?" he relayed with a slobbery smile. "Dog got your tongue?"

---

xhausted, hungover, Wally longed for sleep, but his racing mind kept him awake with tortured visions of his drunken escapade with the notorious Vanderhausen. *Jealous fool!* He lay in bed scolding himself with a whipping Jill might have relished, until finally, after hours of guilty suffering, he at last fell asleep. But sleep was no escape. He dreamed he was back in the saddle of sin, back in the twisted tangle of illicit sex, consumed by nightmares so disturbing they jolted him awake, his heart pounding. Tangled in sweat-soaked sheets, he pushed the debauched images from his mind and caught his breath. Soon his regret spilled over into a review of his past—a woulda, coulda, shoulda highlight reel of all the decisions he had made, all the actions he had taken, or not taken, that had led him here, to this lonely room over Bear's garage. Worn out by the anguish of it all, he finally fell asleep. Soon, Mama Betty appeared in a dream, and his torture took a new turn.

His muse had entered his dreams before, but never with such immediacy or force. Usually, his big-eating Southern grandmother-in-law showed up with a plate of roast beef or a bowl of peach cobbler. As she shoveled in forkfuls, talking with her mouth open, she shared ideas and encouraging words about his day at the keyboard, along with glimpses of meat or pie crust.

"You keep goin', Willy Faulkner!" she would declare in her deep Southern accent, a piece of beef clenched between her teeth, her jowls shaking. "Gonna make a name for yourself! Yes sir!"

And then she would vanish as quickly as she had appeared.

But tonight Mama Betty appeared with no plate and no fork, just an expression of disgust. Thick and solid, she wore a housecoat with a lime-green floral pattern, a pair of furry slippers and her trademark silver wig tilted back to reveal an extra inch of forehead. Her deep brown eyes glared at Wally.

"What were you thinkin'?" she said. "Sleepin' with that tart!"

"I was jealous," said Wally. "And I got drunk."

"Lordy me—us Baptists know better. Keep away from the liquor!"

"I know. I fucked up."

"Don't you use that foul language with me!" Mama Betty waved a thick finger at him and shook her head so vigorously her wig nearly fell off.

"Sorry," said Wally, feeling lower than a snake's belly. He sighed from the very essence of his soul. "Do you think Claire hates me?"

"Mighty fine line between love and hate."

"I apologized, but she won't talk to me."

"Give her time. And stop bein' so scared of success! You hold onto failure like a Cuban clutchin' a life jacket!"

"I do not."

"Oh no? How many clients have you lost in the last three years? How many rejection letters have you gotten in your life?"

Wally hung his head.

"You want Claire to forgive you, stop mopin' around, thinkin' about death. It's how you live that matters."

"I don't want to live without her."

"Then zip up and grow up!" Mama Betty pointed at him and dissolved into thin air.

He woke with a start, Mama Betty's words echoing in his head. But despite her rallying cry, for three days he sat at his computer and couldn't write a thing. He had no ideas and no energy and, equally alarming, no appetite. Had she abandoned him? In his dream, she had said he needed to finish his book. Did she mean all by himself? He uttered prayers asking her to return, but his ability to channel her brilliance seemed to have ended. Thanks to his infidelity, he'd lost Mama Betty. Would Claire be next?

On the third day after his dream, he walked onto the first tee for his weekly golf game with Danny Boy, Bear and Harry.

"Hey, Wally," said Harry, "where's your hockey helmet?"

Danny Boy eyed him, rubbing his chin. "You look naked without it."

"Please," said Bear. "That is *not* a good visual."

"I don't need the helmet," said Wally, swinging his driver, loosening up. "I've discovered I am perfectly screwed without it."

"After what you did last weekend," said Bear, "I would have to agree."

Wally proceeded to play his worst golf of the year on the front nine, bludgeoned by the heat and his sense of failure. On the 12th tee, he lit a cigar in hopes of changing his luck. Danny Boy pulled him aside and said in his deep, resonant voice, "You should hear it from me—unlike last time. Claire is living up at the lake."

Wally's stomach did a somersault. "Says *who?*"

"The Professor. Claire invited her up there for a swim tomorrow."

"So she *lied* to me?"

Danny Boy held up his palms. "Hey, don't shoot the messenger. I have no idea what she's doing up there. I'm just passing along the news." His enormously bushy eyebrows lifted. "Whatever you do, just stay away from Vanderhausen, will you? The Professor is still punishing me for that. Like I'm the one who did it! All the wives hate that woman."

Wally finished the round with his worst score of the year and sat on the deck in a daze while his friends talked animatedly about their golf. As he walked to his scooter, Danny Boy came alongside. "You want me to get a report from the Professor?"

"Not especially," he said.

"I'm sure she'll fill me in."

When they reached Wally's scooter, Danny asked, "How's the writing going?"

"It's not," said Wally. "I seem to have lost my muse."

"Sorry to hear that." Danny Boy reached into his golf bag and pulled out a joint. He handed it to Wally.

"That's okay," said Wally. "I'm good."

"Trust me. It will open your mind. You could use a new perspective on things."

Wally doubted he would ever smoke the joint, but he appreciated his friend's gesture of concern and accepted the gift.

"A muse can only take you so far," said Danny, tapping a finger against Wally's chest. "Ultimately, it's what's inside that counts. The way I see it, you have two choices—fear or faith. What's it going to be?"

Wally looked at him, unable to answer. Danny gave him a final tap on the chest. "You'll figure it out." Then he walked to his truck, threw his clubs in the bed and drove off with a wave.

Wally watched him go. He wanted to have faith but felt mostly fear. Fear and self-loathing, a twist on Hunter S. Thompson. Now there was a fuckup who succeeded. On a grand, self-destructive scale. Wally threw a leg over his scooter and pulled on his hockey helmet. Maybe he should smoke that joint. What did he have to lose? Then his cell phone buzzed in the pocket of his shorts, and he eagerly checked it. But it wasn't Claire. It was a text from Lucia Bonaventura.

August ~ The Red Moon

"Three things cannot be long hidden:
the sun, the moon, and the truth."

—Buddha

30

Lucia had a check for him, if he wanted to stop by Sigma Delta and pick it up. "I'm here studying for a physics test," her text ended.

Wally rode his scooter to the sorority—it was on his way back to Bear's—with a golf bag on his back, hockey helmet on his head, just like the morning he had crashed into the car and triggered all his troubles. Lucia sat on the front steps of the grand, brick house, reading a textbook by the glow of the front light, looking as fetching as ever in a pair of shorts and a sleeveless blouse. Seeing Wally ride up the walk, she sauntered over in her bare feet and gave him such a gorgeous smile that he thought he might fall off his scooter again.

"I've always wondered," she said. "Why don't you leave your golf bag at the club?"

"Because there's no locker room."

"I thought every club had a men's locker room. Where the guys sat around drinking beer, smoking cigars and playing cards?"

"Not at Hancock Country Club."

"How boring," she said. "My dad's a member at Riviera. They know how to have fun."

"I'll bet. The Hollywood crowd."

She flipped her long, silky hair from one side of her head to the other, looking eager for relief from the sticky heat, and pulled an envelope from her back pocket. "Sorry this is so late."

He fumbled her handoff, distracted by her beauty, and dropped the envelope onto the grass. He leaned over and picked up.

"I added a small late charge," she said. "So you'll let us order again next year." Then she pointed to the ground, looking at him with a gleam in her eye. "I think you dropped something."

Wally looked down and saw Danny Boy's joint lying in the grass. It must have fallen from his pocket when he bent over to pick up the check. "Whoopsie daisy!" he said, picking it up.

"So that's why you ride around like that."

"No! A friend gave it to me."

"*Sure.*"

"I don't really smoke pot. Would you like it?" He held the joint out to her.

"You don't want it?"

"Nope."

She took the joint and rolled it in her fingers. She held it to her nose.

"I'm sure it's good," he said. "My friend is Captain Cannabis."

"It smells heavenly." She smiled at him. "Thank you."

"My pleasure."

"So how's the novel coming?"

"Not so hot. That's why my friend gave me the joint."

"Oh, well . . . sorry to hear that. I hope you can find inspiration somewhere." And then she leaned over and kissed him on the cheek. "Thanks for the gift."

He couldn't remember the last time his face felt so hot. What a wonderful girl! Way too young and pretty and smart for him. Physics? He never even stepped into the science building in college. He needed to introduce her to his boys.

"Thanks for the check," he said. "And good luck on your test." As he rode away, she waved goodbye, holding the joint in her fingers like a cigarette. "See you later, Wallace!"

He didn't care which one of his boys won her heart, so long as one of them did. He rode back to Bear's, excited to deliver the Sigma Delta check, but when he pulled into the driveway, he saw a car parked next to Bear's pickup. His friend had company, and the house was out of bounds. He would have to hand over the check tomorrow. Walking to the garage apartment, he heard music filtering through the open sliding door on the deck, and heard Bear say, "Can I freshen your cosmo?"

Up in the garage apartment, inspired by Danny's words and Lucia's interest in his novel, Wally tried writing. But staring at his laptop screen, all he could see were images of Claire up at the lake with Sifu. Skinny-dipping on this hot July night . . . sipping cosmos under the stars in his-and-hers lawn chairs . . . sitting on a dock, their legs dangling in the water, looking at the moon's reflection. After an hour of this torture, his mind was jumping around like a monkey. He knew he shouldn't go there, but he got up and walked out of the apartment to ride up to Lake Glory and find out what the hell was going on.

Passing the house, he heard Bear's deep laughter roll out the door above the music and looked over to see his friend waving a martini glass half full of pink liquid over his head, as he danced with a large, brown-haired woman. Wally skirted closer to the sliding door for a better look. The brunette was a Rubenesque beauty—full-bodied and well-proportioned, with lovely features and a pretty smile. She looked like she had come from playing tennis, dressed in a synthetic, sleeveless top and matching culottes, and moved her curvy body with erotic allure. Suddenly, a second woman entered the frame—a willowy blonde in a tennis dress, with long shapely legs and a lean, athletic build—and Wally's heart jumped. *Holy shit!* The blonde joined the gyrations. Bear danced with the two women, his nose pointed to the ceiling, like he could smell fresh honey. Wally watched them dance, feeling like a Peeping Tom, lurking in the darkness. *Bear, you old scoundrel.* He tore himself away and climbed on his scooter.

He rode into Hancock, happy for Bear, arguing with himself. Was he really some crazed ex who was going to stalk his wife? At the light on Main Street, he looked across the college green toward the library tower clock, glowing in the summer night. 11:45. *You're really going up there at midnight?* Part of him said, *Damn right!* But the other part of him countered, *What good will it do? They'll be asleep. And if they're not, are you going to watch them through the window, too?* He turned right, away from the river, Vermont and Lake Glory, and rode around the green, drawn as if by a magnet toward the golf course. The hot night air felt soft against his skin. Hardly any students were out. He rode through the still campus, and when he reached the practice holes, instead of turning into them, he decided to ride his scooter around the empty course. He flicked off his headlight to let the glorious moonlight guide his way. After passing the 7th green, he rode down the 8th fairway, past the pond and the green, then turned down a hill toward the 9th hole, and that's when he spotted them. A couple off to the right—fifty yards away, two dark forms, as if performing a shadow play. A male pulling on a female's arm as she struggled in the opposite direction, fighting against him. He yanked her toward him. She kicked his shin. He threw her to the ground.

Wally gunned his scooter in their direction. *"Hey! **Hey!**"*

The male figure straightened.

"Leave her alone!" Wally yelled as he tore across the grass. He skidded to a stop in front of the guy, dropping the scooter to the ground and stepping forward. "What are you doing?"

"None of your business." The guy shoved Wally. "Old timer."

Something in Wally snapped. Maybe because of Claire. Maybe because he was shocked to see a man throw a woman to the ground on a golf course—a gentleman's sanctuary, a sacred place. Maybe because he'd had enough of everything lately, including his own stupidity. He tucked his chin into his chest and drove his hockey helmet into the guy's face with a savage fury.

The punk fell to the ground and didn't move.

"Come on!" Wally waved at the woman. "Let's go!" He straddled the bike and felt her climb on behind him, wrapping her arms around his waist. He goosed it up the hill and looked back to see the guy rise to his hands and knees. Wally held the throttle open as he raced down the cart path, weaving past tees and greens for a good ten minutes, all the way to the clubhouse. That's when he finally stopped under a streetlight and his passenger climbed off and he saw her face for the first time.

"Lucia?"

She nodded, wiping away tears, and gave him a great big hug as she choked out a thank-you.

"I thought you were studying for an exam?"

"I was," she sobbed, and then she shared her story—how she'd been trying to break up with her boyfriend for a month, but he kept hanging on, wanting to work it out. But she was done. "Wes gets jealous of *everyone*. And *everything*! I feel like I can't breathe sometimes." Tonight he had come by and begged her to go for a walk—to talk it out. He just needed to know why. And then he didn't accept her reasons. "Thank god you showed up," she said.

"Let me take you back to the house."

"I don't want to go back there. Not right now." She reached into her shorts and pulled out the joint he had given her earlier, her hands trembling. "I need to calm down. Do you have a match?"

Wally found his cigar lighter in his shorts pocket, and flicked it on, his hand trembling, too. He'd never snapped like that, never dropped another person to the ground, never rescued anyone. Lucia inhaled deeply and held out the sweet-smelling joint to him, her eyes so grateful and so gorgeous. He accepted it and took a hit. Why not? Maybe it would calm him down, too.

They passed the joint back and forth a few times, and then Wally waved her off.

"I'm good, thanks."

Lucia took a last toke and flicked off the ember with her fingernail. It skidded across the pavement. Licking her thumb and forefinger, she pinched the end of the joint and slipped the half remaining back into her pocket. A veteran pot smoker, apparently.

"How about going for a ride?" she said.

"Okay." If that would help her, he was game. "Where would you like to go?"

"I don't know. You're the local. Show me around."

He started by taking her around Occom Pond, which lay just past the clubhouse and stretched half a mile back toward the campus. Wally steered the scooter and began to feel the effects of the cannabis. The pond twinkled under the milky light of the moon. Towering pines stood like sentries on the western shore, casting long shadows. The entire landscape seemed to glow, pulsing with life. In the scooter's headlight, a dance performance of molecules and particles, insects and moths captured his imagination. Flowing through the darkness caressed by a warm soft wind, he felt as if he were gliding on a cushion of air.

"It's okay if you want to go faster," Lucia said, leaning forward, her lips by his ear.

He looked at the speedometer. The needle read 10. *Oh man*! Danny's weed was so much stronger than pot back in the day. He sped up to twenty and felt like he was speeding. He gave out a surprised, nervous laugh and decided to skirt the campus, knowing his only salvation in his stoned state would be to get out of town into the countryside as soon as possible. He took shortcuts through one neighborhood after another, avoiding the main roads, riding past the houses of kids he knew back in high school. Memories of his days with them flickered before his eyes like an old newsreel. In the moonlight, the houses appeared suspended in time, as if the sun might rise and all his friends would emerge from their front doors and head to school again. As if nothing had ever changed. As if they were all still sixteen somewhere deep inside themselves.

He climbed a road that wound up a hillside, past homes tucked into the woods. A light burned in a room. A night owl relishing the stillness and quiet? Or an insomniac tortured by dread and uncertainty, what they hadn't done, what they needed to do? *Been there, done that.* Wally made another turn up a steep hill and headed for the countryside.

"How you doing?" he called back to Lucia.

"Great! But you can still go faster."

Maybe he should let her drive. But then he'd have to wrap his arms around her, and he couldn't do that. Not as an old timer. Not as her future father-in-law and the grandfather of her children by Josh or Jack—whichever one captured her heart. He broke twenty-five and felt like he was going fifty. They rode past fields and barns, stone walls and houses, one rural property after another. They cruised toward Moose Mountain, its dense green darkness tinted by the moon, and Wally became one with the scooter, the wind, the sky and the night. He rode suspended in time and space down curving country roads that seemed to stretch forever. He opened his mouth to let the air rush into his lungs, and a bug hit the back of his throat. He coughed and heaved and had to pull over.

"Are you all right?" said Lucia.

He coughed some more. "I'm fine. Just ate a bug."

She laughed and slid off the seat behind him. "You've got the munchies. Where are we anyway?"

"In Etna. Near Hancock Center."

"It's gorgeous." She climbed over a stone wall and stepped into a broad field that crested a hill. The smell of freshly cut hay was so strong Wally could taste it. He watched Lucia cross the newly mown field and climb to the top of the hill, where she stretched her arms toward the sky, gazing at the stars, her silhouette shining in the moonlight. A subtle, vibrating energy permeated everything. In the darkness, his novel suddenly lurked among the trees, tucked between the stones, wrapped in the bales of hay. Was it doing the work that mattered or was it the result? Was it the approval of his father he needed or the acceptance of himself?

Lucia sat down on a large rock and gazed at the night sky. She waved to him and called, "Got a light?" He climbed over the stone wall and walked up the hill to her. She put the joint in her mouth, and he flicked on the lighter like the romantic lead in an old Hollywood movie. She pulled on the joint and it sparked red.

"Does your dad know you smoke pot?" he asked.

"We smoke it all the time," she said, exhaling. "It's better for him than drinking." She handed Wally the joint.

He took a small hit and handed it back. *You are plenty stoned, my good man. You still need to fly that scooter home.*

She took another hit and said, "I can show your novel to my dad, if you want. When it's finished."

Was he hearing things? "Seriously?"

"Sure. His production company takes options on novels all the time."

Goosebumps exploded on the back of Wally's neck. "Don't you want to read it first?"

She shook her head. "No. I'm sure it's good. You have a wonderful heart."

Would he wake up and find this had all been a dream? "That's very kind of you."

"Well, it was very kind of you to rescue me."

They sat under the stars, listening to the sounds of the night. Lucia took another toke and blew smoke toward the heavens. "Do you ever wonder what it all means?"

"Sure." He paused, and then chuckled. "But I really have no idea." For the first time since his father had died, that notion didn't bother him.

"I think it's all right there—just beyond our grasp." She extended her hand into the night.

"Whatever it is, it goes by way too fast."

"That's what my dad says." She smiled at him. "You old timers."

Wally smiled back. Beyond her silhouette, he watched a large owl climb above the trees in long, languid strokes and fly across the face of the moon as if in slow motion. *Ah, Danny, you wizard of weed!*

"I should get back," said Lucia, standing up. "Can I drive?"

How could he say no to his new literary agent? Especially when he was too stoned to be driving again, anyway? When they reached the scooter, he took off his helmet and handed it to her, climbed on the back and grabbed a strap across the seat behind him. There would be no wrapping his arms around his delicious driver. Not at her dad's age. "Go straight," he said. "And in about a mile, turn left."

"Okay," Lucia cried, "hang on!" She accelerated and the scooter surged forward. "Yeeee haaaa!"

*   *   *

Fifteen minutes later, the scooter sputtered to a stop in the breakdown lane of Route 10, three miles from campus.

"What's wrong?" said Wally.

"No idea," said Lucia. "We just lost power."

Wally slid off the seat and walked around to look at the dash.

"*Shit!* We're out of gas."

Lucia laughed. "You really aren't the best stoner, are you?"

"No," said Wally, "but the guy who lives up there is." He pointed to Danny Boy and the Professor's home, 150 yards up the road, tucked off the highway, by an inlet of the Connecticut River. "At least I know where to run out of gas."

He pushed the scooter down to the driveway, where Danny's truck was loaded for his early morning fishing expedition with a kayak and several poles. The bays of the attached garage were open as usual, one holding a motorboat and a trailer, the other containing the Professor's car. Wedged in between were piles of accumulated clutter. Wally rummaged around the packed garage, trying to find a can of gasoline, and knocked over a shovel that hit a rake that clanged against a wheelbarrow.

"*Shhhhhh!*" said Lucia.

Where was the gasoline? He found the lawn mower against the back wall, and then he kicked a can of gasoline in the dark, making another racket.

Suddenly, a light flicked on and the mudroom door opened and the Professor stood on the step in a bathrobe, holding a BB gun.

Wally raised his hands over his head. "Don't shoot!"

"*Wally?*"

"We ran out of gas."

"Who's *we?*"

Lucia stepped into the light. "Hi, Professor Bryan."

"*Lucia?* What are you doing here?"

"I've been riding with Wallace. It's been the most gorgeous night!"

The Professor looked at Wally. "You really are on a roll, aren't you?"

Wally held up the can of gasoline. "May I?"

"Help yourself," said the Professor.

"I'll buy Danny a few beers."

"I'm sure you will." The Professor turned to Lucia. "Can I give you a ride back to campus?"

Lucia shook her head. "Oh, no. Thank you, but that's not necessary. The scooter will be fine."

Wally filled the tank halfway and put the gas can back in its place. He stepped over and gave the Professor a little hug. "Thanks, Professor, you're a lifesaver."

She gave him a neutral squeeze. "You're walking a fine line these days, you know that?"

Wally gave her a stoned grin and launched into Patsy Cline's hit. "I go out walkin', after midnight, out in the moonlight, just like we used to do, I'm always walkin' after midnight, searchin' for yooouuuu!"

"Goodnight, Wally," said the Professor. She waved to Lucia. "Be careful, honey. You don't know what you're dealing with."

When Wally dropped Lucia off at Sigma Delta, he said, "Don't forget to speak with campus safety about what happened."

"I won't."

"And if you need me to tell them what I saw, just let me know."

"Thanks, but I don't think that will be necessary." She ran her fingers through her windblown hair. "There are a couple of Sigma Deltas who date football players and they'll make sure Wes doesn't bother me anymore."

"Good."

"Thanks for the lovely ride." She kissed him on the cheek and started up the steps. At the door, she turned around. "And don't forget about my offer."

"Don't worry," said Wally. "I won't."

31

"I'm not kidding," said the Professor the next evening on Sifu's porch after a swim with Claire and Roz. "He was riding around on his scooter with probably the prettiest girl I've ever seen at Hancock College."

"At two in the morning?" said Roz.

"I thought a raccoon was trying to get into the garbage. Wally was banging into everything, looking for a gas can. I think they were stoned. He looked pretty giddy."

Claire took a drink of her wine and tried to absorb what she was hearing. First Jill Vanderhausen, now a beautiful coed? What was Wally doing? While she uncovered a firecracker without a fuse and held off a silver-haired squire nearing seventy, he slept with a woman ten years younger and got stoned with a college student? Maybe she should start flirting with her handsome young Push Hands partner at the dojo. Let him win for a change and trigger his interest. She could keep him after class for some private tutoring. Show him a thing or two. *Right.* She was as geared to being a New Age cougar as Roz was to becoming a nun.

"I've had Lucia in a few acting classes," said the Professor, "and she's very talented. She gets it honestly. Her mother's an actress and her father's a screenwriter. They live in Hollywood. But evidently she's not interested in an acting career. I think she wants to work for NASA or do physics research or something. She's a real smarty-pants."

Oh for cryin' out loud! "How smart can she be," said Claire, "riding around on the back of Wally's scooter?"

Roz looked at her. "I had no idea Wally was such a stud."

"Screw you, Roz."

The Professor raised her hands, playing the peacekeeper. "Hey, let's talk about something else, shall we? How is the Labor Day event coming along."

"Oh we're in *great* shape," said Claire, her voice laced with sarcasm. "We don't have a band, we don't have a caterer and our special guest is a veterinarian from the Northeast Kingdom who does magic tricks."

Roz's jaw dropped. *"WHAT?"*

"That's right," said Claire, finally coming clean with her. "I'm completely on my own. Millicent has not done a single thing and the other two people on the committee are useless."

"Why didn't you tell me?" said Roz.

"Because you have enough to do with the fundraising and invitations and PR and everything else you're doing. I didn't want to upset you."

"Well you just did!" Roz cried. "The event is four weeks away! Do you even have Porta Potties?"

"Porta Potties?

"The septic system at that old farmhouse can't handle two hundred people!"

"Shit," said Claire. "I never thought of that."

"Shit is right," said Roz.

Claire looked out at the lake and saw Yin crouched by a stump. More shit. She would collect it later. Or let it decompose, like Gus suggested, in a more eco-friendly solution. Enough with poop-filled plastic bags going into larger plastic bags, going into landfills. This was rural living.

"I have an idea for a special guest," said the Professor, sounding upbeat.

"And who is that," said Roz, glaring at Claire.

"I can't tell you. That could jinx it."

Roz threw up her hands. "You two! Oh my god!"

"He's perfect, though," said the Professor. "I don't know if I can get him, but I'll try. I'm pretty sure I can get him. But I don't know. He's a friend of a friend."

"Aggghhhhh!" said Roz. "I need wine."

Claire filled her glass and took a deep breath. Sitting on Sifu's porch was usually very peaceful and calming. In the days since he had departed for Ladakh, leaving her in charge of his house, his pets and the dojo, she had enjoyed being on the lake, especially at dusk, following class. She would go for a swim with Yin and Gus, while Sifu's Siamese cat, Yang, watched from the shore, and then watch the sun slowly disappear behind Tug Mountain, leaving streaks of color melting in its wake. Now, as Gus and Yin rollicked on the lawn, the evening sky was resplendent with purple, red and orange swirls. A breathtaking sight worth relishing—until Roz started breathing down her neck again.

"What about Max?" snapped her friend. "Have you followed up with him at all?"

"No, I haven't," said Claire. "And stop prostituting me!"

"It's not just about the money, honey. It's about *you*. You deserve a man who has his shit together. Who treats you nicely and lets you enjoy some of the finer things in life. Instead of some self-absorbed adolescent who's chasing the impossible dream."

Claire sipped her wine. What could she say?

"You need to give Max a chance," said Roz, her voice softening. "Not just for the shelter, but for *yourself.*"

Claire sighed. "Maybe you're right."

"Of course I'm right." Roz patted her thigh. "Give him a call. You'll thank me later."

At the dojo the next evening, Claire led the class weighed down by thoughts of Wally and Millicent, Roz and her Max mania, the fundraiser debacle. At one point, as she wandered around the dojo in a daze, and Joan took her by the arm and pulled her aside.

"Who died?" said Joan in a harsh whisper.

"Nobody," said Claire, wiping her brow. "I'm just feeling a bit overwhelmed today."

"Well, so are lots of other people in here. That's *life*. That's why they come to class. You need to check your troubles at the door if you're going to help anyone." Joan gave her a slap on the butt. "Come on! Be a leader! Get with the program!"

The little pep talk shook Claire out of her self-pity and put the hint of a smile on her face. She conducted class and lost herself in the process. Afterward, she saw several people smiling as they chatted together.

Joan stepped over and this time stroked her arm. "See! You are *good* at this. Don't ever forget that."

"Thank you, Joan."

"Whatever's going on out there, you're a star in here. Everyone loves your classes. Have you seen *any* attrition since Sifu left?"

Claire thought about it. "No."

"What's going to happen now is you're going to see new people coming in. Because of *you*. So be proud of yourself, lady." Joan winked and strode off. What a fiery little blessing!

Before teaching her first class the week before, Claire had been so nervous she almost threw up. But she had made it through with the support of the students, and in every class since, she had grown more confident and relaxed.

With every tip she shared on technique and posture, breathing and movement, she discovered she knew more about tai chi than she realized. Sifu had been right, as usual. She was ready. And she loved teaching. A part of her felt guilty that his great misfortune had led to her great good fortune. But she did not dwell on that. She kept moving forward. Or trying to. Because teaching tai chi had also made it clear just how tired she was of giving massages. Not just physically tired, but spiritually and emotionally spent. Eager to please and always willing to listen, she could be left haunted by a client's challenges for days, even weeks. But she struggled to set boundaries and brought the problems on herself. Hadn't that been the issue with Wally? Wasn't it the problem with Millicent? And Roz? And pretty much everything and everyone? Others didn't pose the problem, she realized more acutely than ever after teaching for a week at the dojo. She did. The question was, would she ever do anything about it?

She found Max on a far court practicing serves. Dressed all in white, wearing a visor and sunglasses, he looked like a tennis player until he threw the ball into the air and morphed into Gumby, twisting like rubber in every direction. He hit a vicious serve straight down the middle. She smiled at his unorthodox style, a bit surprised by how happy she was to see him.

"Good morning!" he called, as she made her way onto the court. "Thanks for reaching out. I'm so glad we could finally do this."

"Me too," said Claire.

They began to hit, and she struggled to find her rhythm. Max was like a crazed artist, hitting the mark with one effort, missing entirely with the next. A few balls screamed toward the back fence like missiles.

"Incoming!" he cried as Claire twisted out of the way. "Sorry!"

Coping with his unusual game, she took forever to find her groove, racing around the court, chasing down his erratic shots.

"You're like a jackrabbit over there!" he called after fifteen minutes, beaming at her. He looked so cool and composed in his all whites, while she dripped sweat.

"How about playing a set?" said Max. "And don't worry, my fragile male ego can handle a spanking from a beautiful woman." Max laughed at his double entendre and tossed her two balls. "Ladies first."

Thanks to his wild fluctuations between pure genius and god-awful, Claire kept the match close. But at 5–4, when they switched sides with Max leading and about to serve for the match, she wondered if she should let him win. *For the sake of the rescues!*

On his first two serves, he unleashed his eccentric firepower and aced her twice. And that's when her old competitive college juices took over. *She couldn't throw a match! Not even for the dogs.* She bounced on her toes, anticipating another powerful serve, but this time Max fiendishly dinked the ball over the net. A drop shot serve! She scrambled over the clay and lunged for the ball, barely getting it back over the net. Max raced forward, quite quickly for a Gumby nearing seventy, and lobbed his return over her head. Backpedaling like Bernie Sanders about being a socialist millionaire, Claire jumped up and hit a smashing overhead.

Right into his groin.

"Awwwgghhhhhhh!" Max dropped to the clay, writhing in agony.

Claire rushed around the net and knelt by his side. "I am *so* sorry! I didn't mean to do that!"

"Well, you did," he said and groaned.

She brought him water and a towel, and after a few minutes, helped him to his feet. She escorted him to his car, and he slid in gingerly behind the wheel. He looked up at her and flashed a wan smile.

"Smashing good fun," he said.

"I am *so* sorry," said Claire. "I hope you can ice it when you get home."

Max winced. "Ice?"

"Pour some whiskey over it," said Claire, eager for him to do something, *anything*, to feel better.

"I'll be fine," said Max with a grimace. "Nothing a few Advil can't cure." He started his car and drove away with two quick honks of his horn.

Mortified by what she had done to end yet another outing with him badly,

Claire slumped into her front seat. Max was such a gentleman. Such a good sport the way he absorbed all her unintended abuse. He really was a kind soul. She would have to check on him later. For now, she checked her phone before driving home and found two texts from Roz and one from Wally. What did *he* want?

"Tennis with Max McClure?!" said Wally's text. "Are you dating him?" How did Wally know she was playing tennis with Max? Had he ridden past the courts on his way to or from the golf course just down the street and seen them playing? Or did one of his friends spot them and send Wally a note? Small-town life. Was it completely devoid of privacy?

She fired back. "Scooter ride with a coed?! Are you dating a girl young enough to be your daughter?!"

"No! It's not like that!"

"Neither is tennis with Max!"

That seemed to shut him up. She moved on to check Roz's messages.

"Any update on food & band & Porta Potties????!!!!" Followed by, "You DO realize the event is TWO weeks away!!!"

That did it. Enough was enough. Claire drove to Woodstock, speeding with fury along Route 4, making record time. She pulled into a long gravel driveway after following her phone GPS and almost hit a cat as it darted under her wheels. Skidding to a stop in front of an immaculately restored old Cape, she couldn't believe her eyes. Everywhere she looked, she saw cats. Cats by the trees, cats in the garden, cats near the barn, cats encircling the entire house. The place looked like one of those classic George Booth cartoons in The *New Yorker*, bursting with cats of all shapes and sizes, some with crazed expressions, next to equally eccentric-looking humans. Claire leapt out of her car and marched to the front door. She knocked. No answer. She knocked again with greater force. And waited. And waited. Just as she was about to rap on the door again, it swung open and Millicent Fernwater stood facing her in a silk kimono, an eye shield hanging around her neck. She squinted and said, "*Claire?*"

"I can't believe you're a *cat* lady!" snapped Claire, pointing an accusing finger at her. "No wonder you never *do* anything for Doggone Right!"

Millicent stepped back, aghast.

"Is that why I have to do *everything* alone? Because you don't like *dogs?*"

"Goodness!" said Millicent, placing a hand on her chest. "I've been on

Martha's Vineyard. I couldn't be much help from there."

"You weren't much help before you *left!*"

Millicent tugged on her eye mask and straightened it.

"All you do is send emails ordering everyone around. But you never *do* anything!" Claire barked, the weeks of frustration pouring out of her. Finally! She was sticking up for herself. No more bending over backwards. "I can't do it alone! We need a band and we need a caterer and I have two Porta Potties but we need four and it's wedding season and everything and everyone is already BOOKED!"

Millicent looked shell-shocked and stammered a meek reply. "I . . . my . . . well . . . I just . . . . Goodness gracious! Can we discuss this over a cup of tea?"

Claire took a deep breath and unclenched her fists. *Take it easy!* Didn't Sifu tell the class more than once: 'Anger is misplaced energy, and misplaced energy is wasted'?

"Please," said Millicent, waving a hand, "won't you come in?"

Trying to calm herself, Claire followed Millicent into the kitchen. She had gotten so worked up on the drive, by the time she confronted Millicent, her heart was pounding. *Breathe in, breathe out. Calm down.* They sat at an antique table that looked as old as the Cape. The house and its appointments were quite lovely in a rustic Yankee way. Millicent stood by the stove as the kettle heated up.

"You're absolutely right, Claire," she said, looking forlorn. "I really don't *do* anything—except tell other people what to do." She sighed and fiddled with the eyeshade around her neck. "I don't blame you for being angry. When Chester ran off with his secretary, I felt so abandoned. I was quite incapable of handling my own affairs because he had done *everything*. I was probably your age," she said. "Not over the hill but approaching it."

Claire shuddered. That was her, all right. What was she doing about it?

The whistle blew and Claire thought she saw a tear roll down Millicent's cheek. Or perhaps it was steam, condensing on her face.

"Soon after Chester left, a friend invited me to join a volunteer board," Millicent continued, brewing their tea. "To take my mind off my troubles. And I must say, it worked. I loved seeing everyone at meetings and being part of a group. Soon, I began to volunteer on another board and then another, and pretty soon things snowballed, and I was volunteering *everywhere*. But really, I didn't have any skills, so I just became very adept at delegating. And, of course, writing checks. Chester left me a rather sizable fortune for all his philandering.

She poured their tea, looking distraught, and sat down across from Claire. "I'm ashamed to say, I still feel quite incompetent. But I've gotten away with it for so many years. No one has ever challenged me because they're all too scared to lose my donations."

Now tears were clearly flowing down Millicent's cheeks. "I'm terribly sorry to have burdened you with so much work."

Claire felt awful about making her cry. At the same time, she felt liberated by clearing the air. "It's okay, Millicent. Please don't cry."

Millicent dabbed her eyes with a cloth napkin. "Forgive me," she said, trying to regain her composure. "I'm afraid vacation was not very restful. Being with family can be very trying at times. My niece is getting married in three weeks, over in Pomfret, and all hell seems to be breaking loose. Apparently, her fiancé is a bit of a playboy scoundrel. Not unlike Chester."

"I'm sorry to hear that."

"Yes," said Millicent and sipped her tea. "Me, too."

Claire straightened in her chair. "May I ask you a question?"

"By all means."

"Do you even *like* dogs?"

Millicent smiled for the first time since Claire's arrival. "Yes, I am *very* fond of dogs. But cats are rather more self-reliant, and my legion seems to have taken on a life of its own. Not unlike my volunteering. A bit out of control— but they do keep me company." She lifted her cup of tea. "And when you get older, it's nice to have a bit of company. If not a battalion!" She laughed.

What a sweet and gracious woman. Quite the opposite of the imperious royal who had dispatched one email decree after another as if perched on a throne, removed from all the work. Claire felt her scorn melting into sympathy, and as they drank their tea, she shared all the details of the event planning and how dire things had gotten. The event loomed and so far Claire had failed to do her job. She felt like such a failure.

"My dear," said Millicent, "you've had no help! You have every right to call me out. No one else has ever had the courage." She patted Claire's hand and took a sip of her tea. "You know, as I think about it, I may have a solution for the band and the food."

"*Really?*"

"Yes. Let me get back to you." She pointed a finger for emphasis. "And *soon*, I promise!"

"That would be wonderful," said Claire. "Thank you! And thank you for the tea."

"Thank *you* for the talk," said Millicent, a sparkle back in her eyes. "Money is always useful, but people like you who devote your time and energy to a good cause—you are *priceless.*"

Claire drove back to Sifu's house on Lake Glory feeling lighter and more relaxed than she had in weeks. She opened the sunroof and felt the wind stir her hair. Smiled at the glorious day and gave herself a virtual pat on the back. *You did it, Claire! You stuck up for yourself—and it worked!* Setting new boundaries was good! And might not be so hard after all.

But when she arrived back at Sifu's and spotted a bouquet of pink and white lilies by the front door, resting on a small box, her immediate reaction was, "Oh, no! What has Max done? He shouldn't be sending me flowers. I should be sending *him* flowers for smashing that overhead into his groin!" She reached down and collected the bouquet of lilies and spotted an envelope taped to the box. That's when she recognized Wally's handwriting. *What was he doing?* She opened the envelope and read the card.

"*Supersonic Girlfriend,*" he wrote, using a nickname he had given her in their early days, "*I have almost finished my novel and present it here with the hope that you will: a) accept my apology for hurting you; b) view me as a working writer, not a midlife fuckup; and c) enjoy it and possibly even love it as you once loved me, your one and only Wallace J. Rabbit.*"

Boy, he had a lot of nerve! Throwing pet names at her from the days in Greece when they made love all night and slept in a twin bed, merged in each other's arms like a Reese's Peanut Butter Cup. And leaving her favorite flowers!

Could he be any more infuriating? She kicked the box across the slate entry and marched inside, calling for Gus and Yin. *Damn you, Wally!*

She decided to go for a swim, joined by the dogs, while Yang sat erectly on the dock, looking majestic, turning only her head as she followed their movements in the water with her luminescent eyes. Claire noticed clouds were rolling in, passing in front of the late afternoon sun and casting a gray pall across the lake. The breeze carried the smell of freshly cut hay from the farmer's field across the street, behind Sifu's house, and she heard the hum of a distant tractor engine trying to get the hay collected and baled before any rain began to fall from the darkening skies. Some people tended to romanticize farming, but it was nothing but hard work. Claire swam a few laps around the raft, working off her anger at Wally. *The nerve!*

The swim refreshed and restored her, and after a quick rinse in the outdoor shower, she headed into the kitchen, where she gave the three animals a treat and then filled their bowls with dinner. The flowers lay on the kitchen counter, crying for attention. Just because she wasn't going to think about Wally didn't mean she couldn't take care of the lovely lilies. She trimmed the stems and put them in a vase. Part of her was surprised to feel disappointed they had not come from Max. She wondered how he was doing and quickly sent him a text.

"Hope you're feeling okay," she wrote, and then fixed herself a salad with slices of chicken breast. She carried her meal onto the porch, where she settled into a rocker and began to eat.

A minute later, Max replied, "Feeling fine! No more swollen tennis balls!"

"So you iced?" She shivered at the thought.

"Yes! Lots of ice . . . in a large G&T. Excellent medicine."

"Ha ha."

"You should come have one."

"Another time," she replied. "Get some rest & feel better."

He sent her back a thumbs-up.

And then a final note: "You looked smashing today!"

She sent back two emojis—a thank-you and a smile. He really was a sweet fellow.

After dinner, Claire felt a deep fatigue overwhelm her, a profound cumulative weariness that had built up in the months since Wally's departure. She headed upstairs for a hot shower and bed. But slipping under Sifu's silk sheets, she found herself unable to sleep. A blustery wind blew through the open windows facing the lake, waving the thin linen curtains like flags, and in the distance, she heard the rumble of thunder as a storm rolled in. The eaves hung well over the windows, and she liked the sound of rain on the roof, so she left the windows open. Gus trotted in and sat on the braided oval rug at the end of the bed.

"Are you going to leave Wally's manuscript out in the rain?" he relayed telepathically.

Claire shot up. "Oh, crap!" She dashed downstairs, out the front door and scooped the box off the slate stoop. It weighed more than she expected. Was that because it was full of shit? Densely packed rubbish? Or because it was a work of real substance? She was in no rush to find out, partly because she couldn't bear another failure. She brought the box inside, tossed it on the table in the hall and marched back upstairs to bed.

"That wouldn't have been good," Gus communicated as she settled back under the covers.

Oh Wallace! Why were the traits that endeared you to someone when you first met and fell in love the very qualities that eventually drove you crazy after years of marriage? And just to make matters even more complicated, those qualities were often the ones you lacked. It was as if you were trying to become whole, thanks to the other person. Wally didn't care what other people thought. But Claire wanted to please everyone. Wally was cavalier and made a joke out of everything. Claire was earnest and took things seriously. Wally thought of himself. Claire thought of others. Wally chased dreams. Claire had nightmares. She lay in bed and thought of the note he'd left with the flowers and manuscript. What a blatant attempt to soften her up—conjuring a magical time of unbridled joy in Greece, along with her favorite candy! Did he really think he could make up for everything simply by summoning that era of endless possibility and total infatuation? That sacred keepsake stored in her heart forever? What an adman, trying to pull her strings! They had been through so much since; it wasn't fair or right. And that was another thing: after years of marriage, each partner needed to be right. To be the one who could sit smugly, knowing they hadn't fucked up, the other person had. *Why?* She had seen this phenomenon ruin other marriages. The blame game could be lethal. Oddly, she also knew of couples that had divorced and then found they got along better than ever. A few of these couples were her age, recently parted after the kids were grown and gone. They got together at holidays with their kids and grandchildren, one big happy family after years of strife within the marriage. How was this possible? If she was right and Wally was wrong, she wouldn't want to drink eggnog with him at Christmas. She'd rather roast his nuts on an open fire.

Breathe in, breathe out. Calm down, girlfriend. Wasn't she a tai chi practitioner? She certainly wasn't a tai chi master, overreacting like this. It was all well and good to talk about being balanced and grounded, able to go with the flow, to sense oncoming energy and deflect the negative, absorb the positive and live in a state of grace. But in real life? Way too hard! And marriage was hard. Incredibly, you didn't need to pass a test to get married. Anyone could do it. That's why there were all kinds of marriages. They worked, or didn't, in their very own ways. And the truth was, successful marriages often came down to luck. Because invariably people changed over the course of a lifetime, and if those changes didn't coincide with your spouse's evolution, or you wound up on different tracks through no fault of your own, and suddenly your priorities and goals and needs and wants no longer aligned—well, then you were shit out of luck. And whose fault was that? *Wally's, of course!*

Claire's eyes welled up and she blinked back tears. Why could he still unhinge her so? What if he had written something mediocre? Could she bear the disappointment? Hadn't she always harbored the same dream as him—that he would write good books instead of ads and be a successful author? After all this time, if that dream were broken, could their marriage be restored? If only she had a Reese's Peanut Butter Cup to bolster her courage, she might go downstairs, collect the manuscript and bring it back to bed to read as the rain fell on the roof and tears rolled down her cheeks.

"Does depression run in your family?" Gus relayed from the floor. "Because if it does, I'm locking the wine cellar."

"No, I'm just having a little cry," she said.

"I think you miss Wally."

"I miss what we had. And what might have been." Claire rolled onto her back and kicked the sheet off her. "When we first met, it was magical."

"It usually is."

"Now all I have with Wally is frustration. And a shared history we can never change."

"Having a history with another person can be a beautiful thing," said Gus.

"Maybe," said Claire, "but lately it's been painful." She sighed and rolled onto her side as the curtains swayed in the breeze and the rain drummed on the roof. *Such a complicated situation.*

"Here's another way to look at it," opined Gus. "It's a privilege to bear witness to another person's life. It validates your feelings. Your thoughts. Your experiences. You and Wally have done that together."

"Are you trying to make me cry even more?"

"Crying is cathartic. Let it rip." Gus got up and walked over and looked at her with his deep brown eyes, partially covered by a flock of his Rasta hair. "Nobody's perfect," he relayed and licked her face with a big, wet kiss.

"Eeewwwww!" Claire cried, wiping off his slobber.

"Love you, too."

He trotted to the door, turned and delivered a parting message: "And my love is unconditional, by the way. You might think about that."

Gus left her alone, and Claire wiped her eyes. She thought about her shared history with Wally and how they had validated each other's life. But now, she was nearly over the hill—*thanks a lot, Millicent!*—and her days were more precious. How much time did she have left? And how did she want to spend it?

She lifted her head to a dry place on the pillow and told herself to get some sleep. As she had always consoled the boys after a tough day or a disappointing event, "Things always look better in the morning."

32

When he didn't hear back from Claire, Wally grew gloomy. Didn't she like his book? He had been flying so high before dropping it off. Spurred by Lucia's offer to forward his completed manuscript to her father and overjoyed to learn from Danny Boy that Claire was house-sitting for Sifu—*not living with him!*— he had spent two weeks writing at a fever pitch, piling up pages and finishing Act Two. *Finally!* He had overcome the loss of Mama Betty. He still followed their original outline, but now, as the narrative progressed, new events evolved, driven by the characters themselves, and this thrilled him. If he didn't know what was coming, how could the reader? He began to wonder if Mama Betty had been an illusion. A crutch to help him over his fear and his doubt. A way past the perfectionism and achievement of his father and the bar he could never equal. Finally free, he could see the finish line. Creative completion. Work for the work's sake. Except that his ultimate goal was to be reunited with Claire, and since she wasn't responding, he had lost confidence once again.

He moped around Bear's house for a week, wondering if she was *trying* to torture him, while his golf game matched his mood—down and out. The only bright spot was the trust fund hippies from Olive's Organic Farm Stand, who finally sent along their payment with an apologetic note and a humorous illustration of a goat eating their invoice. The day it arrived, Bear thumbtacked the cartoon to the kitchen bulletin board and walloped Wally on the back.

"Great job, Hector!" he said. "Just one more to go!"

But how would he ever extract payment from the weightlifting, crotch-crippling, gone-gambling Jerry? Nothing he had thought of so far seemed worth the risk of further personal injury, and he was in no hurry to get pounded by the little muscle man. Three nights in a row, Bear asked him if he had been to Jerry's Gym yet, and three nights in a row, he said, "I'll get down there tomorrow." Finally, on the fourth day, he screwed up his courage and paid Jerry a visit. He found the sturdy small fry sitting back in his office, feet propped on his desk, leaning back in his chair, smoking a cigar the length of his forearm. Little Fluffernutter sat in his lap. Apparently the lone weightlifter out on the floor didn't care if the place reeked of cigar smoke.

"It's the hired muscle!" said Jerry, grinning at him. The lapdog barked at Wally. Jerry waved at a sagging couch. "Have a seat, mister loan shark."

Wally sat down and was almost swallowed whole. A statuesque blonde appeared at the door—as tall as Jerry was short and equally well built. She looked like one of the professional female wrestlers from the WWE. Lots of makeup and a prodigious cleavage.

"We have company," said Jerry to his lady friend, waving his giant stogie at Wally. "A big, bad bill collector."

Wally waved at the blonde bombshell from his deep seat.

"Nice to meet you," she said, chewing her gum and batting her long, fake eyelashes. She extended her hand. "I'm Tiffany."

"Wally," he said, and tried to stand to greet her, but he couldn't climb out of the depths of the couch. He reached up to shake her hand, trying to avoid looking at her chest as she bent over. But it was impossible. She caught him and smiled. "My pleasure, *Wally.*"

His face burned, and she winked at him.

"I'll leave you boys to your business," she said, spinning her bountiful backside in front of Wally, in what struck him as a practiced maneuver. She took the dog from Jerry and clutched it to her chest. "That's a good Fluffy," she said, and gave the dog an air kiss.

Jerry craned his neck, watching her go. He turned to Wally and smiled. "That, my friend, is my lucky charm." And he launched into the story of his latest foray to Foxwoods, where he wound up meeting Tiffany in the gentlemen's club and invited her to accompany him at the tables when she got off work. "I got hot at the roulette wheel, thanks to her," he said. "And then she licked my ear and blew on my dice and said, 'Put it all on red, Arnold.' So I did. And I won. And then she made me walk away."

Jerry smiled and took a puff of his cigar. "I never walk away. But I did with Tiffany. I already had a lapdog. Why not bring home a lap dancer? She was lookin' for a new career, anyway. We're gonna have her teach some fitness classes. Tell me guys won't wanna take instruction from her! She might give some special clinics for the ladies, too. Teach 'em a few tricks for the fellas. Ha! I dunno, we're playin' it by ear. But I gotta reconfigure my business somehow and Tiffany's a real people person."

"Sounds like a plan," said Wally, wondering if this would be a good time to ask for the money.

But Jerry beat him to it, pulling a thick wad of bills from his pants pocket.

"I suppose you want your cabbage."

"That would be nice," said Wally, doing a crunch to lean forward in the deep, low couch. The old thing was like a killer piece of exercise equipment.

"Whatta I owe you, again?"

"Twenty-six hundred dollars."

Jerry counted twenty-six Ben Franklins onto his desk. Then he slapped down another hundred. "That one's for you," he said. "Hope the family jewels are okay."

A sense of triumph catapulted Wally from the couch to his feet. "Thanks, everything seems to be working just fine." *Just with the wrong woman.* He swept the bills off the desk. "Appreciate the payment. Good luck with your new business model."

"Thanks," said Jerry, and waved his cigar expansively. "Spread the word."

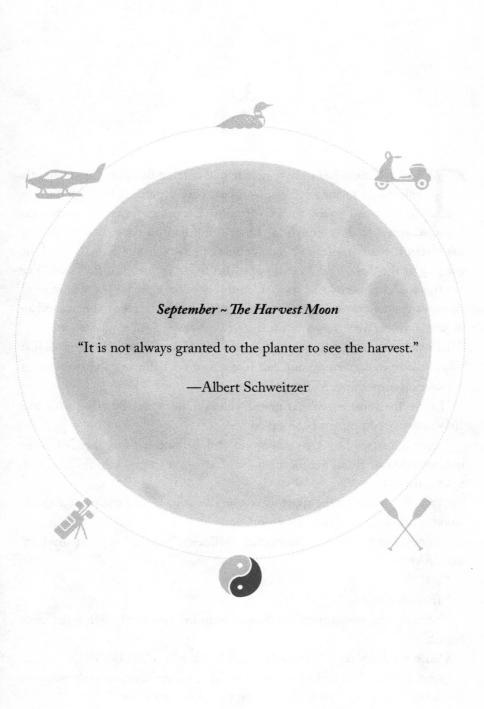

September ~ The Harvest Moon

"It is not always granted to the planter to see the harvest."

—Albert Schweitzer

33

The call came just in time. Claire had entered full panic mode, hardly sleeping, massaging like a robot, barely getting through tai chi classes and trying to keep Roz from coming over to shoot her (as she threatened to do a couple of times). She had no time to read Wally's manuscript, even if she had the inclination—which she still didn't. One evening at the dojo, Joan Marsh pulled her aside before class and said, "I've got this tonight, you take a breather," and conducted class for her. Claire went downstairs and stepped outside. Looking toward the heavens, she uttered an urgent prayer: *Please, **please**, universe, give me a sign. Send me a solution!*

Miraculously, soon after she returned to the lake, the answer arrived. Just when Claire had given up and felt like a fool for believing she would ever actually do something, Millicent called.

"I have the most *wonderful* news," she said, her voice bursting with life. "My niece's wedding has been called off!"

Claire didn't see how that was wonderful, beyond the fact that Millicent had reservations about her niece's fiancé. "And that's a good thing?" she said, a bit confused.

"Yes! Now we have the most *marvelous* dance band and the most *delicious* wood-fired pizza truck for the event!"

Claire almost dropped the phone. "Millicent!" she cried. "Oh my god! *Seriously?*"

"Yes!"

"That's incredible!"

"I finally *did* something!" Millicent sounded absolutely delighted with herself.

Claire suddenly felt a hundred pounds lighter. "You're a hero!"

"I must say, it does feel like a win-win. That young man was only going to break her heart. I just pushed things in the proper direction."

"I can't believe it, Millicent!" *You broke up your niece's wedding and saved my ass!* "I need to call Roz right away. Can we talk details tomorrow?"

"Of course."

"Great job, Millicent!"

"Thank you, my dear."

Roz nearly blew a gasket when Claire told her about Millicent's coup.

"*Oh my god!* What a relief. Now we won't be flipping burgers."

"And the band—Road Apple—is meant to be great," said Claire.

Over the following days, she and Roz and Millicent and the members of every other committee worked with renewed energy to put the final pieces of the event together in brilliant fashion. The only remaining wild card was the special guest, which the Professor told Claire looked "ninety percent certain, but I won't know for sure until the day of the event." Fine, said Claire, knowing they had a backup with the magician vet, and feeling much more relaxed now that everything else was in place. Even the weather forecast looked promising for the whole Labor Day weekend.

When the guests began to arrive at Doggone Right at five o'clock on Saturday night, the weather was nothing short of glorious. Thin strips of clouds floated over the hillsides, reflecting the late afternoon sun in hues of orange and yellow, while farther west, the peaks of Pico and Killington stood majestically purple. The sloping field beyond the farmhouse radiated a golden tint after a recent haying, and the old, large barn that housed the kennels stood gloriously red, tilting slightly. On a wide, flat area below the farmhouse, the large, white tent shimmered like a lure, drawing guests inside with its shining strings of lights. Inside the tent, Claire and other volunteers had set up a small stage for the band, a dance floor, tables for dining and a bar area with a selection of fine wines and local craft beers on tap. Off to one side of the festive tent, smoke curled from the wood-fired pizza oven ready to cook gourmet pies with fresh ingredients from local farms. Beyond the pizza truck in the field, a few of the younger volunteers had dug a large firepit and stacked wood for after the sun went down.

Claire stood next to Roz on the front porch of the farmhouse, watching cars pull into the field to park, directed by volunteers into tidy rows. Roz took a deep breath and stroked the sides of her dress. "I can't believe it's finally happening."

"Neither can I."

Roz gave her a hug. "Great job, partner." She looked Claire up and down. "You really are quite a piece of ass when you get all dressed up, aren't you?"

Claire blushed and shook her head. "I know Max is looking forward to a few dances."

"And you might be surprised to hear," said Claire, "so am I."

Roz squeezed her arm and gave Claire a peck on the cheek. Then she turned toward the line of people streaming into the park and said, "It's go time."

Claire watched Roz make her way down to the procession of guests. Certainly, there were moneyed elites among them, some attired in eye-catching fashion, but all kinds of other local residents were also arriving to support the rescues, some outfitted for a casual night out in the north country, others adorned to the hilt. She spotted one couple in Hawaiian shirts and shorts. A pair of well-groomed men wore crisply pressed Oxford shirts and khakis. Another couple looked like they were dressed to go hiking. But her favorite sight was a short, stocky man with muscles popping out of his neck, dressed in a tuxedo, reaching up to hold the hand of a towering blonde bombshell wearing a revealing evening gown. She smiled at the odd juxtaposition of this striking couple—a mini Arnold Schwarzenegger and his statuesque date—looking ready for the red carpet at the Oscars. *Dog lovers come in all looks, shapes and sizes,* she thought. *Just like the dogs.*

She made her way down to the tent to join the lively crowd being serenaded by Road Apple's lead singer, who played the piano with the flair and energy of Elton John, and spotted Max in line at the bar. He smiled at her and gestured, as if raising a glass to his lips, 'Would you like a glass of wine?' She nodded yes. The Professor appeared and whispered excitedly in her ear. "He's coming!"

"Who?"

"Our special guest!"

Claire looked into the Professor's shining eyes. "Who is it?"

"She won't even tell me," said Danny Boy, leaning over the Professor's shoulder. "Doesn't want to jinx it."

"Seriously?" Claire sighed and shrugged her shoulders. "Fine. Then I don't need to know, either."

Max appeared with her wine and she introduced him to the Professor and Danny Boy.

"Look at this crowd," Max said, beaming at her. "You've done a terrific job, Claire."

"Everyone has," she said.

Max raised his glass. "To a wonderful evening."

"I'll second that," said Danny Boy, and they all clinked glasses.

The music stopped and the lead singer spoke into the microphone: "Ladies and gentlemen, if I could have your attention please." Voices in the crowd fell to a murmur. "We're all here tonight to support a very special cause, thanks in large part to the efforts of a very special person. May I introduce your event chair—Roz Peeler!"

The crowd whooped and clapped, and a few people started barking like dogs. Roz stepped onto the stage and the front man handed her the mike.

"Thank you, Lee," she said to him, and lifted a hand to silence the crowd. "Thank you all. We are SO fortunate to be here tonight on behalf of our wonderful rescues. Our furry friends give us SO much joy and unconditional love. They are our best friends and our loyal companions. All of us are richer, wiser, healthier and happier thanks to them. So on behalf of Doggone Right, our sincere and heartfelt thanks to ALL of you for supporting our mission to save these dogs and place them into loving homes. Thank you!" The guests all clapped and cheered, and Roz raised her hand again.

"I may have been the chairperson for this event," she continued, "but it would NEVER *EVER* have happened without the help of so many *deeply* committed volunteers." She paused for more applause. "And one person in particular literally came to the RESCUE of our rescues to make this party the *rockin'* great time it's going to be—and that is MILLICENT FERNWATER!" Roz looked into the crowd, trying to pick out Millicent. A tall, young couple lifted their arms and pointed at Millicent, who raised her wine glass, smiling from ear to ear. The tent echoed with applause.

Suddenly, the cheering was drowned out by a whirring sound in the sky, and everyone streamed outside to see what was happening. A helicopter hovered overhead, its tail wagging.

"He's here!" said the Professor. "I can't believe it!"

The chopper slowly descended into the field, spraying cut hay as it touched down. The Professor trotted over, bent at the waist, holding her cocktail hat adorned with flowers, and welcomed a tall lanky figure as he opened the cockpit door. A Black man with dreadlocks and dark glasses, dressed in a white blazer, slacks and sneakers stepped down onto the field. An excited buzz electrified the crowd as he bent over and gave the Professor a hug. She led him by the hand back to the tent and onto the stage, where she took the mike and announced, "Everybody, say hello to our very special guest, the ultimate dog of dogs—SNOOP DOGG!"

The crowd went wild. Snoop Dogg smiled and waved and bowed. He took the microphone from the Professor. "Everybody ready to party?!"

The crowd roared.

"*Damn!* You north country white folk don't get out much, do you?"

Everyone laughed and hollered, and some people started barking again. Roz hopped on stage and took Snoop Dogg's hand. She pulled him close and rose on her tiptoes to whisper into his ear. When he smiled and nodded coolly, she took the mike from him.

"We're going to have a special raffle," she said. "For a starlight helicopter ride with our SPECIAL GUEST!"

The crowd erupted.

"So please sign up back at the table where we have a number of other wonderful auction items. You can buy as many tickets as you want. So load up and GOOD LUCK!"

She handed the mike back to Snoop Dogg, who immediately launched into a rap, accompanied by the brilliant keyboard player, who was gifted enough to play anything. The crowd pressed close to the stage, dancing and waving. Claire and Max stood at its perimeter with Danny Boy, where Roz and the Professor soon joined them.

"OH MY GOD!" Roz hugged the Professor for the third time. "*How* did you get him here?"

"I have an old friend who owed me a favor. From my acting days. Snoop won't be here for long. He's giving a show in Boston at nine o'clock."

"Who CARES!" said Roz. "He's here NOW and he's going to help us make A BUNDLE with my raffle idea."

The Professor and Danny Boy joined the dancing crowd. Max turned to Claire, looking a bit embarrassed. "I'll have to ask you to dance later. When

I have some idea how to move appropriately."

"Don't worry," said Claire, with a laugh, "you're not alone."

Snoop Dogg performed three songs and then left the stage to Road Apple and mingled with the crowd, escorted by the Professor. With the Dogg done performing, half the audience dispersed to get another drink or fill a plate with food, while others continued dancing. At the back of the tent, the line for the raffle tickets snaked all the way to the bar. Every time Claire looked over, another person was buying tickets from a volunteer stationed at the table. She spotted Roz working the room, all smiles, her charisma oozing like an aura. People sat at tables, eating and talking, drinking, and laughing, while others mingled outside by the pizza truck—a help-yourself festival of wood-fired flavor. A few folks strolled over to check out the helicopter, while others wandered up to the farmhouse and kennels to tour the facility. Max offered to get Claire something to eat, while she went to the bar to fetch them two more glasses of wine.

"Awesome party, Claire," said Harry Thrall, sidling up behind her.

"Thank you, Harry. And thank you for coming."

"We're adopting another dog next week. Dogs love the company of other dogs, but you probably already know that. We're getting Spike a companion."

"That's wonderful, Harry! They'll both be very happy."

"I hope so," he said. "Did you hear that Wally finished his book?"

Claire said, "I haven't spoken to Wally in a while."

"Yeah, I'm sorry about that. I guess he's sending it out to somebody in Hollywood."

Claire thought of Wally's manuscript from years before—the local detective story that was optioned for film by an independent writer/director. No film was ever made and no novel was ever published.

"Well," she said, "you never know."

"Yeah," said Harry, "you never know. Wally might be the next Chris Bohjalian. Discovered by Oprah all the way up here in Vermont. I know he misses you. Not that it's any of my business."

Claire patted his arm. "You're sweet, Harry." He was so sincere and genuine.

She got two glasses of wine and stepped outside the tent, headed to find Max by the pizza oven. She hadn't wanted to think about Wally tonight. She had wanted to just make sure everything went smoothly, to spend some time with her friends and have a dance or two with Max. But after Harry's comments, she thought she should probably read what Wally had left her. She would have the time with the event finally over. She spotted Max as the first stars were emerging in the darkening sky. A slash of crimson tickled the peak of Killington, the sun's last hurrah from below the horizon. Just as she handed Max his glass of wine, Millicent appeared at her side, pizza in hand, looking happy as a lark.

"I must thank you again," she said to Claire.

"For what?"

"That scolding. It was *very* good for me."

Claire smiled. "It was good for me, too, Millicent. I'm learning how to stick up for myself these days."

Millicent eyed Max, who looked resplendent in a sky-blue linen blazer that highlighted his eyes. "Are you going to introduce me to your husband?"

Claire stepped back, caught off guard. "Oh, no! Max isn't my husband. He's a friend."

"A *good* friend?" asked Millicent. Claire turned to Max, who appeared as eager for her answer as Millicent. Claire looked into his eyes. "Yes, as it so happens, he's becoming quite a good friend."

Millicent gently touched her forearm. "Well, good for you. I won't try to hit on him then." She laughed and extended her hand to Max. "Very nice to meet you, Max. You have a wonderful lady friend here."

"Yes," he said. "I'm a lucky fellow. Or hope to be!"

Was he expecting this to be his lucky night? Claire wasn't sure she was ready for that.

Millicent surveyed the crowd. "Oh! If you'll excuse me, I need to go say hello to the Keanes. They are *such* a power couple, you know." She smiled warmly at Claire. "Thank you again, my dear—for *everything.*"

She and Max ate their pizza and salad, and Claire kept an eye on the party, making sure everyone was having fun. The Professor squired Snoop Dogg around the tent, proudly introducing him to everyone. He was gracious and smiling, generous with his spirit and his time. Claire learned later he was also generous with his money, making a $10,000 donation to the cause on top of flying in at his own expense. At one point, Claire saw Danny Boy slide in next to the Professor and whisk the Dogg out for a walk in the field beyond the tent. In the deepening shadows of the night, a flame flickered and a glowing red ember passed between the two lanky silhouettes.

"Shall we have that dance?" asked Max after they had finished eating, extending a hand to Claire.

"Sure."

They made their way onto the dance floor, packed with people enjoying Road Apple's brilliant repertoire, and Max immediately turned back into Gumby from the tennis court, wiggling and swaying like a rubber figure in a wind tunnel. Claire danced with almost equal abandon, relieved that the party was going so well after months of work and worry. Everyone looked like they were having a wonderful time. Out of nowhere, Ginger and Jack Hughes swooped in like contestants from *Dancing with the Stars*, Jack gyrating madly, spinning Ginger around like a top. Somehow the two whirling dervishes stayed in sync, cutting a wide swath through the crowded floor, and people stepped back to make a circle as they put on a show. When the song ended, everyone clapped and Jack took a deep bow, loving the attention. Ginger stepped over to Claire.

"Fan-*tas*-tic party!" she said. "I just *love* the pizza—what a great idea! And the band—they're *incredible!*"

"Thank you, Ginger," said Claire. She had always liked Wally's old girlfriend, even if she was married to Jack Hughes.

"We'll be making a big donation—won't we, Jack?"

"Abso-fuckin-lootely!" said Jack. He wobbled slightly, clearly lit, and looked at Max. "This your new boyfriend?"

"This is my *friend*," said Claire. "Max McClure."

Jack stepped back. "Max! *Jesus*, I didn't recognize you without your mustache. Finally decide to leave the eighties?"

"About ten years ago," said Max, dry as dirt.

Jack turned to Claire. "Sorry to hear Wally's out of favor. He's going to be out of luck on Monday, too."

Claire's heart skipped a beat. *Was Jack going to fire him?* "What's happening on Monday?"

"It's mano a mano for the senior club championship. And I'm going to beat him like a drum! Ahhh ha ha ha!"

Ginger rolled her eyes at Claire. "Men and their golf. *Honestly.*"

Claire wanted to say, "The only way you'll beat Wally is if he lets you," but Wally always let his obnoxious client win, so what was the point? *Ugghhhh!*

She didn't want to think about Wally. She was having such a good time. "If you'll excuse me, I need to go check on the raffle for the helicopter ride."

The line for raffle tickets had died down, but she kept walking toward the back of the tent, eager to get as far away from Jack Hughes as possible. She felt badly about leaving Max, but he was a big boy and could fend for himself. A familiar voice called her name. She turned around and saw Bear, standing with his date. A younger woman, who looked a lot like Julie, his long-lost love who died too young. Where did he find these lookalikes?

"Hello, Bear," she said, hugging him. "Thanks for coming."

"Wouldn't miss it," he said. "The Professor sold tickets to all the golfers. Now, we're gonna win the chopper ride." He held up a string of raffle tickets three feet long and smiled at his date. "Right, Audrey?"

"Right," said Audrey with a lovely smile, looking like the very specter of Julie.

Bear said, "You know, your husband has written one helluva book."

Claire shook her head. "You and Harry. What are you, his press agents?"

"I know he left you a copy of the manuscript. Why haven't you read it?"

Claire waved a hand at the crowded tent. "Maybe I've been just a little busy? Organizing all this?"

"And you did a great job, Claire. Really. It's a fantastic party. But it's killing Wally to wait. He's a mess. And he's playing Jack in the finals on Monday."

"Oh! So now this is all about *golf?*"

"No! No, not at all," said Bear.

"Because he'll just let Jack win anyway. He always does."

"Not this time. I told him if he throws the match, I'm throwing him out."

Claire let out a sarcastic laugh. "It's taken you all of three months. I've lasted twenty-five years!"

Bear took a long pull on his beer and looked at her sheepishly. "I know. He can be impossible. But I'm just telling you, his book is really good."

"And what's the last book you read? *Bobby Orr and the Big, Bad Bruins?*"

Bear took another drink and shrugged his giant shoulders.

"I don't know that you're the best literary critic, Bear. And if you keep indulging him, I'm not sure you're not the best friend, either." Claire turned to Audrey. "I hope you enjoy the rest of your night." And with that, she made a beeline for the bar. *Enough! No more Wally!* She needed a glass of wine and a different conversation. She heard the crowd clapping and looked over at the stage to see Snoop Dogg standing next to Danny Boy, an arm slung over Danny's shoulder. The toked-up homeys. Roz stepped in, holding a baseball hat upside down, and Snoop dipped his long fingers into the cap to churn the raffle tickets contained inside.

"My man Danny Boy is going to pick the winner," announced the Dogg. "And then some lucky mofo is going stargazing in a *HELL-icopter!*"

The crowd roared, and Danny reached into the hat and pulled out a ticket. He handed it to the Dogg.

"And the winner is: 147998."

A hush fell over the tent as everyone checked their tickets. A few "Ohhhs!" rang out from folks with close calls. But no winner cried out.

Snoop Dogg repeated, "147998."

The tent had not been this quiet all night.

"Nobody?" said Snoop Dogg.

The silence endured.

"Guess we'll have to pull another." He reached for the hat.

"Wait!" said Roz. "I forgot . . ." She reached into her dress and pulled a ticket from her cleavage. "What's the number again?"

Snoop Dogg repeated the winning digits and Roz's scream pierced the tent. "OH MY GOOOOOODDDDDD!" She waved the ticket over her head and jumped up and down as the crowd exploded. She threw the hat into the air, sending ticket stubs flying like confetti, and gave Snoop Dogg a big hug. The two of them hopped around the stage like a pair of lunatics. Then they jumped off, holding hands.

"We're going to take a short break, folks," said Road Apple's star. "So you can watch the lucky winner take off . . ."

As the helicopter rose into the starry night, its lights flashing and propellers whirling, Claire couldn't stop smiling. Did anyone deserve to ride with the Dogg more than Roz?

Unfortunately, Claire's euphoria was short-lived. Because after the lights of the helicopter flickered out of sight, she saw a lone headlight make its way up the driveway, past the parking lot, across the grass and toward the tent, where it stopped ten feet away from her. As the familiar-looking figure climbed off the scooter and hung a hockey helmet on the handlebar, her heart quickened.

She toyed with the idea of pretending she hadn't seen Wally—of slinking into the tent and melting into the crowd—but that would only delay the inevitable. She stepped over to him

"Crashing the party, party boy?" she said.

Wally reached into his pocket and pulled out a ticket. "No, ma'am. Thanks to the Professor, I'm legit."

He tried to hand her the ticket, but she didn't want it.

"Why haven't you answered my texts?" he said. "You haven't said a thing about my book."

"I've been *busy*, Wallace. This party didn't happen over*night*—like some *scooter* ride."

"That ride led to some wonderful things," he said.

"I can only imagine."

"It's not what you think, Claire. Lucia sent my manuscript to her dad. He's a screenwriter. With connections to George Clooney's production company. They're thinking about taking an option—but want to see a different ending."

"Then write a different ending."

"I can't." Wally took her hand. "Not without you on board."

Claire pulled her hand away. "What happened to Mama Betty?"

"She got mad at me."

"Well, that makes two of us," said Claire.

"But I'm so close, Claire. *We're* so close."

"We're *not* close, Wally. We're separated! And you know what? Right now, it's good for me!"

She wheeled away, just as Max appeared from inside the tent.

"There you are!" he said. "Did you see Roz take off?"

"I did."

"Wouldn't surprise me if they never came back." Max laughed. "That woman is a force of nature."

Claire helped herself to a sip of his wine and took his hand. "Come on," she said, "let's go dance."

Wally called after her. "Claire, *please!* Just read it!"

She waved him away, as if shooing an incredibly annoying fly, and walked into the tent with Max. They danced for a long time and were among the last couples on the floor, along with the Professor and Danny Boy, Bear and Audrey, Harry and Barb and a few others. Max was right—Roz and Snoop

Dogg never did return—and Claire later found a text from her:

"Backstage in Boston! With my rescue Dogg!"

On stage under the tent, Road Apple played a final slow dance. As Max led Claire gracefully across the floor, she saw the tiny tuxedoed Terminator lift his blonde Amazon over his head and gracefully spin her around like a pairs figure skater. Bear danced with Audrey, hardly moving his feet, hands on her hips, their foreheads pressed together. Next to them, the eternal newlyweds, Harry and Barb, ground their gears like a high school couple in heat. The party had been a grand success in all respects but one. Setting that elusive boundary line with Wally. *He was so annoying!*

34

The next night, on the eve of the senior club championship, Mama Betty appeared in one of Wally's dreams for the first time since she had abandoned him in the wake of the Vanderhausen incident.

"Saw the great amateur yesterday," said his ex-muse, popping a marshmallow into her mouth. "Mistah Bobby Jones. Told him all about your senior club championship match. Said he might like to watch."

"I'd be honored!" said Wally.

"You might need a little help out there," she said, chomping on her gooey white snack, her jowls jiggling. "Wouldn't hesitate to call on him."

"Thanks, I won't."

"Fine fellah, Bobby Jones. Used to see him at Sunday brunch over at East Lake."

"I remember Claire telling me about that."

"Yes sir, great champion. Swing as smooth as buttah. And a mighty fine lawyah, too."

"A real Renaissance man," said Wally.

"You play well out there! And don't you evah give up. *Evah!*"

At breakfast, Bear said, "You better not let that asshole win."

"The way I'm playing," said Wally, "I'll be lucky to win a hole."

"That's the attitude."

"It's true. My game's gone south."

"*You've* gone south. Man up!"

An hour later, when he stepped onto the 1st tee, Wally shook Jack's hand and said, "Play well."

"You too," said Jack with a smug smile. "But not too well."

Wally played well enough to tie the first three holes, thanks to uttering constant prayers to Bobby Jones, getting two lucky bounces and receiving Danny Boy's expert help reading his putts. Danny had offered to carry his bag and showed up wearing a white jumpsuit, just like the caddies at the Masters.

"A little something for good luck," he said of his outfit.

Jack Hughes had his son, a pimply, skinny college sophomore, as his caddy. They shared Jack's customized golf cart with the BMW hood emblem, while Wally and Danny walked. Bear and Harry followed the action in their own cart, while Ginger Hughes walked with the Professor, who marched along under the shade of an old-fashioned parasol. Wally had never played in front of a gallery before, even a small one consisting of people he knew, and the pressure of an audience led him to miss two easy putts. As he walked to the 6th tee, down by two, Bear pulled up in his cart and scowled at him.

"What's going on?"

"I don't know," said Wally, flummoxed by his poor putting.

"You're not throwing the match, are you?"

"No!"

Bear pointed a meaty finger at him. "Then let's go!" He tore off in a cloud of dust as Harry leaned out of the cart, raised a fist and urged, "Come on, Wally!"

By the 9th hole, Wally had lost two more holes. Again, Bear swung by in the cart.

"Your client looks awfully happy."

"I am *not* throwing the match, Bear."

"Plenty of golf left," said Harry. "Keep grinding!"

God bless Harry. Was anyone more optimistic?

As he and Danny walked past the clubhouse, headed for the 10th tee, his supportive caddy said, "Keep the faith. You never know what will happen."

It was prescient advice. Because Claire suddenly appeared on the clubhouse deck with Gus on a leash and waved at Wally to wait. As she walked toward him, he tried to read her expression, but she looked as straight-faced as a poker player. He'd seen that look many times before, and he never knew which direction it might go.

"I finally read your book," she said, sauntering up to him. Gus wagged his tail and smiled at Wally, his tongue hanging out of the side of his mouth. Claire looked so serious it threw him off.

Wally's mouth went suddenly dry. *"And?"*

"I have to say," she said, and paused, toying with him. "I think it's great."

She gave him a big smile. "I love it."

His heart did a half gainer with a full twist. *She loved his book!*

"Oh, Claire, that's great!"

But she didn't seem eager to dwell on his book. She looked over at Jack on the 10th tee and asked, "Are you winning?"

"No, I'm down by four."

"You're not *letting* him win, are you?" She gave him one of her intense, college-tennis-player looks.

"No! I'm just playing badly."

"Well, start playing better!"

"Excuse me!" Jack called from the tee. "Can we have a little quiet, please? I'm about to drive another ball straight down the middle."

Claire rolled her eyes at Wally and said in a hushed voice, "You can't lose to that loser!" Everyone stood quietly as Jack addressed his ball and took his swing. For the first time all day, he pulled his drive deep into the left rough. He stormed off the tee and kicked the tire of his golf cart, glaring at Claire and Wally. Gus barked at him, as if scolding his poor sportsmanship.

Wally stepped onto the tee, where Danny handed him his driver.

"Tempo," said Danny. "Nice and smooth."

Wise advice. Especially with how jacked up Wally felt after Claire's positive review. *She loved his book!* He stood over his ball and striped his drive deep down the middle.

"Attaboy," said Danny. "Back nine is all yours."

Striding down the fairway to his ball, a new bounce in his step, Wally suddenly found himself with headphones on his ears and a large microphone in front of his face, as Terry Gross resumed their conversation.

"Wallace Scott, welcome back to *Fresh Air.*"

"Thanks, Terry, it's good to be here again."

"I guess there's something to be said for being an obsessive personality, consumed with writing even after all the rejections. I mean, what are you, like a multimillionaire now?"

"Ha ha . . . yeah . . . I guess so. I never expected the book to do this well. And the television adaptation hasn't hurt. But I'll take it. Claire and I are *very* happy. I thought I was going to lose her there for a while. Things seemed pretty hairy."

"Between writing and golf, you are pretty fanatical."

"Nothing gets accomplished without commitment, Terry. Both writing and golf take a lot of practice and dedication. They're solitary and you can't master either one of them. You're basically competing against yourself. When they go well, it's incredibly rewarding. But when you're struggling, it's usually because you're getting in your own way. Kind of like life."

"Speaking of life, I'm curious how true to life your book is. You know, did all this stuff really happen? Or did you just make it up?"

"Well, as a fiction writer, I lie to tell the truth. I want people to say, 'I recognize that feeling ... or I've been in that situation ... or that is *so* true!' If you strike that chord, the reader will gladly suspend their disbelief, and you have a chance to keep them until the end. Especially if they don't know what's coming."

"I'm curious, how many characters in your book are based on real people."

"No one is an exact replica, although a few are pretty close. I merged people to create the characters. It's what fiction writers do. We mix and match."

With the word 'match', Wally suddenly became aware of Jack Hughes pulling up in his cart to hit his next shot.

"Wallace Scott, I want to thank you for taking time from your empty schedule to talk with me. You're actually more sophisticated than I imagined. And you're not bad looking for having that receding hairline. Are you thinking of spending some of your earnings on hair replacement?"

"No, Terry, you have to play the ball where it lies."

"Well, I do think you'd be twenty-seven percent better looking with hair."

"Thanks, it's an honor to sit across from you on that stack of pillows. What are you, like, five one?"

"I'm actually four feet eleven inches tall."

"A body made for radio."

"Ha ha ha. My guest has been Wallace Scott, the surprise bestselling author of a book people are reading in droves—which just shows, you can never account for taste."

On the next tee, Jack Hughes drove his ball wildly into the woods and out of bounds—a two-stroke penalty.

"Son of a BITCH!" he said, slamming his driver into the ground. He threw the club at his cart, nearly decapitating his son.

"Jesus, Dad! Take it easy!"

"*You* take it easy! And stop yelling at your father! Have some RESPECT for your elders!"

Wally won his first hole of the day and capped off this triumph by spotting Claire and Roz following the match, each walking a dog on a leash. Roz sported a new look, her usual sexy apparel replaced by a pair of baggy cargo shorts, a loose-fitting shirt with its tails out, a baseball hat cocked sideways on her head and a pair of red high-top sneakers. She rolled along with a rhythmic strut. What was that all about? Ginger Hughes and the Professor continued to stroll together, chatting amiably. Thrilled to see that Claire had joined the gallery, Wally hit his best drive of the day.

By the 17th tee, spurred on by Claire's presence, he had tightened the match and was only down by one hole. As he uttered a prayer to Bobby Jones to help him tie it up, he spotted Claire and Roz, Ginger and the Professor huddled together on the cart path, surrounding the beverage cart. What were the women talking about, anyway? They'd been tight as a knot for several holes, marching along, smiling and chatting, petting the dogs. Claire and Ginger acted more like teammates than rivals. Didn't they appreciate what was at stake? Didn't they understand their husbands were at war!

"Have you ever been so bored?" Roz said to Claire.

"Only when Wally describes a round of golf shot by shot."

"Oh, I hate it when Jack gives me all that tedious detail!" said Ginger.

"Four Bloody Marys, please," Roz said to the cart girl. "And don't spare the vodka."

"Or the horseradish," said the Professor, opening her purse. "This is my treat."

"At least it's a pretty place to walk," said Roz, looking around.

"If you like chemicals," said Claire.

"I know," said Ginger. "Why can't they be more natural, like over in Scotland?"

The cart girl handed them their drinks and they all took a pull on their straws. "Just what the doctor ordered," said the Professor.

They strolled along the cart path that curved down the hill of the 17th fairway, beneath a stand of tall pines, chatting away while the men hit their tee shots.

"This stupid game takes *forever,*" said Roz.

"That's because they agonize over *every* shot," said Claire.

"They would have a lot more fun if they took it less seriously," said the Professor.

"Good luck with that," said Ginger.

A minute later, Jack Hughes roared down the hill in his flashy custom cart, his gangly son holding on for dear life, and squealed to a stop in front of Ginger.

"Did you see my ball?" he said, leaping out of the cart.

"No," said Ginger. "We didn't see anything."

"And you probably didn't *hear* anything because you're always *cackling* like *hens!*" Jack stormed off to look for his ball as his son scrambled in his wake.

Claire looked at Ginger, who was trying not to laugh. Here was Jack proving everything they had been talking about—life or death over a little white ball! Was anything more hilarious?

"I don't know how anyone plays this game sober," Roz said, and sucked on her straw.

"And they say *we're* moody!" said Claire.

She watched Wally and Danny march down the hill, Danny in his white caddy jumpsuit, Wally's bag over his shoulder, a wisp of smoke in his wake.

"Danny has the right idea," said Roz. "He and the Dogg . . . they're so chill."

Just then, Jack, Jr., found his father's ball nestled in a hole in the rough and called his father over to look at it.

"God-DAMN-it!" said Jack. "How am I supposed to hit THAT!" He grabbed an iron and lashed at the ball like he was trying to kill a snake. The ball sliced across the fairway and disappeared into the far rough.

"FUCK a DUCK named CHUCK!" He stormed back to his cart with Jack, Jr., hustling after him like an anxious water boy.

"You know why they call it golf, don't you?" said the Professor.

"Ask me if I care," said Roz.

"Because fuck was already taken."

They all laughed and touched cups.

When Wally won the hole, Bear hollered, "The match is all even!" And tore off in his cart for the 18th tee, leaving a trail of dust in his wake.

Roz groaned. "This is the last hole, right? Otherwise, I'm going to need another drink."

Wally stood on the 18th tee and looked over the ravine toward the fairway. He tried not to think about the last time he dumped his tee shot into the ravine, watching it nose-dive into the thick underbrush out of bounds.

"Got some new Solaras arriving next week," said Jack, from behind him. "You'd look great in a convertible, Wally."

Wally stuck his tee in the ground. "Out of my price range, Jack."

"I'm sure we could work out a little *bonus.*"

Wally turned around. "Are you trying to bribe me?"

"Oh no! Not at all! I just thought . . . With your new single lifestyle, having a nice car could help you impress the ladies. Since it looks like Claire is impressed with someone else." Jack tilted his head toward the gallery.

Wally looked over to see a new spectator had just joined the ladies—Max McClure. He looked like he had just stepped off the tennis court in a pair of bright white shorts, a yellow polo shirt and aviator sunglasses. The aging interloper looked more virile and athletic than Wally would have liked.

"You do know Max McClure?" said Jack.

"Yeah, yeah," said Wally. "I know Max." He watched Max take Claire's hand and kiss it. *What the hell!*

"Apparently, he's taking Claire to Italy. At least, that's what Ginger heard."

Claire demurely pulled her hand out of Max's grasp and smiled at him. Was she being polite? Or persuaded?

Danny grabbed Wally's bicep and tugged him across the tee box. "Hey! Don't fall for his gamesmanship! That could be fake news."

Wally looked at Claire, standing next to Max, and felt the same wave of jealousy that had led him into Jill Vanderhausen's clutches. Was she really going to Italy with him?

Danny said, "She came to watch you, didn't she?"

Wally didn't reply. He just saw Claire flirting with Max.

"You gotta keep the faith." Danny's gigantic eyebrows rose to the brim of his hat. "Otherwise, you're toast."

Wally turned away. He looked back across the ravine toward the fairway on the other side. Claire said she loved his book didn't she? Didn't that mean she loved him, too? He thought of Mama Betty urging him, *"Don't you evah give up—evah!"*

He turned to Danny and banged his driver on the ground. "Okay," he said. "Let's win this."

Danny's face lit up. He clapped Wally on the back. "Atta boy!"

Wally stood over his ball and suddenly felt very calm. As if he had entered a sanctuary where all he had to do to achieve his goal was to stay out of his own way. Relax and let it go. He took his club back and swung, hitting a perfect tee shot over the gully. On his second shot, he followed Danny's instructions to play it safe and left himself 110 yards to the hole. When he stepped up to his third shot, Danny handed him his pitching wedge.

"I need my gap wedge," said Wally.

"Trust me," said Danny. "Just put a smooth swing on it."

But Wally insisted on the gap wedge.

"I hope you know what you're doing," said Danny, handing him the club.

As soon as Wally struck the ball, he realized Danny was right. He needed more distance. His ball landed just short of the green in the sand trap.

"Dammit!"

Jack Hughes hit his third shot onto the green twenty feet from the pin and grinned at Wally like a hyena. "Don't skull that sand shot!" he called and tore off in his cart so abruptly that his son nearly fell out.

"Dad! Slow down!"

Danny Boy strode alongside him on their way to the bunker. "You know the secret to making a good sand shot, don't you?"

"What?"

"Luck." Danny Boy laughed. "And when you turn through, let all your weight stop inside your left thigh." He patted the spot on his own leg. "Works like a charm."

Wally took a few practice swings outside the bunker, getting a feel for Danny's tip, and stepped into the sand. Looking up at the flag, he saw Claire standing on the rise behind the green, Max beside her, Bear and Harry, the Professor and Roz and Ginger all standing in a row, waiting for him to play his shot. It was as if his entire personal history was reflected back at him in their faces—each one knowing different aspects of his nature, his being, his life—and each with their wish for what would come next, some rooting for him, some not.

"Hello!" called Jack. "Are you lost down there?"

Maybe so, thought Wally.

Danny said, "You got this. Trust it."

Wally dug his feet into the sand. *Get out of your way. Stop thinking.* He closed his eyes and took a deep breath in the way Claire had taught him—up his spine, over his crown, down his chest and into his groin. He opened his eyes and took his club back and swung down through the sand just behind the ball, and when he followed through he stopped all of his weight on the inside of his left thigh, just as Danny Boy had instructed. The ball climbed out of the bunker, landed on the green and bounced twice, rolling toward the cup. When it kissed the pin and dropped into the hole, Wally looked at Danny and cried, *"Oh my god!"*

Danny Boy jumped into the bunker and wrapped him in an epic hug. "Incredible!"

On the hillside, the crowd erupted—Bear the loudest, whooping and hollering, while Harry kept pumping his fist. Across the green, Jack Hughes shook his head in disbelief. His son collected Wally's ball from the cup and tossed it back.

"Nice shot, Mr. Scott," he said.

"Lucky shot!" cried Jack, scowling at his son. "Lucky as hell!"

Jack paced around the green mumbling to himself and shaking his head, looking at his putt from every angle. Finally, he stood over his ball, crouched and intent. But he never had a chance. There was so much energy flowing in Wally's direction that when he stroked the ball, it missed the cup and stopped three feet past it. Jack kicked the air in frustration, picked up his ball and hurled it into the large maple tree beside the green. A squirrel fell to the ground and scrambled away.

"Rocky and Bullwinkle!" he hollered, apparently referring to the squirrel. Shaking his head in disbelief, he turned and walked over to Wally. He extended his hand, and Wally shook it.

"Didn't see that coming," said Jack. "I thought you were going to fold and take the car."

"Not today," said Wally.

"I should fire you."

"That won't be necessary," said Wally. "I quit."

"*What?*"

"I'm done, Jack." He brushed his palms together. "Finito."

"You can't *quit.*"

"I just did."

"Your new jingle is the earworm of all earworms! You're about to do a new direct mail campaign. And print ads. You can't quit now. We're killing it!" Jack stepped in and wrapped an arm around his shoulder. "How 'bout we get you that new Solara, anyway, and you stay right where you are. We go way back, Wally," said Jack, giving him a squeeze.

"We do. But now I'm headed elsewhere."

Jack let go and took a step back. "Let's talk tomorrow. When the heat of battle has cooled. No need to make any rash decisions now." He flashed Wally a smile and pointed his finger at him like it was a gun, turned and walked to his cart.

Wally watched him go and spotted Claire hovering at the edge of the green with Gus on the leash. Apparently, Max had moved on. She stepped onto the green and wrapped her free arm around his neck.

"Congratulations, Henrik! You did it!"

Gus gave a yelp and jumped up on his thigh.

Wally petted the dog and hugged Claire back, soaking in her scent. "Thanks, honey chile," he said. Mama Betty had played such a big role in his success, he wanted her in on the celebration, too.

Claire said, "Did you just quit Hughes Auto?"

"I did."

"Are you *crazy?*"

"It's all good. With you back on board, I can write the new ending and sell the option, and—"

"Whoa, wait—what do you mean, with me *back on board?*"

"You love the book."

"I do, but that doesn't—"

"EVERYONE!" bellowed Bear, cutting Claire off, "Time for the trophy presentation on the deck!"

They all gathered on the deck behind the 18th green and Malcolm Toole, the assistant pro, waddled out of the clubhouse with crumbs of popcorn clinging to the front of his shirt, carrying the trophy—a cheap replica of the

Claret Jug presented to the British Open champion.

"Here you go, Mr. Scott," said Malcolm, handing Wally the trophy. "You can take it down to West Longmont and get your name engraved on it. It costs about seventeen bucks. Congratulations." He shook Wally's hand, his fingers covered with salt from the popcorn, and shuffled back into the pro shop.

The group applauded and Bear poured beer from a pitcher and handed cups around, while Danny Boy ordered a White Russian and Roz got another Bloody Mary.

Bear lifted his beer. "To the champion!"

"And his caddy," said Harry, clapping Danny Boy on the back and raising his glass.

"To keeping the faith," said Danny, smiling at Wally like the Cheshire cat.

35

As the celebration broke up and everyone headed home, Bear wrapped Wally in a hellacious hug. "You rode in on that stallion, Henrik. Really proud of you."

"Couldn't have done it without you, Bear. Thanks for everything."

His friend beamed and stepped over to give Claire a kinder, gentler embrace. "Glad you could make it," he said.

"Me too, Bear," she said. "Thanks for the text."

He lumbered off to the parking lot, leaving Wally and Claire seated alone at the table, the trophy in front of them, Gus and Yin on the deck at their feet. A couple approached the 1st tee.

"There's your friend," Claire said to Wally.

He squinted, trying to make out who it was.

"You really do need glasses," she said. "How do you see your golf ball?"

"A lot of times, I don't. I'm always asking the guys where it is."

"Well, let me help you—it's Jill Vanderhausen."

Wally stiffened. Jill spotted them up on the deck and gave a happy wave. Wally waved back less enthusiastically. A man accompanied Jill, carrying two golf bags. He put the bags down on the cart path next to the first tee, and then Jill took him by the hand and led him up toward the deck.

"Looks like she wants to say hello," said Claire.

Wally took a drink of beer. *Oh shit.*

"Don't look so guilty," said Claire.

When Jill stepped onto the deck, Claire was surprised to see how young her companion looked—and how handsome.

"I want you to meet someone," Jill said, looking at Wally. "Richard Gordon, this is Wallace Scott." She looked at Claire. "And his *wife*, Claire."

Wally stood and shook hands with the young man, who then reached over and shook Claire's hand. Claire eyed Jill, who returned the favor.

"Richard is just finishing at the Buck School of Business," Jill said. "And . . . he's asked me to *marry* him!" She held out her left hand and proudly waved her ring finger at them. A diamond the size of a cat's eye marble sparkled in the sun.

"Wow," said Wally. "Congratulations!"

"How exciting," said Claire, sounding ready for a nap.

"I just want to thank you, Wally," said Jill. "For helping me prepare for Richard's visit last month."

Wally's face went ashen.

"You know—for brunch."

"Ohhhhh . . . right. *Brunch.* I'm glad that worked out."

Richard smiled. "We have you to thank—for *tying the knot.*" He winked at Wally.

Wally's face went crimson.

Jill turned to Claire and said, "Maybe we can all get together sometime—and play a little *paddle.*"

Claire felt her face flush, the Catholic schoolgirl in her taken aback.

"Oh!" said Jill, spotting the trophy on the table. "Did you win the member-member, Wally?"

"No," he said.

"It's for the senior club championship," said Claire, finding her voice. "Wally just beat Jack Hughes to win."

Jill gave a little jump and clapped her hands. She stepped over and kissed Wally on the cheek. "Good for you! Ginger will be *so* happy. Apparently, Jack does nothing but *brag* about his golf."

"I got lucky," said Wally.

"I'd rather be lucky than good," said Jill, and gave her fiancé a sultry look.

"Well, we better be going," she said. "We're next on the tee. And I should stretch. I've been so *tied up* lately, there hasn't been any time for yoga."

Claire watched them go. "Sounds like you had quite a night, Champ. Tying the *knot* and playing *paddle.*"

Wally fidgeted in his seat. "You wouldn't have done the same thing?" he said, turning to her. "If Seafood was able?"

"What's that supposed to mean?"

"I heard about his little issue from Danny. The Professor told him everything."

Claire blushed.

"So how's he doing?"

"It sounds like he's making progress," said Claire. "But there's still a lot to sort out. He's located his first love and finally met his son—after thirty years. And his son has a child of his own."

"So Seafood's a grandfather? Damn." Wally shook his head. "What about the curse?"

"Evidently, his master is now an old man and remorseful about what he did."

"So no small penis anymore?"

"It sounds like he is circulating his chi in a most effective manner. But these things take time. He's asked me to keep running the dojo. The tai chi and Qi Gong part."

Wally straightened. "That's great, Claire." He looked genuinely happy for her.

"He wants me to stay in the lake house as long as he's away—to watch Yin and Yang and be the caretaker. I'll get a salary."

"Are you *serious?*"

She nodded and smiled. "I'm giving my last massage at the end of the month."

"Wow," said Wally, "it *is* the end of an era." A look of concern crossed his brow. "When is he coming back?"

"I don't think he knows. For now, he's trying to reestablish old ties and reverse the curse. And money is not an issue."

"Yeah. I got that impression." Wally drummed his fingers on the table.

"It's not an issue for Max McClure, either."

"Evidently not."

"Are you going to Italy with him?"

"I don't know. I might." Claire looked into his eyes and continued to set her new boundaries. "I'm quite happy living at the lake, Wally. And I love teaching tai chi. I don't want to live through you or your writing anymore. I did that for too long. I'm on a different path now."

Wally sat quietly, looking at the trophy.

"Don't get me wrong," said Claire. "I'm really happy your writing has gone so well. But I think a lot of readers are rooting for me to be with Max."

"Max Schmax. If I sell a movie deal, I'll look pretty good, too."

"What are the odds of that?"

"Not bad, if they like the new ending."

"Then you better write the new ending."

"I'm trying," said Wally. "But you're not making it easy."

"Good stories aren't about things being easy, Wallace. You should know that."

Wally sighed, looking forlorn. "So what am I supposed to do?"

"Come over once a week and cook me dinner—and we'll see where things go." Claire rose to her feet. "You can start tomorrow night. I'll provide the champagne for the club champion."

Wally stood and extended his arms, looking for a hug. "Does this mean we're living apart together?"

"Call it whatever you want." Claire stepped in to embrace him. "All I know is, the past is not the future. And the future is not the past."

She gave him a little squeeze. *How's that for a little tai chi magic?*

Epilogue

"And the moon said to me—'My darling,
you do not have to be whole in order to shine.'"
—Anonymous

That night, Claire sat on the dock with Gus, watching a waning moon cast its shimmering reflection across the lake. The air was warm and still, fragrant with the damp, earthy scent of water merging with the shoreline. Soon the leaves would begin to turn and the surrounding hills would blaze with color. But tonight, the early September air was more like August than October, when the foliage would hit its peak. Claire relished the warmth and stillness and milky light of the moon, so calm and peaceful, making it easy for her to home in on Gus's frequency. She sat beside him as the plaintive call of a loon rolled across the lake.

"Sounds like Wally," Gus intoned. "So sad and lonely."

"Nonsense," said Claire. "He's going to be fine."

"You're breaking his heart into a million pieces."

"That's not true. I just don't want to go back to the way it was."

"Isn't that a movie?"

"It's *The Way We Were*. With Robert Redford and Barbra Streisand."

"I think he was a writer."

"He was. But I am *not* the Barbra Streisand character."

"That's for sure. I've heard you singing in the shower. It's painful."

"And your howling is any better?"

Gus sat up and arched his back, raised his snout and howled at the moon. Twice. He turned to her and smiled, his eyes soft, his tongue hanging out of the side of his mouth.

"I rest my case," said Claire, patting him.

Gus nestled in next to her and she scratched behind his ears.

"I can't help it," he shared. "I just like Wally."

"So do I."

"And I'm all about reconciliation."

"Is that right? You'd want to be returned to your original owners?"

"Hell no! Those people were cruel and selfish."

Claire swung a foot gently through the warm, soft water. "Well, Wally's not cruel, but he can be selfish."

"So you're choosing Max, instead?"

"If I'm choosing anyone, I'm choosing me."

Gus straightened, cocked his head and looked at her. "A life alone?"

"A life *of* my own. There's a difference. I'm done pleasing everyone else all the time. I'm going to spend some time pleasing me."

Gus lay back down and put his head in her lap. "Can I ask one more thing?"

"Fire away."

"What happens if Sifu returns? Without his old flame? I mean, she's probably had a husband for thirty years."

Claire considered this, and not for the first time. "I don't know. Why does it have to be all about men? Why can't it be about discovery on its own terms? About awakening. Transformation. Dancing with the universe."

"Oh for cryin' out loud."

"I'm free, Gus. Free to Push Hands with life. And I gotta say, it feels pretty sweet."

Gus stood and shook from head to toe. "Yowsa!" he declared telepathically. "I need a drink!" And he dove off the dock into the water.

Acknowledgments

My heartfelt thanks to Rootstock publisher Samantha Kolber, who has a great sense of humor (obviously) and an even better editorial touch to coax the best out of a piece of writing; to Abby Clark for her brilliant cover design and artwork, as well as my author website; to Eddie Vincent for his handsome interior book design and final cover arrangements; to Lesley Allen for her eagle-eyed copy edits; to Peter Lincoln, Mary Lincoln, and Ned Waters for catching issues in the galleys; to Greg Hubbard for my good-as-plastic-surgery photo; and to the members of the Rootstock team who expertly oversaw every detail on the path to publication.

I have been blessed over the years to have the support of some exceptionally generous patrons who have brought this book to life—Mark & Lisa and Steve, I can never thank you enough. Others have been in my corner forever, including the True Believers, Carol ("I see a 30-year, overnight success") and Gail (who drank the Kool-Aid and washed it down with wine); my old boss, D.G. Chinaski; the HHS boys; the Midd crew; the Golf & Ski gang; the JVs; my ancestors and writing guides (JEL, MB, Queenie); our supersonic sons, Nolan and Nick, and their wonderful partners, Christy and Tony; and our colorful extended family—my love and thanks to you all.

As for Cecy, my deepest gratitude for your enduring love and faith over decades of the quest, and for the brilliant ideas and belly laughs in the writing room. Who's the author, anyway? xo

About the Author

Chris Lincoln is an award-winning copywriter and creative director who has been recognized with a Clio, advertising's Oscar. He is also the author of the widely praised non-fiction book, *Playing the Game: Inside Athletic Recruiting in the Ivy League*. His articles on sports, recreation, and the arts have appeared in New England-based magazines and newspapers. A graduate of Middlebury College and participant at the Bread Loaf Writers' Conference, he lives in Vermont with his wife. *The Funny Moon* is his first novel. Visit his website www.chrislincoln.net.

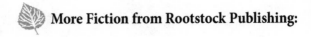 **More Fiction from Rootstock Publishing:**

All Men Glad and Wise: A Mystery by Laura C. Stevenson

Augusta: A Novel by Celia Ryker

Blue Desert: A Novel by Celia Jeffries

Granite Kingdom: A Novel by Eric Pope

Hawai'i Calls: A Novel by Marjorie Nelson Matthews

Horodno Burning: A Novel by Michael Freed-Thall

The Hospice Singer: A Novel by Larry Duberstein

The Inland Sea: A Mystery by Sam Clark

Intent to Commit: A Novel by Bernie Lambek

Junkyard at No Town: A Novel by J.C. Myers

No Excuses by Stephen L. Harris

Street of Storytellers by Doug Wilhelm

Uncivil Liberties: A Novel by Bernie Lambek

Venice Beach: A Novel by William Mark Habeeb

To learn about our titles in poetry, nonfiction, and children's literature, visit our website www.rootstockpublishing.com.

Printed in the USA
CPSIA information can be obtained
at www.ICGtesting.com
JSHW082108020823
45732JS00005B/18